DEADLY

DEVELOPMENT

BY

DL HAVLIN

and J Havlin

ISBN: 978-1-933678-40-5

Palm Pen Press, LLC.
Bokeelia, Florida 33922
www.DLHavlin.com

Dedication

I reserve my largest, most heart-felt thank you for my loving wife, partner, do everything assistant, and Publicist, Jeanelle. Without her support, encouragement, understanding and tolerance I would have abandoned writing long ago.

~ ~ ~ ~ ~

Acknowledgements

I used to read acknowledgements with little or no appreciation and with less feeling for the author and those cited. No more! After my writing journey of the last 30 plus years, I truly know the value of those who vitally contribute to the success of any author on their quest to produce a worthwhile work.

DL Havlin is an eclectic author whose varied experiences and background provide him with a memory chest full of material for writing his novels. He graduated from the University of Cincinnati and attended pre-law at Rollins.

His life has been as varied as his novels. Havlin's occupations have included tasks from systems analyst to worldwide customer service director and from licensed boat captain to football coach. He's in demand as a speaker and seminar presenter for relationship and writing skills.

Havlin's passion for fishing, hunting, Florida's wilderness, and its historical heritage, frequently appear in his writing and his speaking engagements. His tales are just as likely to be set in Kiev, Singapore, London, Sachsenhausen or other places in the over eighty countries he's visited. Their people and customs resonate in his novels. Known for creating memorable characters, his interjection of humor, and his carefully crafted plots, reading a DL Havlin book is always a pleasurable experience.

Titles by DL Havlin

Deadly Development
The Grave with Greener Grass
Turtle Point
Out of Italy
Escaping Skeletons
The Bait Man
Bully Route Home
Blue Water Red Blood
The Cross on Cotton Creek
A Place No One Should Go
The Hangin' Oak
September on Echo Creek
Christmas Story Collection
Story Time-R

www.DLHavlin.com

For information regarding the author contact
PRLady2016@gmail.com or 239.283.3975.

Chapter   1

Heatwaves radiated off of the parking lot pavement outside my office window. It was still hot. Summer blew its breath on the East Florida University campus though the October date on the calendar said it was gone. I took a deep breath and looked at the computer list on my desk. The damned thing was endless. This was one of the parts of archaeology I less than loved. Verifying that the next list entry was, in fact, the one housed in the same numbered cubical, of the same numbered drawer, of the same numbered box, bored me to tears. The hell with the heat! I wanted to be outside, on a dig, let the perspiration be damned.

My eyes closed, my feet found the top of my desk, and my dress assumed a most unladylike position. I didn't care. There had to be a better way to spend the thirty minutes before Reading picked me up for lunch. My brother, never a spender, big or little, offered to buy, so I was sure there'd be a string hanging off of the "free lunch." Clasping my hands behind my head made my eyelids heavier. If I moved the under-wire in my bra, the pinch it created would go away, and it would be easy to catch a mini-nap before Reading arrived. One hand found the annoying sensation, and my nails moved the support. I sighed as I chased the aggravating feeling that bugged me.

"Would you like me to do that for you?" My boss, Dr. Mark Card, joked.

"It depends," I answered.

"On what?"

"How you're going to do it, and with what?"

Mark knew better than to further the conversation's direction. His face flushed, knowing where I'd probably take the chatter. "How are you doing with verifying the catalog?"

"Fine. I guess." I sighed and suddenly realized I was providing him with an inappropriate view of parts of my body. I quickly got my tennis shoes back on to the floor. "I know it has to be done. It has to be perfect and all that, but, one word…boring."

"It comes with the job," he said.

"I know, I know, I know." I pointed to the window. "I want to be out there, sweating, getting bitten by mosquitoes, getting dirt all over me, and smelling like a locker-room at the end of a season. When are we going out on another dig?"

Mark smiled and shook his head, "Not for a while."

"Why, not? We have at least a half-dozen projects in this half of the state that are begging us to start on them."

"Simple. No money. We've exhausted my project budget." Mark pointed to my posterior. "I'm afraid you'll just have to get used to keeping that thing in an office chair until after January first."

I'm sure I pouted. I have a tendency to do that when I don't get my way. It always worked with my Daddy.

Mark chuckled. "I bet you were a cute seven-year-old." He smiled and held his index finger up in the air. "Tell you what. Why don't you find someone out there, floating on the wind, which will bank-roll one of our projects? If you can do that, I'll get you back into the outdoor sauna so quick your head will swim."

"Really?" It sounded good until I realized I didn't have a starting place. If one existed, Mark would have already exploited it. He had a better nose for available funds than the most well-trained, pure-bred, English pointer does for quail.

"Really? Really, what?" Reading stood leaning against the door jam. His green sheriff's uniform had several darker areas that were drenched with sweat.

"I need some money, Bro. Have any ideas?" I quipped.

Reading made a circle with his thumb and forefinger. He peered at me through it for a second. His expression and tone were mock-serious. "Well, Chessie, it depends on what you're willing to sell. I know some good pimps."

I shot him a good-natured bird, and we all laughed.

"Why are you looking for money? You got plenty sitting in the bank. Or are you planning to buy a Maserati?"

"She wants out of the office. Your sister likes playing in the dirt." Mark grinned. "She talked me into using my budget up early in the year, so now she's tethered to a desk."

"Damn Mark, you don't like being stuck here, either." It was my defense. A very weak one, but true. At least, he got in the field to teach some portions of his classes. Mine were campus only affairs.

Mark laughed, "Tell you how to handle your frustration. Think of your office as a site. You can use your trowel to turn the pages of the computer printouts. Who knows what you might find buried in there."

"Smart-ass!" I replied.

"Speaking of finding things, we got a call from one of the cane ranchers south of Florida 60 yesterday." Reading removed his cell phone from his shirt pocket. He maneuvered his fingers until he found what he was looking for. "One of the field hands found this." Reading held the screen so we could see a picture of a skull and several more bones. "These were scattered over ten acres. I'm guessing these are all from the same skeleton, but how can I tell for sure?"

We answered together, "DNA."

Reading shrugged his shoulders, "Is there a cheap way?"

Mark asked, "And still be one hundred percent sure?"

Reading nodded.

"Sorry. You might get close by being sure all the bones are the same gender, same race, same general size. Make sure there aren't any bones that would indicate there was more than one body involved. If all those went right, you could figure you've got an 85% chance of having one person. A *good* examiner can come close and tell you a lot." Mark drummed his fingers on the desk. After a few seconds, he asked, "Who has the bones in the coroner's office?"

"Barry."

Mark shook his head and looked disgusted. "Talk to Frenchie. See if you can get her to do it or have her assign Melvin to the job. Barry *is not* the person you want examining them if you want to learn a damned thing."

"I can do that." Reading looked at his watch. "We're eating into my lunch. Let's go, Chessie. You don't need your purse, remember I'm buying."

"Where are we going?" I asked. "Riverside Café? Ono Luau?" I was hopeful.

"Moe's Deli," Reading replied, "Unless you want to go halves."

"Is it true you breed moths in your billfold?" I asked.

Reading grinned and held his hands in front of him, palms up.

"I'll get my purse," I said. Eating with my brother underlined the saying, *There is no such thing as a free lunch.*"

Chapter   2

"How's your steak?" I asked.

"Very good." Reading eyed the bleeding T-bone on his plate like it was a beautiful girl in a bikini.

"Jon-Jacquez has wonderful food." I sighed and looked at my chef's salad. Reading was eating like Genghis Kahn. I was chowing down like Bugs Bunny.

"Yep." Reading attacked the steak with the finesse of a bulldozer operator. He definitely wasn't ready for the society page. After disposing of his mouthful, he commented, "They keep it nice and cool in here. That's good, particularly today. It was so damned hot out at the Buehl Ranch this morning while we were wrestling that bunch of protestors, I thought I'd burn up. I bet I could have wrung a quart of sweat out of my underwear."

"Reading! I don't need that visual while I'm eating soup and salad."

"Sorry." He grinned, confirming he wasn't interested in any discomfort he'd caused.

"What's going on out there?" I asked.

Reading chomped his mouthful of T-bone and swallowed hurriedly. "Some development company is buying Buehl's operation out on Blue Cypress Lake. The ranch lands, the meat cutting facility, everything. They're planning on making it a kind of Villages South. Country clubs, golf courses, community centers...I heard they expect to end up with more than 20,000 folks living there. The development company has an option on it and was fixin' to cut a temporary road back in there to survey it. The word got out somehow. There were folks from the Audubon Society, the Florida Conservation Knights, the Seminole Tribal Council, and three or four more groups I never heard of. They laid down in front of the construction equipment, threw cow pies at the workers and development people. It was tense."

"What ended up happening?"

"A process server showed up with an injunction the Seminoles got issued. They claim there may be multiple burial sites on the property. Old Carl Buehl took one look at it and stopped everything. Weird thing was he almost looked happy." Reading hacked a piece of rare meat off his steak. He held it up in the air, stuck it on his fork, waving it like a battle flag. "The development people were some kinds of pissed. They yelled at Buehl and his partners, his partners yelled at him, the contractor folks yelled at the protestors, and the protestors were screaming at everyone."

"How did you get it settled down?" I asked.

"I didn't. Nature found a way. While everybody there was concentrating on being assholes, a big rattler crawled onto the middle of that white sand road. Made it look more like nine feet than six feet. It coiled up and sung out. I pointed it out to everybody, warned them there are bunches of those crawling around out there. I had the place to myself in twenty minutes." Reading chuckled and said, "Your high school buddy was one of the first to go."

"My high school buddy? Who?"

"Millie Lane. She's the real estate agent handling the sale." Reading grinned. "You know if she's married?"

I stopped listening when Reading mentioned Millie was the real estate agent. Maybe there was a way to turn Millie's real estate debacle into an archaeological dig.

"Hey, Chessie, what part of space are you traveling in?" Reading growled.

"Sorry. Where were we?"

"Is Millie married?"

"I don't know."

"Find out for me. She isn't that skinny twig she used to be."

I shook my head. "My, my, Reading. You're on the wrong side of thirty-five. Isn't it about time to stop chasing and settle on one person to share sheets with?"

Reading didn't smile. "No, Sis, not until I find that special lady. One that won't let me see a girl like your buddy and wonder what it would be like to go ten rounds in a four-poster. When I put my violin in its case, I intend to keep it there." Reading was as serious as cardiac arrest.

I cocked my head to the side and stared at him. When my brother made a statement like that, he'd do exactly as he said. I had to ask, "You've had some really cool ladies, Bro. None of those would do?"

"Yes, a couple would have. The ones that would have worked for me," he paused, "I didn't work out for them."

"You aren't getting younger," I observed. It was a bad observation.

"Chessie, I don't need to remind you you're three years older than me. I don't mean to be unkind, but…you're still shopping."

I sighed, "Okay, I'll give Millie a call. I haven't seen her in a few years. We'll go to lunch or something."

Lunch with Millie would be a good thing and possibly a *twofer*. I'd find out her marital status for Reading and if she could use bonafide expertise to determine if her deal would survive or be flushed in the porcelain bus.

"Thanks," Reading disposed of the last of his steak. Then he said, "Put your professional hat on for a moment. Why would someone steal part of a skeleton?"

"Part of a skeleton?" That didn't make much sense. "What part? The skull? Why would anyone want a skeleton?" I answered my own question to a degree. "Other than for a Halloween decoration or use as a gag to scare someone with…let me think." I put my hand over my eyes as I concentrated. "To frame someone for a crime, that's about all I can think of."

"They didn't take the skull, so I think it's less likely to be a prank or a decoration." Reading removed his cell phone and looked something up. "Here's what was stolen." He cleared his throat before he recited. "One humerus, one ulna, one radius, one femur, one tibia, one fibula."

I chuckled, "Someone has a sense of humor. They stole an arm and a leg. That doesn't help me any, though."

"If we recover them, do you think you or Mark can match them to the skeleton?"

"Yes, sure. Where were they stolen from?" I asked.

"From a retired anthropologist's private collection. He lives over on the beach." Reading reached for his billfold. "Oh, shit. I left my wallet in the squad car. Do you mind, Chessie?"

There is no such thing as a free lunch!

Chapter   3

"How long has it been?" Millie asked, though I knew she probably knew to the day. She was a detail person. Millie was the quiet girl-next-door type, with doe-brown eyes and a China doll innocence that repelled suitors despite her attractiveness. She'd added considerable curves to the body with which she'd graduated from Vero Beach high.

"Let's see," I backed my way through time. I'd seen her after my time in the Marines. On the beach…yes, it was just before I'd taken the job as a mate on a fishing boat. "I'd say a little over five years. Down on Atlantic Avenue. You were there with Annabelle and some other gal."

"I think that's right," Millie's half-smile was a major show of emotion for her.

"You see Annabelle much? I think that was the first time I saw her since we graduated."

"No. Not since she got married. She's got seven kids." Millie spoke as if she was speaking of the dear departed.

"Wow! How long has she been married?" I asked. I didn't remember Annabelle as being the type to have a brood. She'd been suspected of being one of the last virgins in our class.

"Six years." Millie looked uncomfortable talking about Annabelle.

"So, are you married?" I asked.

"No."

"Going with anybody?"

"Not really. Ben Torrey calls me occasionally." Millie looked down at the Pizza Hut table. "I saw your brother the other day. Did you call me because of him?"

Millie was smart. I tried not to show my surprise. "Not exactly. He said he saw you out at Buehl's place. It reminded me we hadn't seen each other in a spell. Walla, I gave you a call."

"Oh. I was hoping he was interested in taking me out." She blushed. "I used to fantasize about going out with him when we were in high school." Her look asked the question her words wouldn't.

I smiled. "I'll tell him to give you a call. He is single."

"I know." The half-smile reappeared.

"Reading tells me you're a real estate agent, now."

Her countenance returned to expressionless. "Uh-huh. Century 21. I'm working for the Larry Regnillos' agency."

I smiled broadly, "Old Larry's the best."

"He is. I just don't want to let him down on the Buehl ranch deal. It's getting complicated. That's why I saw your brother. There were a bunch of activists trying to stop what the developer wants to do."

I said, "You mean bunny-huggers?"

Millie shrugged her shoulders, "Activists."

There were no bushes to beat around. "Reading told me that a lot of the argument was over claims there were either Seminole or Ais burial grounds on the property. If you need an impartial source of expertise, I can provide it for you. Did you know I'm working and studying at East Florida? I have my undergrad degree in archaeology and plan to go for my doctorate. My boss is Dr. Mark Card. He's respected by both sides…activists and developers. He's always truthful. I'm sure he has contacts with the decision-makers in all the groups. He's good at getting compromises that work. I'll talk to him if you'd like me too. I'm sure he'd do it, but someone would have to pay for the survey."

"I heard about what you're doing. I was hoping you'd ask, so I didn't have to. I didn't want to impose on you. As far as paying, Dillon Development would do it. Gladly." Millie appeared relieved. I was surprised.

"Dillon Development? As in, Beth Dillon's father's company?" The Dillons were among the wealthiest families on Florida's East Coast.

"It's Beth's company now. Her daddy retired, and she's running it. President and CEO." Millie saw the shock on my face an added, "She is doing a real good job."

My shock was real. Beth was the only girl in my senior class whose reputation had been as tarnished as mine. I'd been figuratively accused of doing the basketball team. Beth was a football type of girl. "Really!" was the best I could muster.

Millie nodded her head. "A…how do you two get on?"

"Not one way or the other. We lived in different circles. I can't remember any problem we had." I remembered Beth was noted for her strong opinions, likes, and dislikes. "I don't believe I was ever on her blacklist."

Millie looked relieved. "I can set up a meeting if you'd like?"

"Okay. Do it."

"One thing. I'll have to bring Beth. She signs the checks. You'll need to bring whoever approves you going out there." Millie was being as delicate as possible. "We don't want to count on something happening and then not." Her tone was apologetic.

"Dr. Card will be with me. He has the power to approve his own work." I lied a tiny bit. He'd have to get Dr. Andrews to rubber-stamp his decision. That would not be a problem. I asked, "When do you think you can get us together?"

Millie looked nervous. "I'm not sure. Beth usually has a full schedule. This is a high priority project for her so…but…well…there is one other thing." She took a deep breath. "Buehl's group is a problem. Three of the four are all for selling. If it comes to a vote, it will change hands. The problem is, the one fighting this thing is old man Buehl. Beth may or may not want one or all of them to attend. I don't know how she'll react."

That made sense. Beth never was unprepared. I asked, "Does she still quote that old American Express slogan?"

Millie blushed. "Yes, she still tells everyone she doesn't leave home without her credit card and her birth control." Millie shook her head sadly. "I guess there are some parts of people that never change."

Chapter   4

"Remind me of this the next time I shoot my mouth off, casually." Mark Card had that *I know something you don't* look. It always infuriates me when he plays that game.

"You told me if I could line up the money, we'd go play in the dirt…that's the way I think you said it." I put my hands on my hips and scowled at him. "You aren't going back on your word, are you?"

"No, you know I wouldn't." Mark smiled, emptied his lungs, and slumped a little. "We'll get to go play in the dirt. But, if you want to surprise me, you need to be quicker. You had lunch, what, three hours ago?"

"Yes, that quick?" I said.

"That quick." Mark waved for me to sit down at the conference table in his office, as he slid into one of the chairs surrounding it. "Dr. Andrews called me two hours ago, telling me he'd approve the request to do the survey on the Dillon Properties Development." He paused, held his finger up, indicating there was more, and chuckled. "My phone hadn't settled in its cradle when it rang again. It was Beth Dillon." He got that, *yes, I did* smile and confirmed, "We have some history. Beth told me not to worry overspending whatever she authorized. She's paying the school $40,000 for three weeks plus any out-of-pocket expenses. She'll furnish her company's vehicles and backhoe, plus an operator for the dig."

"Any strings?" I asked.

"No. She wants an honest evaluation. The only thing she says she'd like us to do is to determine if part of the property can be separated if we do find anything of consequence. Beth's a straight shooter; she tells it like it is. If we find there's a significant site, she'll donate it to the state with the understanding it becomes a restricted park." Mark leaned back in his chair, nodded seriously, and said, "So…you'll get to go play in the dirt."

"So…our job is to isolate anything that's there so she can build around it?" It was cynical and sarcastic, and I regretted saying it. My mouth runs on automatic too much.

"No…our job is to see what's there. Period." Mark waited for a reply. When he didn't get one, he said, "We meet with her, Carl Buehl and his partners, her assistant, and the real estate agent Millie somebody."

"Lane. She's a high school friend." I prompted.

"Does two and two make four?" He asked, I nodded, he continued, "Beth suggested Jim McMillan from the state. He'll be fair. She named a couple people from the groups who are fighting the development to be there. I added a couple more and Terrie Tall Pine from the Seminoles. Some Beth named are extreme. One of them thinks the cavemen were environmental unfriendly because they wore animal skins."

I was sure I knew who he was talking about. Those animal skins would have served a better purpose if removed from the cavemen and shoved into her mouth. She'd be a problem whether included in meetings or not. It wouldn't affect me, I hoped. I asked, "Who is Terrie Tall Pine? I don't know him."

"You don't know, *her*. I think you'll like each other. She has some quirk's and doesn't trust people easily, but when she gets to know and like you, she's great." Mark chuckled. "You two are a lot alike in some ways. If there are two women in this world, I don't want mad at me, it's Terrie and you."

"Sounds like a good woman." I ignored my cell phone's rendition of Dixie and asked, "When does this kick-off?"

Mark said, "Monday, 10:00 AM, at the gate to the Buehl's ranch.

After a pause, I removed my cell phone, but before answering, I asked, "Any type of bonus in this for you?"

Mark just smiled.

Chapter   5

I was running late. Stopping at the Dunkin' Donuts and a chance run-in with a couple old friends put me twenty minutes behind schedule without a valid excuse. Compounding the problem was driving my brother's four-wheel-drive truck. It made speeding to make up some time uncomfortable. It didn't handle a bit like my F-150. I'd borrowed it because I was sure to get stuck in mud or loose sand without four-wheel drive.

The wash-board surface was interspersed with huge holes that made me glad Reading volunteered his vehicle. He had extra heavy-duty, shocks, springs, and accessories for the type driving I was doing. My mind appreciated that, even if my kidneys and rear did not! Regardless, the road was rugged. I seldom could get the speedometer to register twenty. The vision of cars and trucks lined up on either side of the road was a relief as I rounded a cypress head. My cell phone told me I was twelve minutes late.

The road between me and the vehicles bisected a pine barren. Barbed wire fences on either side had been there long enough to have acquired a "curtain." Birds perch on the wire, drop seeds, and all manner of weeds, brush, and trees sprout outside away from the teeth of grazing cattle.

As I got closer, I counted nine trucks and cars. A knot of people was gathered under the gateway made from pine timbers framing the steel gate below. The cross pole was ten feet above the ground. Three cattle skulls were mounted on it. Below them, a wooden sign swung from eyelets. Craved on it was, *Buehl Quality Beef, Ranch #1.*

I recognized Mark Card's Jeep, Millie Lane's Edge, and what I knew was the ranch all-terrain vehicle. The two HUMV's were clean and without "field rash," so they probably belonged to the development people. The other two pickups and jeeps were a mystery. As I neared, one thing was certain; some type of hostility had already begun. Another hundred yards, and I understood why. I mumbled to myself, "Oh shit, Billie Mulhee."

The woman stood in the middle of the road, waving her arms and gesturing. Millie, Mark, and the others gathered around her in a semi-circle. Her loud voice was audible after another two hundred. If there was one person on the East Coast of Florida that could make a shambles of any event, it was Billie. I parked the truck behind the line of vehicles in queue on the right side of the road.

When I opened the door of my truck, I wouldn't have had to see Billie to know it was her. Her voice and choice of words were both distinctive. The high-pitched screech that carried a steady stream of four-letter words was annoying and loud. She seldom uttered more than ten consecutive words without "fuck" being among them. Shit and damn were close frequency seconds with more complex curses liberally utilized. Her general behavior made vulgar an understatement.

As I joined the group of four women and seven men, I noted the sharp differences in dress. I knew all but one of the women. Millie was dressed in a plain gray dress with flats. Beth's grab was out of an outfitter's catalog for an African safari, topped by a pith helmet. I assumed that the lady who wasn't familiar was Terrie Tall Pine. We were dressed the same…long khaki pants, tee shirts, ball caps, and snake boots. Billie fell into the discard box at Goodwill and emerged in clothes most likely to be converted to rags by anyone else.

I only recognized three men. Carl Buehl, the primary owner, was of slight build, fifty-sixth, salt and pepper hair, piercing brown eyes, high forehead, and a distinctive hooked nose. His clothes, more suited for golf than ranching, hug on his 6'3" frame like it was a coat hanger. Dr. Card was dressed in his usual field garb…that of an extra in a WWII film featuring Australian soldiers.

Jim McMillan, the Florida representative for the Council of Native Affairs, was perspiration soaked and miserable in a navy suit with polished black shoes. Jim was average everything. Height, weight, features, the type you were sure not to notice, until he spoke. The man was brilliant, a lawyer, and thirty-five.

I knew Mark would do the introductions if he could get Billie's mouth closed long enough to do it. I got within twenty feet, and he tried.

"Ah, we're all here now." Billie cut Mark off.

"Bull-shit you worthless fuck!" Billie was in fine form. "None of the good fucking people who represent fucking nature are here. Where the fuck is Wendall from Audubon? Or Cathy from the Nature Conservancy? Did your piles of shit ask them to be the fuck here? How about Willow and Johnathan from the Knights of Nature? Where's—"

Dr. Card cut her off. "Billie, I've already explained I contacted each of the organizations you discussed, and they are happy to see the results of our field research, then make a decision on whether to support this or not."

"Why in the fuck didn't you contact me?" Billie was back to screaming.

"Because of the way you are acting this second," Beth Dillon spoke calmly but with assured authority. "You've heard me tell you I won't disturb one inch of archaeological rich ground, and even if there isn't a single bone or piece of pottery here, I'm going to make one-third of this property a park and sanctuary."

"Losing one fucking acre to you shit-heads is too much." Billie renewed her rant.

"Tough shit!" One of the men I didn't know spoke. Harshly. He was big, muscular, fortyish, and wealthy looking. I found out his name was Stanton Griggs. "This is going to happen. You keep your uncouth a…rear out of here and out of our way. I'll keep you in court so much you'll have to move in there if you don't."

Billie sneered, "That's why I *am* a lawyer."

"I do not have time to waste." The woman I believed to be Terrie spoke in a commanding voice. "I will see what these people propose. My people have the greatest interest in what was once ours. If you wish to come, keep your words and thoughts to yourself. I'm sure a place can be found. If not, *shut up and go away.*"

The two women stood ten feet apart, eye-balling each other. Neither spoke, and it was silent except for the chattering of mockingbirds and the whistling of quail.

Finally, Billie croaked feebly, "They buy you off?"

Terrie immediately moved toward the woman who insulted her. When she was a foot from Billie, the Seminole said, "Repeat that, and I will have your hair." As she spoke, her hand felt for the handle of a fourteen-inch Bowie knife stuck in her waistband, behind her back.

Billie shook her head. There was terror in her eyes and fire in Terrie's. "Go with us or leave this place," Terrie commanded.

"Go with you?! You'll bury me out there!" Billie took two steps backward.

Terrie made no sign to confirm or deny the woman's claim. Instead, she said, "Think what you will. You will not listen to those who speak to you."

Billie stood her ground, though her bravado had fled. The Indian woman ground her under with her steely eye-contact.

"How did you find out about our meeting here?" Beth Dillon looked at Billie then glanced at the rest of us. "I contacted everyone myself, except Partin," she pointed to me. "This is a closed meeting. Mulhee, you weren't invited…or shouldn't have been. Leave."

Billie forced her eyes away from Terrie's fierce stare and looked at Beth defiantly. As her eyes moved, I noticed a flicker of response as they passed Carl Buehl. It told me a lot.

When Mulhee showed no intent to leave, Terrie moved close to the woman and thrust her head forward, so their noses were less than an inch apart. She said something in such a low voice, no one but Billie could hear. The woman shrieked and took two quick steps away from Terrie.

Terrie turned and saw the shocked faces surrounding her. She took one hard step toward us and yelled, "Raaahhhh!" Everyone flinched, and she laughed. Billie ran for her truck and was in it and gone before Tall Pine's prank wore off.

~ ~ ~ ~ ~ ~ ~

Before we climbed in the Jeeps and all-terrain vehicle, Mark did a round-robin introduction of us all. Besides Millie Lane, Beth Dillon, Jim McMillan, Carl Buehl, and Mark, all of who I knew, I met Beth's assistant, Issac Steinman, who looked like the CPA he was. Stanton Griggs and Bill Wheeler were two of Buehl's three partners, or as they could better be described, his financial lifeboat that saved his business several years back. Stanton was the man that had threatened Billie Mulhee. Wheeler was an obese fellow that wanted to flee to the nearest bar, and dispose of a few pitchers. Terrie Tall Pine looked the part of a Seminole. Her raven black hair, short, stocky build, and fierce, piercing eyes closely fit the stereotype. The last man introduced himself as, "Wilbur Carson, I'm the happenin' man. If'n it's gonna happen, I'm the man that does it. I'm the foreman here at the Bar B." Carson was like a hundred Cracker cowboys I'd known. As hard in body and mind as a lighter knot, he'd be stubborn, cantankerous, even vicious if he or his felt threatened. He would be our guide for our first glide over the land. Carson loaded Beth, Mark, and me in the "Gator," and we were off in the all-terrain with Buehl driving a four-wheel Jeep Waggoneer stuffed with the rest of the party following in our wake.

It was our first glimpse and taste of what the property and our primary host were like. We would get to know both *very* well.

Chapter   6

Though I had seen it hundreds of times before, and will hundreds of times more, the splendor that is the raw Florida backwoods holds my love and fascinates me. This trip into the wilds was a racing panorama blurred by the speed our driver pushed the all-terrain vehicle. Wilbur Carson knew the land, and it was good that he did for at the speed he drove the Gator, if he hadn't, we surely would have ended up in a serious accident. He avoided stumps, logs, bogs, loose sand, even gopher tortoise and armadillo holes that could have killed us.

The cattle herds we passed changed as we went from pasture to pasture. There were black Angus, white-faced Herefords, and mixes of the two breeds. Huge bulls occupied their own domains. The vehicle meant feeding time to the cattle. We had to reassure Beth they were looking for a handout, not her head when they loped after the vehicles.

A myriad of wildlife scurried from in front of us. Deer scampered away as we neared them, snakes slithered out of our path, and an assortment of small guys…raccoons, rabbits, squirrels, etc., fled in terror. We saw a variety of birds…herons, buzzards, woodpeckers, quail, turkey, mockingbirds, crows, sandhill cranes, and the list went on.

Nothing was new to us, so we drove in relative silence, enjoying the show. The exception was some shouted editorial comments by Carson. His words were meant to be helpful for the future but were meaningless since we had no idea where we were. So, "There's a bunch of rattlers in that area," or "That's all loose sand over there," though important, lost relevance.

Carl Buehl hugged the rear of our vehicle. That told me, though he owned the property, he wasn't anywhere close to having Wilbur Carson's familiarity with the land. It also made me fearful that if we stopped sharply, the Waggoneer would leave tire tracks over the little Gator. The twists and turns we traveled since leaving the county sand road made the distance through the open pastures difficult to judge. After what I guessed was nearly a mile, we came to ruts serving as a ranch road that would take us deeper into the ranch. The only thing I was sure of was it was morning, and the sun was in front of us, so we were heading east.

The ruts led us toward and in between cypress heads that increasingly dotted the landscape. Those ruts made it possible to weave through the dense wooded, ponds. We exited the cypress and came to a sand ridge covered with huge old live oaks. As we approached, Wilbur slowed the Gator to a crawl and shouted, "Up ahead is the first spot you wanted to see. Since I was a young un,' I been told the mounds up ahead was made by Indians that lived here afore the Seminoles. They ain't real big, but I'd say they're the only ones on this ranch most folks know about."

The vehicle crept up the gentle seven-foot grade. Five mounds appeared as we neared the top. They sat in open ground and formed a semi-circle at the edge of what I guessed to be a twenty-acre lake. They were situated in a beautiful spot. Located thirty yards from the crest of the ridge, I could see how the spot had been chosen. Good source of water…check. A natural high point to escape Florida's seasonal flooding…check. Plentiful food animals and plants…check. The thick leaf and Spanish moss canopy provided cool shade and prevented almost all underbrush from growing. It would have been a comfortable place to live using their standards.

Wilbur eased the vehicle to a halt next to one of the mounds. He asked, "Want to get out for a look-see.?"

"Sure," Mark answered. He swung his legs out of the Gator, and I followed him.

Beth Dillon asked Wilbur, "Are there snakes here?"

"If'n you mean snakes that can hurt you, ain't none to speak of. No rattlers I've seen. Might be a moccasin or two at the edge of the lake. Ya can't tell about them." Wilbur saw her expression and grinned. "Course they's always a bunch of black snakes, pine snakes, rat snakes, and such a crawling."

"Oooohh! I'll stay here," Beth said.

Terrie Tall Pine and Jim McMillan joined us from the Wagoneer, the rest stayed in the AC. The four of us walked up the side of the sand hillock. Wilbur followed a few steps behind. The growth on it and its configuration had all the hallmarks of an Indian midden.

"What do you think, Terrie?" Mark asked.

"It looks like they are. Let me nose around more." She walked up to the top of the mound and carefully was inspecting the surroundings.

Jim McMillan kneeled down and examined a hole three feet wide and two feet deep on the side of one of the mounds. After carefully running his fingers through some sand and further examination, he said, "I vote they are middens, probably Ais, and probably often disturbed. If I had to guess, I'd say the people who did this digging were just curious and had no training."

"I agree," Terrie said. "The question I have is, how extensively have they been disturbed. What do you think, Dr. Card?"

"Let me take a look at the last two." He walked around and over them as we watched. While waiting, I decided to take a closer look at something that caught my eye at the bottom of a hole near the top of one of the middens. I walked up the incline and looked into a hole that was a couple feet in diameter and a foot in depth. What I'd noticed was the bottom of the hole was convex; not concave as one would expect. I knelt next to the depression.

Gently, I rubbed my fingers through soft, powdery sand. There was something hard and curved under them. It was the right shape to be part of the top of a skull. Carefully, I brushed the loose sand away. It wasn't a skull, but it was interesting. It was a large piece of pottery with a unique coloring not found in local artifacts. It was 'clean' for something buried for hundreds of years, and a minimum of vegetation grew at the hole's bottom. There were markings on it! I felt I could identify the source. After examining it carefully, I did! Navaho!

I stood up and called out to the rest. "Hey, folks. I got something here you all have to see. It's either a great archaeological find or a sign we may have a problem."

~ ~ ~ ~ ~ ~ ~

It looked like a daisy whose center was the hole and whose petals were made of human butts. Terrie, Mark, Jim, and Wilbur joined me on my hands and knees. We circled the hole, evenly spaced, staring at the piece of pottery.

Mark said, "You're right, Chessie, that's Navaho." He pointed to the shiny flecks around the hardened clay. "That looks like mica mixed in the sand. Mica sure in hell isn't from here. I think we have a planted piece. My question is; who would salt this place? And, who would do it so poorly?"

It was obvious to me. "Someone who doesn't want this development project to go forward or someone who wants these middens excavated."

"Or both," Terrie added.

"Find something, Dr. Card?" Carl Buehl spoke as he approached the middens accompanied by Stanton Griggs.

Mark folded his arms and parried the question. "I'd rather not say until I can do a bit of research."

"What's that mean?" Griggs asked.

"It means this is an archaeological site. It will have to be protected. These will all have to be dug up. Isn't that right, Dr. Card." Buehl's tone was almost begging.

"Not necessarily. We'll do a sampling to see if a total dig is justified." Mark said something Buehl did not want to hear, and it reflected in his face. Mark added, "What I can tell you, is just from what we've found here, doing the three-week study of the property is indicated. I don't need to see more today. This definitely looks like it was an inhabited site. Now there is the probability that there are more sites scattered about the property. I'll get some aerial photos, and we can get good ideas of where to look."

Buehl looked concerned. "You aren't going to be tearing up my ranch all over, are you? Just around here?"

"I can't answer that until I do the survey." Mark shook his head. Then he asked Terrie and Jim, "We all agree we need to do the survey?"

The answer was a unanimous yes.

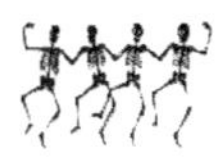

Chapter 7

There is a unique smell I associate with the storage room where we keep our field equipment. Trying to describe it is hard. It incorporates the smell of the earth we dig in, the odor of grass and weeds, a certain amount of mustiness, and a faint whiff of the WD-40 oil we use to care for some of our tools. I've come to connect it with the excitement of starting an excavation. The aroma surrounded me as I checked and prepared field kits for use.

Our equipment was spread over four large tables and the floor space around them. A table was dedicated to the tools required for each phase of the excavation. One table contained the equipment we'd require for surveying and preparing a site map. Spread out on it, were our theodolite, transit, rods, tapes, levels, and chains. A drafting board and some instruments were in a large rectangular plastic case.

Table two was stacked with innumerable clearing and excavating tools. There were spades, root cutters, machetes, axes, trowels, brushes, brooms, rakes, dental picks, and many others. On the floor surrounding that table were a portable generator, air compressor, wheelbarrows, hoses, and a pump. Piled next to the wheelbarrows were our screening boxes, ten of them with various sizes of mesh. Three pop-up tents gave the equipment and us relief from the elements. Water containers, coolers, folding chairs and tables, tarps, stoves, and a combination shower/potty room completed our camping equipment.

Equipment required to record our findings filled the third table. I'd placed our cameras—video and still, measuring tapes, rulers, graph paper, waterproof notebooks, I-pads, labels, and a dictating unit on it. Our GPR, Ground Penetrating Radar, units were pushed against that table.

The last collection of paraphernalia consisted of items we'd need to collect and preserve artifacts we might find. Included in this menagerie of items were plastic bags of all sizes and configurations, boxes, vials, plaster of Paris, various preservatives, chests and vats, and polyurethane.

I was busily engaged in listing anything that needed replacement or repair when Mark tapped me on the shoulder. He said, "Be sure to put some waterproof markers and pens on the list. I don't want to rely on ballpoint pens that won't write half the time."

"Okay." I scribbled them on my 'to purchase' list.

"What kind of shape is our equipment in?"

I nodded and smiled, "Good. Really, good. When do we start?"

"Humph!" I heard Mark exhale. "We're ready to go. I have all the aerial photos and maps we need. Terri Tall Pine has some information from some tribal elders that will help…it's typed and in our possession. Beth has a backhoe, a bobcat, and two trucks at our disposal to use as we wish.

Slave labor is lined up. Four of my students have volunteered. I have everything, but Carl Buehl's go-ahead to start."

"What's his problem?"

Mark shook his head. "He said he has to redistribute the cattle away from the area we're working in. That's bull-shit. I think he doesn't want to part with the ranch. I can understand that. The property has belonged to his family since right after the Civil War. Problem is, he only owns 40% of it now. Whether he likes it or not, chances are Dillon Development will own it soon."

"What do you think? Are we doing all this for nothing?"

"No. I spoke to Beth Dillon a little while ago. She said all three of his partners are going to put the pressure on him at a meeting tomorrow. Buehl told her he couldn't be there. Beth told his partners…Stanton Griggs called Buehl and told him if he didn't show, the other three would take a vote and go ahead anyway. She thinks we'll have a date tomorrow." Mark set his jaw. "I'm sure enough, I'm scheduling us to start next Monday. That's six days. We will be ready by then, and he should be."

"I bet I know how to get him to beg you to go ahead," I said. My comment also served as a hint that I wanted to see the aerial photography of the ranch.

"How's that?" I had Mark's full attention.

"Tell him you will be examining the aerials of his property in the time you're waiting for approval. Then say the more you look at them, the more different places you want to look." I smiled at Mark, and he returned it.

"That's a good strategy, Chessie. A little devious, but it has a high probability of success." Mark scribbled words on the notepad he always carried. His seriousness returned. "That's kind of true. I found four locations I want to visit from the photos, and Terri told me of two places the oldest members of the tribe told her had either small villages or individual families living on them."

"You going to check that out first?" I asked.

"Yes. I want to make these three weeks as meaningful as we can. I don't want to spend all my time in one place that ends up being a waste. Two spots on the aerial look promising. Both have strong indications humans have disturbed the area. Would you like a copy of the aerials to familiarize yourself with the land? I have three copies."

"Yeh, I would." My hint worked. It would give me something to do for the next few evenings. TV is so terrible. "How much time do you intend to spend on the prelim?"

"A couple days. If we find anything promising, I'll go over the area with our GPR. If there isn't anything significant in the sweeps we make at the different locations, we'll devote most of the time to those middens."

"You find out anything about the pottery we found out there?" I asked.

"Plenty. Everything we surmised was true. It's Navaho, not terribly old, and was probably originally stolen from a museum in Sante Fe, New Mexico, nine years ago. Something really is odd. When we tracked it down, we traced it to an anthropologist here in Indian River County. Guess what? He just reported that robbery in the last couple of weeks."

I thought for several seconds. "You want to make a bet?" I asked.

"On what?"

"I'll bet we find the bones from one arm and one leg somewhere out there on Buehl's property. And, *they won't belong to anything else we find there.*"

Dr. Mark Card looked at me, quizzically. He said, "What! Where does that come from?"

"Oh, I'm just good." I grinned. "Very, very, very good."

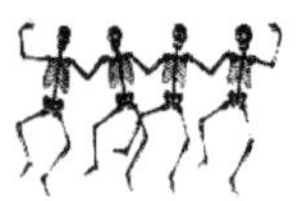

Chapter   8

My calculator's screen's green LEDs showed 326,880,000. That was square feet. I needed to divide that by 43,560 to determine the number of acres within the Buehl site. I entered the number and divided. My answer: 7,449. I did the last calculation in my head. Eleven and a half square miles, plus or minus a bit. "Holy shit, just riding that property to see what's there could take a week and a half." I returned my attention to the aerial photographs and the topographical map spread out on our dining room table. I'd been studying them and had taken measurements from the map to calculate the acreage.

"What are you *holy shitting* about?" Reading, my duplex mate and brother was looking over my shoulder.

"I was going over the photos and map of the Buehl place. It's a lot bigger than I thought." I looked up at him. Reading's eyes were focused on the documents. I said, "I never thanked you for telling me about the Buehl thing, thanks."

"Hey, you already did." Reading took his eyes off the map long enough to peer into mine while he said, "I'm taking Millie Lane out Friday."

"Good for both of you!" I hadn't told him about Millie's high school crush on him. Some things are best discovered, not relayed.

"Mind if I point out a few things to you? Remember that seminar I attended about using maps and photos to help solve cases? Let me show you a few things I learned. It might be helpful." He nodded toward a chair.

"Sure. Pull it up and park."

Reading eased into the chair and repositioned the largest of the photos in front of us. "You look for areas that have been cleared and have a different generation of growth covering them." He pointed to an area on the photo. "See how that spot is almost a perfect rectangle with another rectangle over it? I'd be willing to bet you'll find that was a ranch at one time, way back when." He perused the photo. "Here's another. This one is more likely what you're looking for. See the circular area here?" He pointed,

"Yes, I see exactly what you're talking about." Once you were aware of what to look for, traces of human activity were evident. I was learning a very useful skill that would be helpful in surveying sites. "It's like finding old trails and roads. You use a similar logic. If you find where people traveled, eventually, you find where they lived." I pointed to what had been a trail or road in the past that was now abandoned. My finger moved to a small round spot where the vegetation was greener, thicker. "This is some type of water source. A sink…maybe a spring. If you find naturally occurring water, there is a good chance you'll find that people have lived there at some time. See how close this spot is to where that cleared round area was?"

"Another thing they taught us is that you find graves primarily in high spots, very seldom in wet areas. Recent graves are often sunk areas and have nothing but weeds over them. Of course, you won't have any—" Reading stopped talking, and pointed to a spot on the aerial on a ridge close to a ranch road. "They look just like that."

I marked the spot with a red check.

"It probably is a dead cow. They bury them in the pastures where they die," Reading tried to downplay the potential gravesite. However, he didn't stop examining the photo. If anything, he intensified his focus. My brother's increased interest was something to take note. His nose for any type of shady or criminal activity was bloodhound sharp. I saw his eyes stop on a couple of more areas.

As he turned to leave, I asked, "Okay, are you going to make me ask?"

"No. I see three other areas that look like they'd be worth either you or Mark making a visit." He pointed to them one after the other. I marked each one before I let him move his finger. At the last place he pointed, he tapped the photo emphatically. "This one here." Reading rubbed the tip of his finger over it. "This one interests me. The shape is the size you'd dig if you buried a human body. Check the location. It's close to that tractor trail that connects to the county road. It isn't far off of the road, but it's located with that cypress head between the ruts and whatever is buried.

No one could see…well, I'm a cop, and that's the way I think."

"We're taking our GPR units with us. I could run the radar over it for you. Want me to do that?" He nodded while still staring at the map. I decided to needle him a bit. "A…Reading, you are supposed to say, why that would be very kind of you, Chessie. You are the best sister ever. The next time I invite you for a free lunch, I'll actually pay for it."

"Want a beer or a soft drink? I'm headed to the fridge," Reading said. He showed no sign he'd heard my zinger. He wandered toward the kitchen.

I sighed, "A Pepsi."

I scanned the map looking for more locations that deserved scrutiny. The landline phone rang. And rang. And rang. I yelled at Reading, "Answer that damned thing! I'm busy."

Reading's mumbling was followed by him yelling, "Hey Chessie, it's for you…I think."

Snorting in disgust, I got up from the table, stomped into the kitchen, and snatched the handset out of Reading's hand. He had a weird smile on his face.

"Hello," I demanded.

The phone was silent. I looked at the screen and read the numbers. It was a local call. I repeated, "Hello." No one spoke. I hung up and asked, "Did you recognize the voice, Reading?"

"No. It was a woman's voice. But I'm sure it wasn't one of your friends." He shook his head. "You dating somebody's boyfriend or husband?"

"No! Why?"

"The lady's choice of language indicated she doesn't much like you." Reading wasn't smiling.

"So, what did she say?"

Reading grimaced before he said, "She asked me if my slimy cunt sister was around. She said more, but that gives you the flavor." He waved a slip of paper. "I wrote down her phone, and I'll check it out."

The phone rang again. It was the same number. I picked it up and answered angrily, "Hello, asshole!"

The laugh was distinctive but was one I wasn't familiar with. When it stopped the woman said, "Don't go desecrating all the graves on the ranch of those who rest there. The ghosts of the old ones and the new ones will haunt you forever. I will put a curse on you. You will wish you were dead." There was a click, and the line went silent. I hung up.

"You have any idea who that was?" Reading asked.

"Not really." I thought for a few seconds. "The only person I can think it might be is that nut, Billie Mulhee. It sounded like an older woman, and she has a trash mouth on her. If it was Mulhee, she disguised her voice well." After reflecting a few more seconds, I said, "No, I don't think it's her. It just wasn't right."

"Did she make a death threat?" Reading asked.

"No. She just said she'd make me feel like I wanted to be dead."

Chapter 9

The stack of artifacts to be documented and stored didn't seem to get any smaller. One of our student interns just delivered another computer printout. That meant another load of bone fragments, pottery shards, chert, etc. would soon find its way to my desk. I took a deep breath, mumbled, and prayed that Dr. Card would get the phone call allowing us to proceed with the Buehl Ranch survey.

I looked at the pile of paper, the stacks of plastic bags, bottles, and small plastic containers. It was endless. The biggest problem associated with our field trip; it was sure to deepen those very stacks and piles. My mind rebelled, so I let it wander.

How could something so simple become contentious? If I had known it would spur arguments and discord, I'd have thought twice about getting Mark and I involved. I looked for someone to blame besides myself. How could those involved become so incensed? It wasn't like we wanted to stop the development. The piece of property was huge. Anything of archaeological value would only occupy a minute portion of the land. Why would people who wanted to protect what might be there be more opposed to our survey than the developers? Nothing made sense.

I shook my head. It was symptomatic of our every-day culture. There were no moderate viewpoints. Battle lines were drawn on everything. People in our society were happier in a confrontational mode, willing to fight over everything, large or small, to get their way. Common sense and compromise had died. It seemed many individuals would prefer to accomplish nothing rather than concede anything to those with an opposing viewpoint. Worse, many of the "generals" leading these battalions of discontent were hypocrites of the highest order.

My mind selected Beatrice "Billie" Mulhee as my prime example. The woman dressed and acted like a flower child from San Francisco's Haight-Asbury district, transported to today from the 1960s. She represented environmental and woman's causes from the needed and legitimate, to the far-out and obscene. An example was two organizations she was heavily involved in: Florida Wetlands Preservation Association and EEL, or Eliminate Electric from our Living. One fought to preserve nature, the other to return man to the stone-age. Her law firm was the leader in procuring grants from governmental agencies. That firm's sister group represented mining operations, off-shore drilling, and firms importing illegal exotic animals. She'd been a professor at a liberal college before becoming a lawyer. She proudly proclaimed that's where she learned her 'right thinking.' Billie flew on corporate jets, owned a silent partner's interest in a series of motels and bars suspected of having involvement in the lucrative human trafficking trade, and lived in a 2.5 million dollar home on the beach, built on a sensitive turtle nesting ground.

"It's a go," Mark Card sounded relieved, but there was some reservation in his tone.

"Great, Mark. Do we start Monday?"

He nodded, "I'll talk to Beth Dillon about having the equipment there to meet us." He opened his mouth as though to speak, but nothing came out.

"Yes?" I prompted.

"I was wondering. Did you get any strange calls last night or this morning?" I read concern in his countenance. I wondered.

"If by strange, you mean someone who called and threatened me to stay away from the Buehl ranch, yes, I did."

Mark's face became angry. "A death threat?"

I shook my head. "Not a death threat. She just told me I'd wish I was dead."

"Yours was a woman, too?"

I nodded.

"I didn't recognize her voice or the phone number. Probably should have written it down." Mark smacked his palm on my desk in a rare display of anger. "People can be such assholes. Could Reading have traced the number if I'd gotten it?"

"Yes," I said. "He was at home when my call came in. He got the number and traced it."

"And?"

"It came from a payphone in the Ft. Pierce airport." I held my hands out, palms up. "Dead end."

"That's truly a dead end," Mark chuckled, "I thought pay phones were dead."

The word 'dead' triggered an idea. Maybe… I spoke as I thought. "Mark, Reading looked at the aerial and saw some things that he said might be graves. It occurs to me that the real reason someone doesn't want us poking around on the Buehl land isn't because of archaeological items we'd disturb or the development. We could find something else they don't want us to." I hesitated. "Reading asked me to run the GPR units over a couple spots."

He sighed and said, "The same thought occurred to me. I have a military friend who was in graves registration looking at the photo. He was an expert at locating undocumented battlefield graves."

Chapter 10

"That's what the slaves are for," Mark was grinning.

I watched the three girls and two boys unloading equipment from a rented box truck and stashing it on four-wheel-drive trucks provided by Dalton Development. A few years before, I'd been one of the 'slaves' in Dr. Card's cadre of site volunteers. The thought occurred to me, I should have sympathy for them or at least feel some guilt for idly watching them sweat and labor. I didn't. Not one bit. What they'd learn while digging in the dirt, with Mark Card as their mentor, was indescribably valuable. Only part of it was the archaeological knowledge they'd acquire. Devotion to planning, meticulous attention to detail, the use of critical thinking, human relations savvy, and learning the value of patience were skills they'd absorb without being aware of their "education." These skills were passed to his field assistants as he tutored by action as well as word.

"Bobby, when you're loading that truck, think about what you'll need first when we unload at the dig location. You don't want to handle stuff twice, right?" Mark suggested.

A big blonde fellow with biceps that fought with his shirt sleeves for maneuvering room grinned. He looked like a cast member from a Bergman directed 1950's movie.

"Gottcha, chief!" he answered and barked orders at the other four students. They grumbled but complied.

I asked, "Hey Mark, why can't we drive out to the middens? Looks to me you have an overseer who knows what you want."

"You are a digger!" Mark shook his head. "You'll have to be patient. My instructions are to wait here for Buehl's foreman. He's our chaperone here on the property. Beth Dillon told me that was the only way Buehl would allow us to go ahead immediately. She said the meeting they had got hot. She thought Griggs and Buehl were five words away from swinging at each other. Jim McMillan suggested Carson accompany us to calm Buehl down. The old man has it in his mind we're going to make his ranch into a strip mine. That's BS and I believe Buehl knows it."

"What's his real problem?" I asked.

Mark shrugged his shoulders. "The grave thing? I don't think so. Carl isn't the type to go around snuffing people out. I haven't the slightest…on specifics. My guess is there's something he doesn't want us to find."

"You have an idea as to what that might be?" I was still thinking of a body.

"Yes, I do. Carl Buehl's family has run a slaughterhouse and meatpacking operation here for years. Over thirty, I'm sure of that. My guess is that he has some dumpsites out here. What's in them? Hazardous materials? Who knows? Could be a lot of things." He pointed behind me at a "Gator" ATV bouncing through the field of palmettoes and pines. "Wilbur Carson has been foreman here forever. He'd know where stuff was dumped and where to keep us away from."

There was a second person seated next to Carson. As they came closer, I recognized the man under the gray Stetson sitting next to Wilbur. It was Carl Buehl. They drove straight at Mark's Jeep, where he and I sat. Wilbur smiled as they got close. Carl didn't.

"Hey, folks." Carson nodded as he parked the ATV ten feet from the Jeep. "You got a good day to start. It ain't so damned hot."

"We got a break. Good morning and thanks for meeting us here," Mark was in his ultra-friendly mode.

Carson said, "No problem."

Buehl nodded a stone-faced response to Mark's overture. When he spoke, it was to half-ask, half-demand a "favor." He said, "I need the Gator, so I would like it if Wilbur can ride with ya'll today. My wife borrowed my four-wheeler. She's overdue comin' back to the house. I'm afraid she's got herself stuck or the truck is broke down out here some where's."

Mark's smile continued, "Sure. We'll bring him back to the ranch house at the end of the day."

"Thank you, Dr. Card." Wilbur Carson got out of the ATV, removed a backpack and shotgun from the vehicle, and asked, "Can I climb in the back of your Jeep with you folks?"

"Sure," Mark repeated.

"I'll see you, folks, later," Buehl said. He wheeled the ATV around and headed back toward the ranch house.

Carson stowed his gear and gun in the Jeep's rear, but hesitated before he climbed in. He said, "You two ever meet Mrs. Buehl?"

We answered, "No," together.

Wilbur tilted his head to one side, hesitated as he carefully considered his words before saying, "Mrs. Laurie is a kind of special person. She's different. Mr. Buehl is real protective of her. She had some problems back a few years. Alcohol, mostly. He tries to keep her close. Mrs. Buehl ain't normally here at the ranch. Most times, she stays at their home on the beach. Just be patient if she happens along. She does some things some folks think are strange." Wilbur stopped speaking abruptly, his face indicating he believed he'd said too much.

I couldn't resist, "Like, what kind of strange things?"

Wilbur inhaled and exhaled, hard. "Well, she doesn't much like wearin' clothes. Takes 'em off if it suites her."

"Are we likely to bump into her out here?" Mark asked.

"No, Doc, not likely. Carl's huntin' her now." Wilbur didn't sound sure of that.

Chapter 11

While Mark supervised setting up the dig camp, I walked the middens and the surrounding ground. It didn't take long to find evidence that the mounds had suffered extensive disturbance. Ranch roads passed nearby, and several ruts led to the middens where people visited frequently enough to make the tracks. I carried a topo map and the aerial photo for the area. 'Pot holes' were dug in the three largest mounds; not a few…many. Comparing what I observed to the topo map and the aerials disclosed, four of the five earthworks were accurately pictured. One was noticeably smaller. It appeared to have had half of the structure removed. I made notes of what I saw. The five structures were evenly spaced around a center point with one glaring exception. It appeared that a sixth midden was missing from the circle the other five formed. Had it been removed or never built? It was a question worth investigating.

I noticed the lake covered more area in the photo than its current size. That was typical of the small lakes that dotted the flatlands grassy plains whose size varied dramatically. The map showed its depth to be seven feet, a moderately deep lake for the area. Most varied with the season, many becoming shallow marshes or completely dry in the winter. It was when I checked the map to see the lake's depth that a subtle landscape feature caught my attention. A low ridge of land extended from the line of oaks to the point the 'missing' midden should have been. It was almost a straight line, something nature abhors.

The more I looked at the six-foot-wide rise of land the more man-made it looked. It was close to being a uniform two feet higher than its surroundings. Land the middens were located on was also higher than the ground around them. The topo said three feet. When I grasped the possibility, I became excited. Was it a possibility that what I was looking at was a causeway? One that had been built through a marsh to mounds that housed a village and provided a defensive fortification? I climbed the highest of the mounds to get a more panoramic look.

The view certainly supported my theory. In addition, a depression, again in what was close to being a straight line, led from the lake to the outer circumference created by the midden circle. Was it a shallow canal used by the village's inhabitants to pull their dugout canoes close to their homes for safe-keeping?

I felt, rather than saw, someone, staring at me. Instinctively, my head swiveled. Wilbur Carson stood at the edge of one of the mounds. His lecherous half-grin was a look I'd seen many times before. He was mentally paring away my clothes. Having an ample full figure had its disadvantages as well as its perks. I waved to him and motioned for him to come to me. Maybe he would know something about the landscape features that had piqued my interest.

He was spry for a man I judged to have left sixty behind. His eyes wandered unabashedly from my eyes, to my butt, to my boobs. Carson's smile left little doubt about what was in his mind. My face must have disclosed my feeling of discomfort and disgust. His first words were, "Y'all can't blame a man for window shoppin.' I don't mean nothin' bad by it." They were accompanied by an even broader smile.

"As long as you realize the merchandise isn't for handling or for sale, we'll get along," I cautioned.

"Yes, Ma'am." Wilbur's smile remained.

"How long have you worked here, Wilbur?"

Carson averted his eyes upward as he did a mental count. "About forty-seven years. This was the first place I worked after I quit high school."

I asked, "Is this place the same as it was when you started here?"

"No." The smile disappeared.

"What's changed?"

"You know. I saw you a-lookin' at those maps and at that there mound." He pointed at the one where half the soil was missing. "About ten years ago we brought a backhoe in here and loaded some dirt to make an abutment for a bridge."

"Were you the one that did the work?" I asked.

Carson tilted his head to the side and said, "I was there."

"Did you find anything unusual in the earth you removed?"

"Like bones and such? Yes. When we started to find them, we quit diggin' here." His half-smile returned.

I asked, "Did you report what you found to anyone?"

He shrugged his shoulders, "You'll have to bring that up with Mr. Buehl."

It was obvious I wouldn't get any more info on the half-destroyed midden from Wilbur, so I tried another avenue. "Did you build up that land between these mounds and that oak ridge?" I pointed at the area I thought might be a causeway.

"No, Ma'am, it's been that-a-way since I started work here."

Wilbur Carson was a lean, sinewy man of six-feet that looked as hard as the lighter-knots that were scattered all over the ranch. His sunken cheeks, prominent nose, pale blue eyes, and thick brows were a face reproduced from a Civil War portrait taken by Mathew Brady. He smiled at me and said, "Miss Chessie, I'm not one for volunteerin' much, but if'n you ask a question, I'll answer, honest. *Real honest.*"

Carson was telling me something, but I didn't know what it was. I was about to ask him a test question, when Mark shouted at us to come to where he was fiddling with surveying equipment. As I started down the slope of the mound, I heard Carson say softly, but purposefully loud enough for me to hear, "There was a day."

Chapter   12

The meticulous process of surveying the dig site was finished. Dr. Mark Card was a stickler for controlling every facet of an excavation. A carefully processed map of the terrain broken into two-meter squares, each identified with an alpha-numeric identification, was complete. Mark wasn't satisfied. He felt limiting exploratory study to obvious and conspicuous locations on Buehl's ranch was reducing the site's potential drastically. He managed to convince the people paying the bills to allow him to do a little random sample within the area marked for initial development. As he put it, "The sampling is mighty— mighty random and mighty small." Mark wasn't happy, but it was all he could get. The primary site would be the middens we had surveyed, but Mark was determined to do some investigation of other spots that held promise.

What had been the primary use of the mounds? Were they the site of an inhabited village? Were they used as a ceremonial center? Were they used as burial locations? Dr. Card's best guess was they were part of the structure of a village. Pushing GPR units around the area to make a cursory check, didn't disclose any skeletons, but did show many areas where fires had been built, and all kinds of animal bones and pottery fragments lit the radar's screen.

Mark picked two areas of interest. We would begin digging the next morning.

Mark said, "Chessie, you'll have Nick and Lindy working for you. I'll have Bobby and Sheila working with me. Albie will supervise screening and control of the backfill. She has six more from my classes to help her move dirt, etc." He scanned his newly finished map. "You do Buehl-8-NW/SE. I'm going to do Buehl-12-SE/NW." Those were designations for two areas that were each two meters square.

My location was near the center of the circle formed by the middens. If Dr. Card was correct in his calculation that the site was inhabited, I'd find lots of evidence of village life. Among the things I believed I'd find would be pottery shards, animal bones, evidence of cooking fires, remains of tools, and other necessities of life 500 hundred to a thousand years ago. Again, if Mark's surmise was right, he'd find remains of weapons, a sparse smattering of artifacts of all varieties, but certainly not bones. Burial sites seldom were utilized as living space.

"We starting now?" I asked.

He nodded, "Get your site book, gather up the slaves, and start digging."

~ ~ ~ ~ ~ ~

I made the entry in my log:

Site designation: Buehl-8-NW/SE

Recording technician: Chessie Partin

Date & Time: Wednesday, October 14, 2017, 4:32 PM

Weather: Sunny, some clouds, high-humidity

Crew: Chessie, Nick, Lindy

Beginning level: Surface, to down 5 CM designated level 1.

Bag Numbers: 8NW/SE1L1 through 11, NW/SE9L1 through 7. No significant finds.

Comments: Area NW/SE9L1 has had soil deposited in the area in the modern era (reported as 1997-1998). Overburden is sandy, with items expected to be found in soil removed from water-covered areas. Bags 3 and 7 preliminarily ID as rusted fishhooks.

Visitor: Wilbur Carson – on-site 11:38 AM until 3:12 PM. Confirmed soil removed from lake was dumped in the location NW/SE9L1. Estimated depth "10 to 12 inches." Dr. Card confirms overburden to be removed using full archaeological controls.

I sighed. We'd be doing a lot of work that would be of marginal value.

"Don't be discouraged. You're going through the soil from the lake to see if there were any artifacts transferred from there." Mark read my face and body language correctly.

I shrugged my shoulders and asked, "Did you find anything this afternoon?"

"Yes, and it disturbs me," Mark shook his head. "We could be being used, I'm afraid."

"How's that?" I asked.

Mark folded his arms in front of him. "I chose that spot to start, because I was suspicious of it. The ground appeared to be disturbed recently. The spot I started is immediately adjacent to it." He paused and tilted his head before continuing. "Chessie, someone's been digging there in the last week or two. At least, since the last heavy rain we've had. The ground around it is packed. The disturbed area is powder. Either something has been removed or something planted. I'm leaning toward the latter."

I followed Mark's line of reasoning. "Somebody wants us to make a find and stop the development. Sounds reasonable, but why? And, who?"

"The 'why' has obvious choices; the 'who,' not so much." He took a deep breath. "People like Billie Mulhee and her crowd are opposed to just driving over wildlands, so imagine how they feel about building on it. Billie is obviously a suspect, maybe too obvious. I know her. She's too smart to do something like that. The woman is familiar with what we do and knows we'd recognize a plant. That leaves a whole universe of potential suspects." Mark pointed in the direction of the Buehl ranch house. "Carl Buehl and his people don't want to give this place up, that's obvious. I'm sure when he took on partners, he never thought he'd end up getting the place sold out from under him. A lot of the local people sympathize with him. Again, I don't think Buehl is dumb enough to try planting something."

"Where does that leave us?"

"Chessie, in the middle of legal squabble, I'm afraid."

Chapter   13

The dew rag I had tied around my hair did little to impede the rivulets of perspiration from finding my eyes. The red cotton had reached saturation an hour ago, and it still was an hour to lunch. I was on my knees, bent over low, examining the layering on the perpendicular edge of my site, using a trowel to remove more dirt.

I heard footsteps other than Nick's sliding plod, or Lindy's light tennis shoe whisper on the ground. Someone was standing behind me. Tucking my head down under my arm, I saw Wilbur Carson. He was leering at my rear that stuck up in the air. It was clear what he was thinking. I asked as coldly as I could, "What do you want?"

"My wife wouldn't allow me to have it," he chuckled as he talked.

I straightened up, and duck walked on my knees so I could turn and face him. "You a member of the dirty old man's club?" I wanted to zing him.

"Yep. A charter member." The zing rebounded.

"Touche! Let me rephrase and be specific. What information can I provide you on what I'm doing?" I was slightly pissed and didn't care if he was aware that I was.

"Whoa! Let's us start over. I wasn't tryin' to hit on you. Maybe a little adult humor. The smart-ass in me doesn't always come across good."

"I agree about the smart-ass, but the humor is more junior high than adult." My response was caustic, but I'd cooled considerably.

Carson looked sorry. He said, "Didn't mean to offend you, Miss Chessie, what about we start over?"

I stared at him, trying to decide if I wanted to keep him on the defensive. He looked miserable enough to let him off the hook. "Let's try a truce. You keep your eyes up and your comments about my person to yourself. I'll stop being a mean, nasty bitch."

"Agreed." Wilbur was relieved. He changed the subject, keeping his eyes so averted it almost made me laugh. "Did you find anything today?"

"The skeleton of what looks to be duck, a plastic fishing float, and several freshwater mussel shells." I put my hands on my hips and smiled, acknowledging I was willing to forgive his comments. I'd over-reacted but wasn't going to back off or apologize.

"People used to fish in here regular. There were loads of bass and blue-bream in the lake. One old boy that fished back here screwed it up for everyone." Wilbur grimaced and shuffled his feet. "He stole a cow and got away with it. Stole a second one and got caught. Carl hasn't let anybody fish or hunt on his property since. Least, that he don't know real good."

"Did the folks that fished here dig that little cut from the lake to the mounds to put their boats in?" I asked.

"No. Carl never let people bring boats in here. That ain't sayin' there wasn't lots of folks that came down to the lake. Some neighbors did their picnics here. Teenagers used to park up under the oaks." Wilbur motioned to the tree-lined ridge. "I reckon you might find most anything 'round this lake." He shook his head. "Not much a what you'd be lookin' for."

"What do you think would be?"

"Indian stuff. Dinosaurs. That kind of shit."

"You think we'll find anything like that?" I asked.

Wilbur scrunched up his face. "Here? Don't think so. Not unless there's somethin' deep in those mounds. People been scratching in the dirt in this place for close to a hundred years." His face became completely serious, and I noted a tinge of apprehension. "They's things to find. Not here." His eyes glanced around nervously. "You ever done somethin' you didn't think was bad at the time, but sticks in your brain like a sandspur? I have."

He had my full attention. "Is there something you want to show me or tell me about?"

"I'm thinkin' on it."

"Does it have to do with Indian artifacts or something else?" I asked.

Carson didn't answer.

"Is this something you know about or something you did?" The inference of my question was plain. I didn't expect an answer, but got a quick one.

"I know about it and wish I didn't."

"Tell me what—"

He pointed at Rick and Lindy returning with the wheelbarrow for another load of dirt to screen. "I'll sleep on it overnight and tell you in the mornin'…if'n I decide to. Meet me at the gate tomorrow at 6:30. I'll unlock it, so if'n I gotta do something, you won't have to park in the road. I'll either tell you or not tomorrow."

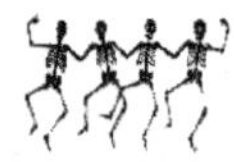

Chapter   14

It was still dark. I turned on the cab light in my truck and checked the time. The dash clock said, 6:47. I was perplexed. Wilbur had been to the gate to unlock it. When I showed up at twenty after six, the padlock was open dangling at the end of the chain securing the gate. When I got out of my truck to open it, I thought I saw fresh tracks from Wilbur's ATV. I'd closed the gate, and sat waiting for Wilbur's return. The rest of the crew would be arriving soon, and the secrecy he sought would be gone.

Headlights on the road appeared at the same time gray, and a hint of pink began showing in the eastern sky. It was a few minutes before seven. The lights were from a pickup driven by Rick. Six of our college student work crew was jammed in it.

After opening and pulling through the gate, Rick asked, "Hi Miss Partin. Is anyone down at the dig?"

"I don't know. Wilbur Carson, maybe. I think he unlocked the gate," I answered.

"Can we drive back there and start getting things ready?" Rick was always a willing worker.

"Sure. If you see Mr. Carson, would you tell him I'm at the gate? He was supposed to meet me here."

Rick nodded, said, "Yes," and drove away…the truck's springs protesting every pothole and washboard in the road.

Ten minutes later, Mark's Jeep separated the dawn mists in the morning's dim light. Carson wasn't going to show up. He'd decided not to tell me I supposed. I opened the gate for Mark, returned to my truck, and followed him to the dig.

~ ~ ~ ~ ~ ~

Mark and I were munching lunch in the shade of a huge oak. The tooting of the truck horn from the vehicle we'd sent Bobby to refill the water supply tank, interrupted our relaxed conversation. He drove straight up to us. Bobby quickly jumped from the truck, raced around to the passenger side, and pulled a limp Sheila from the front seat. He screamed, "Come help me!"

"What happened?" Mark yelled as we scrambled to our feet and hurried to the girl who Bobby laid on the ground. She was out…cold.

"She fainted when we found him,"

"Found who?" Mark asked.

"That Carson guy…the ranch foreman. He's dead. His body is all hacked up!" Bobby was clearly shaken to the point of panic.

"Where?" Mark was searching his pockets for his Jeep keys.

"Back up the road about two-thirds of the way to the gate. Off of the road fifty yards to the right. He's lying in a patch of palmetto." Bobby's eyes were wild. He sucked in a breath. "There's a whole flock of buzzards circling over him. We noticed them and went to investigate. That's how we found him."

~ ~ ~ ~ ~ ~ ~

Seven black harbingers of death circled the earth in lazy, graceful flight. I could see Bobby's truck tracks that had crushed weeds and palmettoes where curiosity had spurred their discovery. Mark followed the path through the freshly disturbed vegetation. One at a time, three vultures took flight as we approached. We were thirty feet away when I first saw the burnt orange color of the shirt he wore through a veil of palmetto fronds.

Mark stopped the Jeep abruptly. "Stay here until I have a look," Mark said.

"Fat chance of that happening." My feet were on the ground before his.

He shook his head and grumbled, "I pity the man who marries you. Getting you to cooperate is like asking a road to change direction." He waved his hand toward his rear. "Follow me, …understand."

I nodded and traced his footsteps. "You thinking of asking?" I tossed a barb at him.

"To marry you? I considered it a time or two." He stopped like he'd walked into a wall. "Oh, God. You don't want to look at this."

Though it was intended to deter me, Mark's words were a challenge, an invitation to see what lay in the bushes. I stepped around him. Visions of Afghanistan returned. Wilbur Carson's body was face up, suspended off of the ground by a thick cover of palmettoes. The first thing visible was the large number of deep wounds inflicted by what was probably an ax or hatchet. I counted twelve in his chest and face and quit. For all the damage done to the body, I was surprised there wasn't more blood. Only small streaks colored his shirt and jeans. One prominent stream ended in his open vacant eyes. I traced it to its origin; a small, neat, round hole in his forehead. He'd been shot to death before his body was savaged. I spoke what I thought, "There was no need for this!"

Mark was fumbling for his cell phone. I stopped him, saying, "Let me make the call."

He nodded. My brother would be among the first to be involved anyway. I tapped his number stored in my cell phone files.

He answered, sounding harried and out of sorts, "Hey, Chessie. I'm kind of busy right now. Unless it's real important, can I give you a call back?"

"It's important. Some kids on our dig team found a body that was killed last night or this morning," I explained.

Reading whistled in his phone's mic. "How do you know he was killed so recently?"

"I was talking to him yesterday afternoon. Someone killed Wilbur Carson, Buehl's foreman."

There were a few seconds of quiet as the shock cleared. Reading said, "I've known old Wilbur for fifteen years. He's a nice guy. Who'd want to kill him?"

Mark leaned over my shoulder from the position where he had been listening and said, "Someone didn't like him. His body has been hacked up like someone was taking out their anger on him."

"That you. Mark?" Reading asked.

"Yes. Before you ask, we're on that ranch trail that goes back to the middens. I'll meet your people at the gate on the county road to Buehl's place." Mark leaned away from me.

"I'll be coming too. You still there, Chessie?" Reading asked.

"Uh-huh."

"Take charge of the murder site until I get there. Stay put. Don't let anyone within twenty feet of the body." He hesitated then asked, "Did either of you see, hear, or know anything?"

Mark quickly volunteered, "No."

I hesitated, bit my lip, then confessed, "Uh-huh. I might be the reason he's dead."

Simultaneously, both Reading and Mark exclaimed, "What!"

I sighed. "Just get out here. I'll tell you about it then."

Reading disconnected before I finished my words.

"What in the hell is this about!" Mark had become his angry Dr. Card persona.

"Not now, Mark. I'll go through the whole thing when Reading gets here." I wiped my forehead and returned the glare he was directing at me. "Don't you think you should check on Sheila and Bobby before you go to meet the sheriff's people?"

"Haven't got time. Reading will have one of his cars here, that's in this area, in ten minutes or less." Mark got back into the Jeep. "You do what your brother said. But, you be damned careful. Come here" He opened the glove compartment, removed a revolver, and handed it to me as I approached him. "We have no idea who did this or if they're still around. Put two in their chest and one in their head if they come back and threaten you."

He drove off at a faster than safe speed. I'd be on Dr. Card's shit list until I explained the situation and begged forgiveness from Mark.

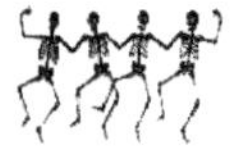

Chapter   15

"Holy, shit!" Reading got his first look at Wilbur Carson's corpse. He shook his head. His face reflected the furious anger he felt inside. I found out he knew the man well. The rest of us stood away from the body as we'd been told. Reading circled the corpse, being exceedingly careful where he placed his feet.

A knot of spectators had gathered. That included most of our team from the dig site, five deputies, detective Bob Wallace, and three ranch hands. Lashann Hargrove…a recently hired criminologist from Appalachian State, and his assistant, were busy cordoning off the scene with bright yellow tape. Reading stopped several times to snap pictures using his cell phone.

When he completed his initial examination, he retraced his steps to us. He said, "Okay, Lashann, it's all yours." Hargrove nodded, motioned for his assistant to bring his crime scene case, and carefully approached Carson's body. "Is everybody here that initially saw Carson?" Reading asked.

"No," Mark answered. "Sheila is back at the dig."

"Who all saw it before we were called?"

Mark pointed to Bobby and said, "This man here, then your sister, and me."

"Bobby, you were the first to see Carson?"

"No, sir. Actually, Sheila was. She got out of the truck and ran over to him before I did. We thought it was a dead cow or a hog."

"Where did you park your truck?" Reading asked.

"There." Bobby pointed to a spot that was fifty feet closer to the ranch lane than the corpse.

My brother nodded to Bobby. "I want you to go to where you parked your truck, walk the same way you did to get to the body, and stop where you did when you first saw it. Watch the ground. Don't disturb footprints." He turned to Detective Wallace and said, "You know the drill, Bob."

Wallace grunted and followed behind Bobby marking each step with a thin rod with a flag attached to it.

When Bobby stopped and pointed to where he'd picked up Sheila, "That's where my friend feinted."

Reading said, "Lashann, see where he pointed?"

"Got it, boss."

"Anything else you need before I haul these folks away?"

"No."

Reading said, "Keep everybody away from the crime scene. Keep them *far* away. That includes Carl Buehl, the man that owns this place. I expect he'll show up any minute. Send him back to where the dig is. I'll be there for a preliminary question session."

Hargrove pointed to the ranch lane. "I'd guess you can tell him yourself."

A pickup truck approached at a high rate of speed. When it was close enough, I could see the printing and logo on the truck's door identifying it as belonging to Buehl Ranch. A tearful Carl Buehl sat in the truck after it came to a stop. He opened the door but stayed seated when Reading ordered him to do so. The whole group, except the forensic people, was soon riding the ruts back to the middens.

~ ~ ~ ~ ~ ~

"That's all I can tell you, Captain Partin. I was watching for snakes when I was walking. When I stopped and looked up, I saw the body and all the wounds. I don't really remember anything after that until I was back at the dig camp."

Reading looked at the girl's terrified eyes. She didn't have anything to tell. "Okay, Sheila, no one should have to see what you did. Just one thing, if you do remember anything at all you haven't told me, I want you to let me know."

The frightened girl nodded vigorously, "Yes sir, Captain Partin."

"Just call me Reading, Sheila."

"Yes, sir."

Reading turned to me. I was the last one to be interrogated. He used my full name to emphasize his neutrality in the interview. "For the record, your proper name is Chesapeake E. Partin, correct?"

"Yes." It was hard for me to keep a straight face, but I managed to restrain the smile that fought to form.

Reading wrote down all answers. His chin rose as he finished his notes. "Miss Partin. Were you with Dr. Card when he viewed the body for the first time?"

"Yes."

"Did you view the body at approximately the same time?"

"I would say we saw it simultaneously."

"In order to save time, did you observe anything that you would describe differently than that Dr. Card described when he answered my questions?" I wondered why we had all been able to hear each other answer my brother's inquiries. I had my answer. We weren't suspects and could be questioned in more detail at the sheriff's office later. Reading wanted a complete statement of the facts so soon as possible after his witness' experience.

"No, not really," I said.

"Not really? What was different?" Reading was like a shark following a blood trail at the slightest hint of inconsistency.

I frowned at him. "Not a damned thing. It was just my way of putting it. Just, semantics."

"Semantics mean a lot in a murder investigation, Chessie." Reading gave me one of his cold stares until he decided I was telling him the truth. Finally, he said, "Alright. I want Dr. Card and Miss Partin to stay, the rest of you can go about your business."

He remained silent until the rest of the witnesses were out of hearing. Then Reading asked me, "What's this about you being the cause of Carson's murder?"

I took a deep breath. Reading was staring at me intensely. Mark was frowning. "I'll be as brief as possible. Wilbur and I were talking about some things. I asked him what he thought we might find in the middens. He said not much where we were. Then he hinted he knew some stuff about the property. I could tell it was heavy-duty by the way he was acting. He wouldn't tell me then…he said he had to sleep on it…he told me he'd meet me at the gate early this morning if he decided to speak. I got here at 6:20. The gate was closed but unlocked. There were fresh ATV tracks on both sides of the gate. I figured he showed, but got cold feet and left. My guess is he asked advice from someone he shouldn't." I turned to Mark and addressed what I knew he was upset about. "I really thought it wasn't something *that* big. Maybe a chemical dumpsite. Besides, the last thing I'd thought he'd do was tell someone else what he intended to tell me. I didn't think it was something that would put him, me or anyone else in danger."

Reading asked, "Did he give you any idea what he might tell you?"

"No, just that it was about something he'd seen or knew about that he wished he hadn't."

Reading rubbed his chin for several seconds as he thought about what I'd just told him. Finally, he said, "What you just outlined…I don't want anyone knowing that. You both have to keep that info locked…no double-locked inside."

~ ~ ~ ~ ~ ~

I watched Reading question Carl Buehl from a distance. One enforced by my brother's deputies. The man was obviously distraught. His head shakes and nods were vigorous, but his slumped shoulders and other body language reflected his grief and despair. After an intense fifteen minutes, Buehl half-stumbled to his truck and disappeared behind the oaks that hid the ranch road from my view. I knew better than to ask anything about Reading's interview with the rancher. That would have to wait until later, and under just the right circumstance.

Reading waved to both Mark and me to come. He pointed at a couple of our camping chairs and said, "Have a seat."

Mark asked, "Is this going to affect our survey? Will you have to shut us down?"

"No, but I'll have to have you clear out until Hargrove is satisfied he's collected all the evidence. He's getting the body removed now. You might be able to get back tomorrow, but I'd count on the day after." Reading jerked his thumb toward the county road. "I'll have at least two deputies posted at the gate to chase off curiosity seekers and news-people. You have to keep the gate locked at all times. The only folks that have access to this part of the ranch are your archaeological team members and Carl

Buehl and his ranch staff. I've told Carl that, and he'll give you a list of who can be here."

"Do you think this is because of Beth Dillon's company wanting to develop this land?" I asked.

Reading shook his head. "I don't know." He sighed. "What I'm pretty sure of is there's something on this land someone is desperate to keep from being found. They've killed to keep that from happening. One of the reasons Carson *could* have been murdered is the killer was afraid what Carson would tell, or has told you, Chessie…what's out here, somewhere. He could reason you told Dr. Card. You both could be targets. That's why I've decided to keep a couple deputies at the dig while you're here."

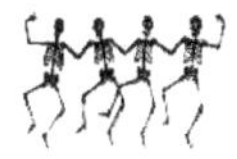

Chapter   16

"What did Lashann find?" I asked. Reading ignored me. He never took his eyes off the chicken-parm that he was inhaling. We sat in our kitchen, our normal "conference room."

"Don't give me that bull-crap that you can't tell me anything because of policy," I said as I finished my second glass of cabernet.

Slowly, Reading put his fork down. His eyes bored into my pupils, and I knew I'd stirred the mud puddle too hard. He lifted one eyebrow, never a good sign. "Well, if I knew anything, I couldn't tell you because the policies you call bull-crap wouldn't allow me. I thought you'd have understood this, but I'll spell it for you. You are a suspect. S-U-S-P-E-C-T. As soon as I wrote that in a report, I had to take myself off of the case. Bill Worthington is handling it. I can tell you that Lashann finished with the site this afternoon…and that's all."

"You're shitting me!" I exploded.

"No, I'm not." Reading leaned toward me. "Do I think you killed the man? Hell no! But let's look at what I have to work with. "You knew the victim, were supposed to meet him that morning, you were at the murder site, that's opportunity. That's about all we have. That makes you a possibility, and that makes you a suspect. You're my sister, that's conflict of interest. Until you're ruled out as a suspect, I can't have anything to do with Carson's murder."

I understood why Reading would have to remove himself from the case. What I didn't understand was his assertion I was at the murder scene. I asked, "Me, at the murder scene? Who told you that, the imaginary clue fairy? I was never near that clump of Palmettoes until Mark, and I visited his body…*after* we were told."

"Chessie, you and Mark already figured there wasn't enough blood there for that to be where he got killed."

"You found where he was killed?" I asked. Reading stared at me with an emotionless stone face. The gears in my brain spun wildly. They provided a guess. "It was near the gate, wasn't it?"

"Sorry, sis. I've said all I can say." However, I could tell I had guessed correctly. The facts Reading spoke of definitely identified me as someone who deserved scrutiny.

"What about Mark and the rest of the crew?" I asked.

"Yes, until they can prove where they were when Carson was snuffed. That goes for the ranch people and the individuals involved in the development deal, too."

That told me something. "You have a time of death."

Reading's silence and stone face told me they had.

I thought for several seconds before asking, "Will I be allowed to rejoin the site team when they start back up?"

Reading leaned away from me. He nodded his head slowly before saying, "I knew it would come up. I asked Bill what he'd decide on that. He said innocent until proven guilty. But, you or no one can get anywhere near the areas of interest we have marked off. This is me speaking: Keep your nosey ass *away* from the taped off areas."

"Did he say when we could get back to work on the site?" I tried to ignore my dislike for my brother's sharp words. My face showed my feelings, but I managed to hold my tongue.

"Tomorrow. I expected that Dr. Card had called you already. He knew late this afternoon." Reading helped himself to more chicken-parm. "Sorry, Chessie, this is serious. I want you to be damned careful out there. My gut tells me we just opened the equivalent to Pandora's Box at the Buehl place." He hesitated then added, "And I think we'll find out that Pandora was a wimp."

~~~~~~~

I received a text, not a phone call from Mark telling me we could resume our operation the next morning. He didn't send it until after ten. That meant something. Dr. Mark Card despised the text as a means of communication. Mark seldom answered his phone after nine. He wanted to avoid a conversation with me. Why was the question. I knew he wasn't happy that I'd arranged a meeting with Wilbur Carson without being told about it. It could be any number of other things if that hurt his feelings. I always saw Mark as a fifteen-year-old if his tender ego got wrinkled. The message read: "got go ahd-8@gate." That meant we'd get a later than usual start. Why? I was puzzled enough to phone Mark anyway.
~~~~~~~

As I reached for my cell, the landline rang and I heard Reading answer it. I listened.

"Yes, it is. Why do you want to speak to her?" Reading's tone was one of suspicion.

"I'm her brother. Why do you want to speak to her?" There was a pause.

"Because it's obvious you're trying to disguise your voice." Reading was calm but assertive. "Hello…hello…hello." The caller had hung up. He appeared at the door and said, "I think you were about to get a threat of some kind. I recognized the number. It was from the same payphone as the first one you got." He took a breath. "Be real careful out there!"

Yes, it looked like Pandora *was* a wimp!

Chapter   17

I could see the line of pickups, Mark's Jeep, Dillon Development's four-wheel flatbeds, and Indian River Sheriff Department cruisers clustered around the gate. There were a dozen in all. In the middle of the road, Mark, Carl Buehl, Beth Dillon, two 'someones' in suits I didn't know, and a knot of Deputies were having an animated discussion. I parked at the end of the line vehicles that were half-in the ditch and half-on the road. When I opened my truck's door, I heard raised voices.

"Your injunction isn't valid." One of the business suit-clad 'someones' spoke in an authoritative voice. A lawyer…I understood why my stomach was upset.

"I maintain it is. I've not been properly informed that your motion to quash was approved." The second suit spoke in an assertive manner. Watching the two, posture, reminded me of a couple of little roosters preparing for battle.

The rest of the group observed. Carl's face was a vivid red, Beth's a few shades lighter. Mark was a disgusted bystander. The deputies looked amused. I recognized three of the six that stood in the road providing moral support for Captain Bill Worthington. One, in particular, I wished wasn't there.

Al Dobbs. We graduated in the same class. Al was history that I wished would go away, and wouldn't. He was a nice boy. Stud football player. He was a scholarship guy who never made it because he had a closer association with a Coors can than the practice field. I'd dated him steady for half of my junior year. I can best describe our relationship as high school lust. I got to know the rear of his Suburban better than I should have. Al was the perfect example of a workman with great tools and no idea how to use them.

I stopped my approach at what I considered a safe distance. Evidently, the arguments had been going on for a while. Worthington spoke, "Folks, there is only one way of settling this. You have conflicting court orders issued by two judges. *They* have to settle this. So, here's what is going to happen. The Sheriff is going to be in their offices when they open at ten o'clock. He'll get a ruling. The gate stays locked until then. Buehl…Card, no one goes in but my deputies. Whatever the judges' rule, will be what happens. One exception, I'm allowing Dr. Card to pick three of his people, put them in his Jeep, and go to his dig site. Mark, you can stow your equipment and protect it and the site, but you can't move any sand. You have four hours, and a deputy will be with you. Not one grain. Understand?"

Mark nodded. He pointed to me, Bobby and Nick. "You three, any problems?" Mark asked.

A chorus of "No's" responded as we all walked to the Jeep.

Worthington scanned his deputies and called for a volunteer, "Who wants to go with them?"

"I will." It was Al Dobbs.

I thought, oh shit, but wasn't sure whether I said it. The day wasn't starting well.

~ ~ ~ ~ ~ ~

Should I let the dog sleep or prod him? Mark showed no signs of being upset with me. Actually, he was his normal charming self. In a way, that bothered me more than if he'd been snarky. One of his favorite bromides is, "The prisoner always gets a great meal right before his execution." I wondered if he was applying that to me. Mark and my relationship was a long, personal, and strong one. But I also knew him well enough to know if he felt something endangered his professional reputation, friendships were secondary.

The safe way was to just let things evolve. Unfortunately, I'm a 'wake the dog,' kind of girl. After we'd tarped everything outside, moved things inside that would fit in the storage tents, and made sure none of our critical gear was missing, I cut Mark out of the herd so the two of us could talk privately.

Prod one. "What was the deal last night? You texted me we'd start today. You never text."

Mark tilted his head to one side, "I didn't want to wake you if you were in bed."

Prod two. "Why didn't you call earlier? Reading told me you knew we'd be able to begin digging again early yesterday afternoon."

Mark grinned. "You saw what happened at the gate this morning. I got a call from Beth Dillon telling me about the injunction right after Worthington called me. She told me her lawyer was in the process of quashing it and would call me back. When she did…I texted you." He smiled, folded his arms, and asked, "Is that all? Or are you dedicated to a strong offense being the best defense? You know, I'm not happy about you agreeing to meet Carson without at least telling me."

"Sorry, Mark. I really am. When he talked to me, I wasn't sure whether he was just blowing smoke to get attention. Getting involved in him getting killed…How could I have possibly seen that? I didn't want to take you looking for wild geese with me." I half-lied about the smoke; I was fairly sure he did know something important. "As far as the offense thing, yes, it was worth a try."

"It's a good story. I'll buy it." Mark turned serious. "Now, this thing is a lot different than we expected. Chessie, we have to stay close on this. You and I don't need bad publicity. East Florida sure doesn't want any mud on it, and Dr. Andrews would be pissed. And very importantly, neither of us needs our asses to end up buried out here."

"Hey, Dr. Card," Bill Worthington approached us from his cruiser.

"Good Afternoon, Captain," Mark's smile was extra broad, extra friendly. He was wasting it on Worthington. Bill's favorite quote was that of the police prefect from *Casablanca*, "my heart is my least vulnerable part."

"Your side won. You're free to resume working immediately." Though Bill was addressing Mark, his eyes were focused on me. He paused for a second then asked, "Doc, may I speak to you in private for a couple minutes?"

The two men left me sitting as they walked ten paces away. I expected there to be a long discussion. It wasn't. They were back after what I guessed was thirty words. However, I felt uncomfortable when Worthington positioned himself right in front of me. Was I being arrested?

"Chessie, we need your voluntary cooperation," he said.

I said, "Sure." I thought, *oh shit*! "What do you want?"

"Where are the clothes you wore yesterday? Have you washed them?"

"No. They're in the clothes hamper in our duplex." I reached in my pants pocket, removed my keyring, took off my house key, and handed it to the captain. "You can give it to Reading when you're done. I'm wearing the shoes I wore yesterday if you need them."

Worthington laughed. "You're acting like an innocent person."

"I am."

"You know this will go a long way to getting you off the list. In fact, you just helped yourself."

"How did I do that?" I was puzzled.

"You had your keys in your right pants pocket and took them out with your right hand, does that mean you're right-handed?" he asked.

"Yes."

"Whoever inflicted those wounds on Carson was definitely left-handed according to our forensics guy."

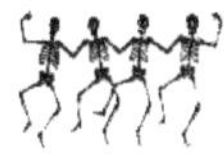

Chapter   18

"Before you start digging in your section, I want you to work with me." The request wasn't an unusual one from Mark. He'd often ask me or one of his associates to work with him when he felt he was on the verge of making a discovery. Mark had a glint in his eye. He added, "Bring your people with you. I want as many witnesses as possible."

"It sounds as if you know what you're going to find," I said.

He grinned his classroom 'Dr. Card' grin, and said, "I don't *know what* I'm going to find. I just know I'm going to find *something*." He pointed to the disturbed sand on the middens surface he was excavating. "I'll oblige whoever is trying to be sure we find some kind of artifacts here."

"What do you want me to do?" I asked.

"Nothing. Be as observant as possible, and take lots of pictures if I tell you." Mark climbed into the shallow pit and carefully began removing soil from the spot adjacent to where he expected to find something. He removed the earth between the pit and the suspect area. As soon as he exposed that soil, the dry powdery sand poured into the bottom of the pit in a stream. Within a few minutes, he grunted and pointed to an object covered with a layer of soil.

"Bobby, start taking video of this," Mark told his student assistant. He motioned for me to stand on the side of the midden so I could get unobstructed still shots of him uncovering whatever lay beneath the sand. Within seconds I was snapping pictures of a human femur as Mark carefully brushed away sand from the bone. Even an unpracticed eye could see that it had been cleaned and possibly preserved before it was clumsily buried for us to find. In another ten minutes, the mating bones of the lower leg were exposed. As Mark was completing his work, he said, "I wonder where these came from?"

"I'll make you a bet. Reading asked me some questions about identifying bones that were stolen from a private collection. Some anthropologist had them in his beach house. I'll give you ten to one odds, that you're looking at them." I pointed to the femur. "It looks as though they were waxed, or coated with PEG, or something."

"I won't take the bet." Mark shook his head. "This whole project is getting stranger by the day. Better get a hold of your brother, Chessie."

"I can do that for you." Deputy Al Dobbs stood behind me like an unwanted shadow. After a brief conversation with my brother, Al said, "Dr. Card, Chessie…Reading told me to ask you to leave what you've found just the way it is until he gets here. He said you can work in a different area."

I mumbled, "Careful what you wish for, Chessie." I remember how the project started. Sitting in my office was looking better…all the time!

~ ~ ~ ~ ~ ~

Dr. Alexander Curtis smiled as he rotated the femur in his hands. "This is definitely mine." He pointed to some scratches in the bone. "There couldn't be two exactly like this."

"You have any idea who stole it?" my brother asked.

"No. Quite honestly, I was very surprised when it was stolen. Seeing where you found it, I can understand why, but who?" He shook his head.

Reading asked, "Doc, was there a reason why you were so surprised it got stolen, other than a human bone isn't something high on most people's wish list?"

"Yes. Whoever stole the bones were specifically after them. Little else was taken and there were some very expensive items laying around. Hardly anyone knows about my collection. At least, I don't think they do."

"Anything besides the bones missing?"

"A couple pieces of pottery and a spear point," the doctor replied.

"Navaho?" Reading guessed.

"How did you know that?"

Reading grinned, "Clairvoyant…Hopefully, I can return some of that to you. Can you make me a list of people who knows about what you do?" Reading asked.

"Sure, but it will be a mighty short list." Dr Curtis asked, "Got a piece of paper?"

~ ~ ~ ~ ~ ~

By the end of the day, Dr. Curtis' collection was intact, every bone, every artifact having been recovered. The list that Curtis made was very short and not one person had a connection with any of Buehl's or the developer's friends or colleagues. Something that should have been a noteworthy clue showed no promise. The only good thing was that Bill Worthington had given us permission to go back to work the next morning. Me included.

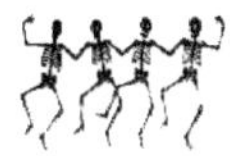

Chapter   19

The only things good about the morning were the cream filled donuts and coffee. We shared these with our bored student volunteers and Al Dobbs as we sat in the shade of an oak that had become our chair-less "breakroom." A week passed. It would be wonderful to report the discovery of significant archaeological treasures occurred. Not happening, not happening. The list of artifacts wasn't impressive. The number of items that were recent history was much longer, but no more interesting. We were able to rule out more than we were able to establish.

Pottery shards, some tools fashioned from deer bones, many animal and fish bones, four iron ax heads, some unidentified steel items, and several shells that had served as tools had found their way into the middens. There were no burials left, though Mark and I were positive two areas probably had bodies buried in them at one time. They had been robbed. Remnants of canvas and plastic attested to the fact "modern man" beat us to the site.

Besides the canvas and plastic in what we believed had been graves, the place was littered with soft drink bottles and various types of cans spanning sixty years. Old, and not so old, shotgun shells were very common. Rusty digging implements, most so abused they were left behind, several knifes of different types, broken glass from many sources, cans of all sizes and a perfectly preserved Mason Jar with a date of 1918 were unearthed. The best find was a cast iron skillet that had somehow been abandoned with fish still in it.

The Indian artifacts weren't ancient. We estimated most were less than 2000 years old, probably from the Ais, or Juegan tribes. I yawned. The prospect of further work in the pit I was excavating wasn't the least bit enticing. There is always the possibility, in archaeology, that the next shovel turn, trowel slice, or brush stroke will reveal something important. It's the gas that fuels us. Unfortunately, the word "probability" exists. It hung over the Buehl site middens like a nuclear cloud.

I was relieved when Mark said, "I've found all the Budweiser cans and Coke bottles I need to see for a day or two. Let's get out the aerials of the ranch and check some of those other spots that looked promising. We can have Bobby and Nick back fill the first two pits we've finished. What do you say Chessie?"

"If you're waiting for me, you're running backwards!" I was on my feet and heading for one of our ground-penetrating radar units. "I'll bring a site journal and the GPR. Meet you at the Jeep," I said.

"Ahhhh…I gotta go with you two." Al Dobbs struggled to his feet. He looked and sounded apologetic.

The week that had transpired between the discovery of Wilbur Carson's body had pushed that into a secondary place in our minds. It remained a very close second.

I was still uncomfortable having an old flame attached to me with shadow-like closeness. The necessity for his protection remained and would until some break occurred in the case. Reading told me they were at a total impasse. Deputy Dobbs constant presence served two purposes. The stated one was to keep the archaeology team safe. The second, more insidious purpose, was to keep us all under observation…we were still low-grade suspects.

He brushed sand and leaves off of his uniform as he spoke into a radio. "Hey, Bill, it's Al. Dr. Card and Miss Partin are wanting to go look at some other places on the ranch. You want me to stick with them?" He nodded, and asked. "Should I wait until someone else gets here, or can I let the college students by themselves?" Dobbs nodded again. He turned to us and said, "Captain Worthington says we can go. He's sending another deputy back here to stay at the site. Dr. Card, you need to tell your people to stay here until the deputy comes."

"You two load up. I'll talk to Bobby and give him instructions." Mark walked away.

"Can I help you load that?" Al watched me struggle with the case the radar was in.

I frowned but said, "Okay."

Dobbs grabbed the other end of the case and we gently placed it in the Jeep.

"Chessie, I'm just another deputy assigned to the case. That's all." Al tried to make me feel more at ease. I appreciated his effort. Some history doesn't vanish that easily. I answered sincerely, "Thanks, Al."

"Let's head over to that spot your brother showed you on the aerials," Mark announced his presence. He climbed into the Jeep, waved for us to get in, and started the engine.

Chapter   20

Mark Card stopped to take another look at the aerial photograph. He nodded. "There is only one way to get a vehicle into the spot. We are right on it." He eased the clutch out and the Jeep began forward, crushed weeds and small bushes beneath it as it remade a twisting, snake shaped path through the Florida underbrush.

I looked at the photo and then at the greenery surrounding the vehicle. Trying to determine where the Jeep pushed toward the spot we sought relative to the photo…that proved impossible for me. I asked, "How old is this?" waving the aerial at Mark.

"Less than a year. Dillon Development had the whole ranch photographed when they became serious about buying it."

"I'm glad you know where you're going." I shook my head. "Other than taking your word we're driving around somewhere on the photo; I have no idea where we are."

"I hope I do! If I'm right, we should come to a large cluster of cabbage palms on the right side of this Jeep in the next hundred yards. If we don't, I'll have to follow the path we made coming in. It means I don't know where I'm at either." The Jeep rolled over a small log or other large bump making Mark, Al and myself grunt and grab for anything to hold us in our seats.

"I hope you do too, I wouldn't want to have to walk out of here." Al Dobbs pointed to a bare patch of white sand fronting a gopher tortoise hole. A four-foot rattlesnake was sprawled on the sand while it digested the lump in its body several inches past its head.

Mark and I nodded our approvals.

The Jeep made several sharp turns before exiting a scrub oak thicket. We entered a field of thickly covered pine trees with a scattering of palmettoes mixed between. Through its center, an obvious trail had been cut, wide enough to accommodate a pickup truck. At the end of the fifty yard 'road,' stood the cluster of a dozen or more cabbage palms Mark had mentioned.

"We are where I thought we were," Mark gloated.

Surveying the pines cut down to make the path, Dobbs observed, "Somebody wanted to keep returning here. You don't go to the trouble of sawing out timber unless you plan on coming back."

"You're right. But for what? There isn't any reason someone would want to come to this place," I observed.

"Just looking at the growth of weeds and saplings, I'd guess it has been at least a year since anyone's driven back here," Mark ventured.

Dobbs agreed, "A year, maybe two."

The Jeep neared the palms, and it was evident a small clearing nestled in the semicircle the cluster created. A huge oak well over 100 years in age walled off the right side of the clearing. Nothing but weeds and a solitary pine, three feet tall, covered the 'open' area created by palms and oak.

"It looks like a campsite," Al observed.

"Could be," Mark agreed, "If you were sneaking on this property to hunt and wanted to stay over-night, this would be a great place to not get caught."

Mark had slowed the Jeep to a crawl as we approached within forty feet. The weeds covering the clearing were so thick it was impossible to see what lay beneath them.

"Look at that," Dobbs pointed to the base of the cabbage palms and moved his finger in and arc. "I'd say someone has used this to camp. See the logs laid in a half circle. They're probably seats used to sit around a campfire."

There were four logs, each long enough to provide seating for two or three butts. They formed 180° of a 360° circle. Neatly placed and evenly spaced, they provided the appearance of an outdoor amphitheater more than a crude campsite.

"I bet we'll find a huge old campfire pit under those weeds," Al said.

Mark stopped the Jeep and commented, "It won't take long to find out. The grass whips are ready, and the weed-eaters gassed up. All they need are humans to use them. Shall we?"

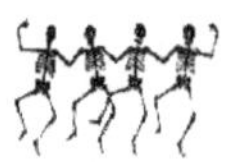

Chapter   21

Mark's training and discipline is evident in everything he does. Before we started to clear the twenty-five-foot diameter circle, he devised a plan. He put both Al Dobbs, Al volunteered, and me to work cutting down the outside perimeter. Mark began his inspection of the site by carefully examining the four logs as soon as we cleared the area around them. In the silence between roars from the weed eaters, he informed us, "This isn't likely any kind of interest to us. At least, in what we've been hired to examine. These logs were cut by a chain saw."

I asked, "Do we keep working? I know there's a 99° chance this isn't Native American, but can we run the radar unit over it?"

"We keep working. All we're liable to find are buried beer cans, but with the setup of these logs, there is the possibility we'll find something else," Mark said.

"A buried whiskey bottle?" Al theorized.

"Probably," Mark chuckled as he spoke, "Ready weed eaters…attack!"

The roar of the gas engines resumed. We rapidly cut the covering grass and weeds down to sand level until Al yelled, "I think I found something." He pointed to two three-inch diameter tree limbs cut at 45° and placed to form a perfect right angle.

"That isn't a freak of nature, that's man made." Mark bent over and examined the find. "There's more here. Cut the weeds away from the outside edges of the wood, but do it very carefully. Cut a foot then look into the weeds to be sure there's nothing in the next foot."

Al and I nodded. We began the surgeon like removal of weeds from the outside of the limbs. Ten minutes later, we exposed a perfect square, three feet on a side. All corners were bevel cut like the first one Al discovered. As we finished cutting, Mark had already began inspecting the square's interior.

"We're definitely going to want to run the radar over this area." Mark was peering at something in the center of the square. He motioned to me, "Hand me your trimmer," I obliged. The little engine roared and Mark was meticulously careful as he cut around the object he'd discovered. The fallen weeds exposed a human skull.

"Damn!" Al uttered.

Mark said, "I'll remove the rest of the weeds inside the square. Al, would you remove the weeds from the rest of the clearing. Chessie, get the radar unit ready."

~ ~ ~ ~ ~ ~ ~

"Good God, there's another one!" Dobb's eyes focused on the radar screen as we made another pass across the clearing.

"That's three and we aren't half done." The 'three' I referred to were skeletons. Skeletons unique in the fact they had commonalities. The skulls were missing, the bones were in disarray…particularly the arms and legs…and all were buried 'face down.'

"I think I should call my brother," I said. "This looks like something the sheriff is going to be all over."

"And Bill Worthington, too. It might have some connection to the Carson case," Dobbs added.

"Call them both. By the time this is over you may need the whole Indian River Sheriff's Department out here." Mark shook his head. "I have a gut feel this isn't all we'll find." He paused and looked at the nine 'lanes' he'd laid out to do our radar search. We were on our fourth one. "Let's get back to work after you make your calls."

~ ~ ~ ~ ~ ~

Reading, Bill Worthington, and an officer I didn't know listened to Mark as he recounted our discovery. "There are seven, at least. In one of the lanes, we found a lot of individual bones but we can't be sure if they're from the other skeletons. We won't know if we have an eighth until they're dug up."

Worthington asked, "Do you have any idea how long they might have been there?"

"Not one I'd share. Common sense says recently. In the last two to fifty years. The setting screams ritual of some sort. But, again, until we dig… I have to proceed as if anything we find is an antiquity or Native American. If you're asking if you can dig these skeletons up assuming they victims of a modern murder case, no you can't. I have to do my thing. As soon as we excavate, prove they're not Ais, or Seminole, or any other tribe, they are yours. And as improbable as it maybe, I have to do that with each individual find."

"How long?" Reading asked.

"It depends. I have to discuss this with the development company. They set my priorities. After I get the go ahead, assuming I can verify what we think quickly, a week to ten days. If we get lucky, I might have one for you in two days, assuming I can put my whole crew on it."

"How big of a problem is it going to be?" Reading's face showed disgust.

Mark stared for a second before he answered, "It will be a problem. Beth Dillon approved enough money for three weeks work to prove if this was a Native American historic site and if parts of it had to be set aside from development. I don't think she'll want to finance work for the sheriff that won't contribute to that."

Worthington puffed up like an angry toad. "We'll just go get court orders."

"It won't be that simple," Mark cautioned. "Everybody in this area's historical, ecological, and tribal communities, know about and have a keen interest in this land and project. For every order you get, they'll get two."

"He's right, Bill. I had to keep both sides apart when this project started. It's like a pack of dogs with rabies.

Let's talk to, Lisa, in the Sheriff's controller's office. I'm sure she can find some bucks in the budget to finance digging this site up." Reading grinned. "I know Beth. If she doesn't have to pay for it, she won't mind a week's delay. That way we both get what we want."

"I don't know why Lisa would approve this. These are college people," Worthington objected.

Reading smiled. "Bill, the sheriff is going to have to pay somebody to do it. We don't have that capability inside the department. Those bones aren't going to float to the surface by themselves." He looked toward Mark. "You won't mind if Lashann Hargrove looks over your shoulder while you're excavating, will you Mark?"

"No. As long as he doesn't interfere."

"He'll be a church mouse." Reading removed his cell phone. "I'll call Lisa and we'll have this thing settled."

Chapter   22

Mark made one last check to see that his dig plan had been properly translated from map to terrain. The stakes indicating the locations were in their proper places. Strings stretched tight designated each excavation area. Screens for straining the dirt removed from the dig were at the place designated for housing that material until it was returned to the site. He announced, "Okay, we are ready to go."

Bobby, Mark, and me would do the digging, Sheila would supervise the screening operations, and five of Mark's students would provide labor to haul dirt and all the other tasks required on a dig site. Al Dobbs had strict orders to only provide security. His presence with a high-powered rifle at the ready, gave him the appearance of a prison chain-gang guard. Lashann Hargrove volunteered to act as photographer and recorder rather than to sit as an idle observer.

The two meter, by one meter rectangles we were each assigned to excavate were pure sand. My attempts to keep edge of the rectangle intact, proved very difficult. The soft sand collapsed time and time again. It wasn't until I reached a foot or more in depth and there was enough moisture in the soil that my trench looked like the wall had been exposed by a person trained in archaeological procedures. Bobby and Mark had the same problem so I felt less humiliated than I would have been otherwise.

Our seven AM start proved wise. The day heated quickly and our frustration with it. One twelve gage shotgun shell, in bad condition, was our total recovery for the morning. We'd penetrated almost two feet when we took a lunch break at eleven.

I ask Mark, "How deep do you think they are?"

"The skeletons?" he replied.

"Yes."

"The radar said they were in a layer from four to five-and-a-half feet down." Mark looked at the pits we'd labored in. "The GPR readings are very accurate in the conditions we're working under. I'd say we're halfway there."

"You disappointed we've found so few items in what we've removed?"

"Naturally, I'd like the effort to be worth it. But I didn't expect to find anything. I'm surprised we didn't at least find some trash. Tin cans. Bottles. My guess, anything we find will be in the same area as the skeletons." Mark raised his eyebrows. "Whoever buried the bodies made sure there aren't traces in what covers them."

"You don't believe there's any chance these are old remains, do you?" I asked.

"Oh, there's a chance. Just not a good one. Maybe one in a thousand." Mark shook his head. "We won't be calling Tall Pine or Nichols. This is last fifty-year stuff."

"You are right about that," Lashann had walked up to us unobserved. "The skull you found had dental work that wasn't available for use until thirty-eight years ago."

Both my and Mark's head swiveled to see our visitor. Mark asked, "Are you trying to identify her that way?"

"Yes. The office is sending out bulletins this morning. I don't have much hope of getting anything positive back. All the work appears to have been done in Eastern Europe, my guess Poland. A friend of mine is a dentist. I showed him the skull. He says the techniques used on it aren't taught in the US."

Mark motioned for Hargrove to sit next to us. He offered the sheriff's crime scene specialist a sandwich. "Tuna fish," Mark explained. "There are drinks in the cooler."

"Thanks," Lashann replied. He sat with us after fishing out a Pepsi to wash down his sandwich.

"What do you think we'll find, Lashann?" I asked.

"I haven't a clue. The one thing I can say is whoever the person or persons are that buried them are probably psychopaths. Hacking the heads off? That's weird!" After a few seconds pause he added, "One thing I'd be willing to bet on. If whoever did that," he pointed to the rectangles, "Isn't dead or in prison, they're still doing it."

~ ~ ~ ~ ~ ~

"Tomorrow, before ten," Mark said as he surveyed the net results of the days labor. Beside the shotgun shell, the three of us and the screen crew found: a can opener, a butter knife, the plastic retainer to hold a six-pack together, a Tupperware container, the clasp part of a padlock, and a house key. Our excavations were all nearing the four-foot depth mark. We would be in the layer the GPR predicted the skeletons rested soon after we returned to work the next morning.

Chapter   23

I found the first one. My trowel hit something solid in the sand. Something of substantial size. After removing more sand with my trowel, my fingers, and a brush, I could identify my find and ones on either side. I yelled to Mark, "We have the first one here. This is a rib cage I'm uncovering." Everyone at the site assembled around my pit within seconds.

I continued to work. The skeleton's vertebrae soon appeared. Mark watched closely but did not interfere with my work. That gave me a great deal of confidence. I worked downward toward the pelvis, filling buckets with the sand I removed from around the bones. Lashann said, "Stop for just a minute. I'm going to get into the dig with you."

He carefully backed down the short ladder resting against the pit's side. "Could you move away for a couple minutes?" Hargrove asked.

"Sure." I moved as far away from the skeleton as I could.

Lashann removed a magnifying glass from a pocket, knelt next to the ribs, and examined one of the bones with intense interest. After a minute, he spoke. "I think we have a murder here." He pointed to a small arc cut from the top of one of the ribs. "That was made by a medium caliber bullet. I'm guessing a .38." Hargrove scanned the people flanking the edge of the pit until he saw Sheila. "You need to be extra careful screening the material Chessie has been pulling out from around the rib cage. A bullet hitting a bone like that would probably keep it from passing all the way through. If we're lucky, we'll find the damned thing."

"You have any quick tricks to tell how long it's been there?" Mark asked.

"None you're not aware of. I'll have to get the body to my lab to get any accuracy." Lashann took another long look at the skeleton. "I can tell you this, *she's* been in the ground long enough there's no hint of soft tissue remaining…cartlidge…anything. I'm guessing two plus years. She's had four ribs broken and healed for a long time. That plus a back surgery fusing L2 and L3 gives me a place to start checking old missing persons reports." He stood and added, "I need to call this in." Within seconds he had scrambled up the ladder and disappeared.

I looked at Mark and asked, "What do I do now?"

"What we all do. Go back to work." He walked toward the screens. "Come on Sheila, I'll work with you."

~ ~ ~ ~ ~ ~ ~

It was my turn to race to someone else's discovery. We hadn't been back to work for fifteen minutes when I heard Sheila scream, "I found it!" I joined a knot of people surrounding Mark and Sheila.

Nestled in her hand, Sheila held a slug that looked to be the right size. She asked Mark, "Does this look like the right one?"

"My expertise is in arrow heads, not bullets, but I'd say it probably is the .38 caliber slug Lashann hopes to find."

"I'll call it in." Al Dobbs already had his phone in hand.

Mark scanned the group that had assembled around him. "All right folks. Back to work."

Most of the crew chanted the last three words with him.

~ ~ ~ ~ ~ ~ ~

As 'my' skeleton became liberated from its grave, the gruesome nature of those who killed the victim became exposed with it. The right arm had been removed at the shoulder. So was the left leg. We already knew all the heads were missing. Lashann arrived and watched the exhumation keeping his camera in action constantly. Hargrove pointed out damage to the pelvis saying he theorized the leg was detached with an axe. Mark released several bones from the foot of the skeleton I'd discovered for Lashann to test in his lab. Then, Mark finally returned to work in his pit.

Within twenty minutes of returning to work, Mark announced, "I have mine." There was another instant replay as we all gathered around the pit in which Mark labored. He had uncovered a femur and part of the pelvic area. Mark worked as we watched. Skillfully, he quickly removed the sand from around the pelvis. As he continued removing over-burden, he remarked, "Our psycho is an equal opportunity murderer. This skeleton belonged to a man."

When Mark exposed the left side of the pelvis, it was clear the left leg had been removed in much the same manner as the skeleton I worked on. Mark stopped long enough to mutter, "Sick," before continuing his task. He looked at the crew gathered at the rim of his dig and drew breath to speak. Before he could the group recited in unison, "Back to work." All left except Lashann Hargrove. I eavesdropped.

"Mark, don't you think it is obvious none of these remains are of archaeological importance? We could speed this up a lot if you can concede that point. I can get you some help to uncover what's here."

Mark thought for several seconds before answering. He sighed and said, "I believe you're correct, but I have to do this right. Get me some dates on the bones from the two skeletons we've dug up. You've got one in your lab now. I'll accept the dating on that for both...so I'll fudge a little. Until you have a date on the second to confirm. I've got Bobby working on the area where random bones, not full skeletons shown on the radar. When he finds something, I can look at, and when I can agree they are of the same vintage, I'll call Terrie and McMillan and get them to allow us to abandon this as an historic site. If they agree, I have to call Beth Dillon...I'm sure she'll be happy. Honestly, my thing is archaeology, not crime scene investigation. I'll be happy to be out of this."

Chapter   24

Day three on the dig/crime scene started with an air of morbid fascination. Lashann returned with the lab report. He stated his lab people could conclusively say the bones had been interred for less than seventy years but needed more time to get an accurate date. I started to ask how Lashann's lab people arrived at the seventy-year figure, but Mark silenced me with a look. He wanted us out of the mess as soon as possible.

Since I'd completed the excavation of my two-by-one rectangle, Mark assigned me to work with Bobby. His turned out to be the hardest task. Everything he'd uncovered were individual bones. Recording, documenting, and preserving these small finds were time consuming. The object, Mark informed us, was to establish that those bones were or were not from the skeletons we'd unearthed.

I quickly discovered how frustrating it was when I uncovered a couple of metatarsals. The time to photograph, describe, and geographically locate those small bones took as much time as the whole skeleton I'd discovered.

"Finally," Bobby exclaimed.

I glanced at what he was brushing sand from, then took a second look. It was a femur...one that could be a match from the skeleton I dug up. The coloring and size were correct. As I watched Bobby work with trowel and brush to remove the bone, he remarked, "These have the same marks that were on some of the small bones I found yesterday. I wanted to point them out to Mark but forgot. You know what they are?" He removed the last earth from the femur and handed to me.

He positioned the bone in my hands and pointed to scratches and gouges on the bones surface. It took a few moments for the right synapses to fire. When they did, I dropped the bone. They were teeth marks. We were dealing with cannibalism!

Chapter   25

"That's one hell of a good reason for somebody to not want you poking around the property." Reading sat across the kitchen table in our shared duplex. He spooned grits on his three sunny-siders. "It's also a reason for you people to be extra careful. You don't have to guess if those people are dangerous or not. Somebody that will chow down on their victims has to be capable of anything."

I shook my body and made a face, "Do you have to be so callous? Those people were somebody's loved ones."

"You? Playing the femininity card? That's not like you, Sis. Where's your 'we can do anything you can do better,' song?"

Staring coldly at my brother, I indicted him with, "I played the humanity card, Reading."

"Touché," he grudgingly agreed.

I changed the subject. "Our discovery furnishes you with a built-in short list of suspects. You going to question old man Buehl? That's so obvious."

"Sure." Reading shook his head. "I've known Carl since Dad took me hunting on his property a time or two. He was in Kiwanis with me for God's sake. I just have such a hard time seeing him as a candidate for Old Sparky."

"I don't know him. I've met him a few times before this, and I've got to say he didn't strike me as Wolfman or Dracula. But…you're always telling me you can't tell by a person's looks." I raised my eyebrows. "Who else is on your list? Lashann told me he believes that it involves some kind of a ritual. Probably a cult could be responsible. It would seem to me that it would take a number of people to catch and kill that number of victims."

"Not necessarily, but probably." Reading finished inhaling his eggs and grits. He stared at the sausage links remaining on his plate and I wondered if the subject made him reticent to eat them. If there was, he quickly overcame it. He drove a fork into one of the links before he spoke, "Those bodies were probably stuck in the ground at different times." He bit off a piece of the sausage and talked around it. "That's what your boss thinks. He says the way the remains were placed indicates whoever planted them didn't want to accidentally dig into a former victim." The rest of the sausage disappeared.

"Then it could have been Buehl by himself?"

"Could. But, I doubt that." Reading stuck the fork tines into the last link, eyeballed it, and disposed of it as if its presence disturbed him. "I'm not sure old Carl killed them. I'm not even sure he knew they were there."

"The way he has reacted to our looking over his property makes me think you're wrong. If he isn't guilty, why so strong of a reaction?"

"Sis, remember when I got rid of your freshman letter sweater when you were in the Marines?" Reading waited for my face to mimic a thunder cloud. I quickly obliged. He continued, "You'd have liked to kill me. Now think of losing your family property. Property that's been passed down for a couple generations because of a bad financial decision you made. How would you react? Afterall, he wasn't upset when you were digging up the middens. He didn't get frantic until Wilson got killed." Reading grinned at me like he does when he wants to get a reaction. "Now, Chessie, I want you to think of old Buehl, munching on that femur you folks found yesterday."

He got his reaction. I made a face and growled, "Gross!" He also made his point. "Who else are you going to look at?"

"Everybody connected to the property. Buehl's family and close friends." Reading hesitated. "The problem is that the property in huge. There are more than thirty gates. Carl has made a couple dozen complaints to us in past years about people cutting off his gate's padlocks. Parts of it are so thickly wooded that anything could go on out there without Carl or anybody knowing. Whoever killed those folks could be someone with no association to Buehl."

"But they would have to be someone who knew about the property. That means it has to be somebody who lives around here," I suggested.

"Or did at one time," Reading concurred.

"Where do you start to look for suspects on something like this?"

Reading leaned back in his chair and took a couple of sips of coffee. It was clear he asked himself the same question. "The first thing I'll do is look for anyone that is associated with that property past or present with a violent criminal record or mental problems." He took another sip as he thought. "I'll look at state records. Both criminals and funny ranch folks that have any history of similarities to what we think went on out there. See if they have a connection with this area. Cults that do those kind of things."

"Cults? What about cults? It could be the first place to check." I suggested.

Reading nodded, "That's a great place to look. The problem is, how? Those people are secretive as all get out. Trying to even find someone who admits belonging isn't going to be easy."

I hesitated a few seconds before I offered. "Reading, I might be able to help. I know a few professors at the university that dabble in occult things and paranormal stuff. I don't think they'd describe themselves as cult members, but... I've heard them discuss some pretty weird ideas. I can give you names, phone numbers."

Reading stared at me for several seconds before answering. "That will be great information. My problem will be how to use it. I can't see them opening up to me, when I introduce myself. 'Hi, I'm Captain Reading Partin of the Indian River Sheriff's Department. I'm investigating a multiple homicide and want to see if your group has a connection.' They won't admit to being born on earth."

"I can see that," I admitted.

After several seconds pause, Reading asked, "Would you consider plowing a little ground for me? See if you can find out a little about the different groups that might be out there? I don't mean join or get deeply involved, just ask around."

I thought about holding the gnawed femur in my hand. And, I had a vague, set up, feeling. "Bro, I'll have to think long and hard about that. Honestly, AOC has a better chance of marrying Rush Limbaugh than me saying yes to that."

"Limbaugh is dead!"

"There you go."

Chapter   26

We all sat under one of the huge oaks that topped the sand ridge by the middens we had first explored. My brother, Worthington, Tall Pine, McMillan, Buehl, Nichols, Dillon, Stanton Griggs, and a man from the State's Attorney's Office listened intensely as Dr. Card recounted our exhumation of the graves during the last three days. He concluded that, "I'm absolutely convinced there are no artifacts involved with the skeletons in the area we have examined. I've relinquished control of the site to Captain Partin of the Indian River Sheriff's Department, pending the approval of this antiquities committee. I'd like to get back to my search of this land to see if there are any legitimate sites that need to be preserved. I'm asking for that approval."

Silence.

"What do you intend to do at the site Dr. Mark has told us about, Captain Partin?" Terrie Tall Pine asked after many seconds. "You understand my concern. The history of such discoveries."

"It's a crime scene and we'll treat it as such. The remains will all be recovered and a thorough search of the area around the bodies will be conducted. No rash decisions or unwarranted information will be formulated. When we're finished, we will return the land to as close to the condition it was before the first shovel of dirt was moved." Reading hesitated for a few seconds then added, "We will restrict access to that spot until we're sure, no additional investigation needs doing."

She nodded then asked, "I would like an observer from our tribe to be present. Do you have a problem with that?"

"Absolutely none," Reading responded.

"Then, I speak for my people. We have no objection so long as the search continues on the rest of the land that might be developed." Terrie looked at Mark. "My questions are about what you will do to be sure any of our graves are undisturbed."

"I have to get approval to return to my survey before I can do anything." Mark made a questioning look in McMillan's direction.

McMillan nodded. "All those in favor of releasing the site to the sheriff and allowing Dr. Card to resume his archaeological investigation, say yes."

Everyone answered yes. Even those that weren't a member of the committee. There was only one exception. Carl Buehl. He remained quiet, and he looked catatonic.

"My question Dr. Card," Terrie persisted.

Mark held up a group of aerial photos and his notes. "Terrie, we've located spots on these photos that I think have the highest probability of having man made changes. We will do a preliminary examination of each. There are fourteen in all. That includes the site we've been discussing and the five middens where we have done some work.

Though it is apparent that the five-mound site has been disturbed…often…I intend to do a thorough review of it. Of the twelve we haven't checked; we believe we've located possible middens at two of them. They and the area around them will get an exacting search. All will get checked with GPR. If anything is shown by the radar at any site, we will set up an exploratory dig. It will get our full attention."

"What if you run out of money," Tall Pine asked.

"That won't be a problem," Beth Dillon volunteered. "My company will pay for any costs associated with determining if there are historical finds. I will also commit to you that the middens and any other area that is connected to Native American heritage will be exempt from development. And a reasonable surrounding area. The sheriff will be responsible for any finds with criminal potentials."

"What do you consider a reasonable area?" Terrie asked.

Dillon hesitated, then answered with a question, "What would you consider reasonable?"

Terrie laughed but didn't answer.

"If you folks had your way, you'd level everything from Miami to Jacksonville," Griggs commented sarcastically.

"That would be a good start," Tall Pine replied.

"This isn't going to do either side any good. Making absurd comments gets us nowhere. You can't change history no matter how much you want to…even if it should be. So do we sit here like a bunch of four-year-olds or respond to Beth Dillon's offer." Jim McMillan had lost patience. "I don't want to be forced into making an arbitrary decision for the state…but I will."

"Your offer sounds well intentioned, Miss Dillon. But understand, many such offers have been made to us through many years. Few have proved to have substance. Understand my suspicions, please." Terrie nodded to McMillan, "I will refrain from future remarks. However, I must re-ask my question; what would you consider reasonable, Miss Dillon?"

"What is reasonable to me is for me to make a good profit on what I develop. I need to utilize two-thirds of the Buehl property for that to happen. My original intent was to make the third I wouldn't use as green areas. A lot of the area is swamp and wetlands. I never considered doing anything with them other than leaving them as is. That equals roughly 20%. That leaves 13% to house your historical sites. I'd be happy to allow you to draw the boundaries around your places of concern, no questions asked so long as the requests don't exceed that amount." Dillon pulled out her phone and used its calculation app. "That means you have up to 960 acres to reserve. That sound fair?"

Terrie smiled, "Fair. You will prepare paper to do this?"

"I'll deed it to your people."

"When Dr. Card is through, we can decide what those acres will be. I will not ask for land for no reason and I believe you will not deny me land my ancestors have made sacred." Terrie nodded. "We can go on." The meeting had ended without McMillan's formal declaration.

~ ~ ~ ~ ~ ~ ~

"What's next? Do we go back to the five middens or look elsewhere first?" I asked after most of the meeting members has disbursed. Mark, Terrie, and my brother stood under the oaks looking at the assortment of four-wheel vehicles bounce along the ranch ruts leading to the county road.

"I'd like to rule out places. We can visit all the sites I have marked on the maps and aerials, run the GPR over them, ones that are barren, we eliminate. Ones that have the most potential we rank and do the highest possible sites first and work down." Mark folded his arms in a defensive posture. "If we think the site has something there, but is modern in origin, it goes to the bottom of the list."

Reading frowned, but I knew my brother wouldn't object. He'd find a way to get his 'prospecting done.'

Terrie nodded her approval and said, "May I see the sites you have located. I have new information from four elders from Brighton who just learned of this." She waved her hand in an encompassing movement. Mark laid the maps and aerials in front of her. Each site was marked. "There are two places to add." She slid an aerial photo of an oak ridge area near the edge of Blue Cypress Lake on top of the pile. Terrie pointed to one end of the ridge. "I have been told three families lived at this spot for many years. Enough for two generations to be born there. Some died and were reported as buried on the ridge." Mark drew a circle in red ink around where Terrie pointed. She shuffled through several more photos before selecting another. "This spot is for you to know about." She traced her finger around an area with a small lake and a large rectangle of second growth vegetation. "My people tell me that a family lived here. They were black. They lived there many years and were friends of the Seminole. After the second war on my people, they all died or were taken away. Many are buried there. The burying place is here." Terrie pointed to one corner of the rectangle. Mark dutifully circled the location.

"Taken away?" I asked.

Terrie looked at me coldly, then answered, "Slave catchers came and took them away."

"That's a horrible thing, but I never did it…so don't blame me for things I didn't do," It disturbed me. The deeds were disgraceful, true. But I firmly believe I'm responsible for my actions, not others.

Terrie looked at me. At first, a trace of resentment crossed her features, then the realization she couldn't change my logic…any more than I could change history. Finally, she said, showing no visual or verbal emotion, "You profess to value people by their actions, regardless of *other things*. Then I would tell you to start looking for those who buried the headless ones and ate them, among those that you know." She walked away.

Chapter   27

Thump…thump…thump…thump, the noise from the windshield wipers provided the sound in my brothers Jeep as we drove on route 60. It was the only response to my question, "Does Terrie Tall Pine know something about the murders at the Buehl place we don't?"

Without saying a word Reading pulled his vehicle onto a dirt road and parked on the shoulder. He looked at me with an expression I knew well. Reading always used it for two reasons. The first was when he legitimately couldn't decide if he should share some information with me. The second was when he tried to manipulate me into doing something for him. At times, they coincide. I thought this was one of those times.

"She may," was his teaser.

"So?"

Reading stared at me, his silence increasing my interest and curiosity.

"Okay, I'll at least consider whatever you're trying to rope me into," I stayed away from a firm commitment.

"When you have something like what happened at Buehl's place, where's the first place to look for suspects?" he asked.

"History. You look to see if you have anything similar in the past and who did it or was suspected." I answered.

"Right. Well, there were two cases I knew about without opening a cabinet or a hard drive." Reading took a deep breath. "What I'm going to tell you is confidential. I have to have your word you will not divulge anything we talk about."

"Agreed."

"This goes back several years. You were in the Marines when it happened…I'm sure that's why it did not come to mind." Reading turned off the ignition. It would be a long story. "We had two cases that are very similar in nature to what you found at Buehl's. They involved decapitated bodies and the strong suspicion of cannibalism. The site of these murders, or at least the discovery of the bodies had another striking similarity. Both were on lands containing Native American artifacts."

"Oh…That's the reason for the convoluted answer you gave to Terrie's question." It hadn't made sense to me when my brother responded to her.

"Very much so. You'll see how as I tell you about the case." Reading took a breath. "I'd been in the department for five years and had just been promoted to detective. We got a call from a rancher who has a place over near Feldsmere. He reported a body dump. The man had two before but not like this one. At that time, a power struggle between three factions of Miami's organized criminals produced corpses weekly and we were a popular disposal area. When I took the call, I figured that was what we were dealing with. When I got there, it only took a few minutes to realize this had nothing to do with Miami's underworld. The body, if you could call it that was female, in a shallow grave, headless, and both arms and legs were gone. We found a square of wood over the grave. That's a signature. Mob executions don't involve any of that. It's a simple bullet in the back of the head. Female mob killings are rare, bodies aren't dismembered, and they just toss them in a field…burials are an exception."

"Cutting off the head, arms, and legs seem to be a way to keep the body from being identified," I theorized.

"Moe Fuller, he was lead detective on the case, started with that reasoning. The body, what was left, didn't give us much to go on. Woman…mid-thirties…average size, average build…based on pubic hair, blonde. She'd had a cesarian section, so we knew she given birth…that's it. I remember it so damned well. The first gruesome corpse stays with you for life my homicide buddies told me. It does. I can close my eyes and still see it."

I remembered my past experience, nodded and said, "Same here."

"We were stumped. Obviously, the press sensationalized the thing. That put pressure on the Sheriff. He put pressure on Moe and the rest of us. But there was nothing to help. No recent missing person's report that fit in the area, in the state, in adjoining states. No domestic violence reports that produced victim or suspect. No DNA on file after we got around to checking it. There were no wounds…gunshot, knifing. The coroner put decapitation as cause of death. The head and limbs hadn't showed up. We were completely at an impasse until we got an anonymous tip. When it came it turned the local world upside down."

"Why?"

"When you think of suspects for a slaughter like what we had, the suspects you think of are mentally deranged or the dregs of humanity. Moe got a letter. Words and sentences cut from newspapers and pasted on a sheet. It read, 'If you want to find parts missing from your corpse, check Professor Lisa Talmadge's freezer.' Moe laughed when he saw it. He thought it was a college prank by one of the woman's students. He filed it and we forgot about it for a week. Then we got another. Exact same wording, but this time they sent a copy to the TV station. We were lucky. The station manager wouldn't allow any release until he ran it through us. He gave us seventy-two hours to investigate it. The Sheriff was furious with Moe and pushed us to question the professor immediately. We tried. She answered the phone the first time. She hung up when we told her who we were. Wouldn't answer again. Moe and I got over there as quick as we could. She'd left and the place was locked. Now we knew it wasn't some fraternity or sorority prank. I stayed there while Moe got a search order issued. Long story short…the corpses leg, part of it *was* in the professor's freezer."

"Damn, did you catch her?"

"Find her, yes. Catch her, no. We did our best to shut off any possible means of escape. All regional airports, bus stations, all public transportation was covered. We set up roadblocks and did thorough checks. Kept watch on her friends and associates, best we could. That lasted five days before we were forced to relax. We didn't know how she escaped other than someone helped her. The earth swallowed her. News folks busted our chops for a couple weeks, it became old news, and then disappeared."

"You ever get any leads on who the corpse was or where the professor escaped to?"

"Yes. The DNA sample we sent off to match got a hit about six months later. A relative of the woman, Juliet Burress, that was our victim's name, became concerned when she couldn't contact her niece in four months. The victim lived in Charleston, South Carolina. She was a waitress. Lived by herself; kept to herself. Had an interest in witchcraft. We immediately started checking. We found a record of Lisa Talmadge being at a hotel there a few days before Juliet last reported for work. She quit eight days before her body showed up here. Talmadge attended a conference in Charleston at a college. Coincidences don't happen like that. Turns out several members of the university staff from our area attended that seminar. Political Science and Literature. Sounds innocent. By the time we finished we had twenty-seven names. Deans and department heads were included. Sheriff Adkins got wind of what we were doing. He had less than two years before he'd retire. The old boy wanted no part of swimming in a cesspool. He set the priority so low we'd have been investigating roaches in restaurants before that case got its turn. Then we found Talmadge…what was left of her."

"Dead and dismembered, right?"

"Dead and destroyed…that's more like it. A hunter's dog dug her up. I won't describe her other than to say you could not lay a hand on any part of her body without touching two or more stab wounds or axe marks. Her head was severed. That was in a cardboard box buried under the wooden square. That's what the dog found. Her left leg and right arm were missing. However, where she was found created a storm, and it is what complicates the crime we found out about at Buehl's. Juliet's body and Lisa Talmadge were both found on property that had strong connections to Native American heritage claims. Pressure to solve the case immediately exploded. Adkins got frantic. He wanted to tear up both properties. He got the idea the killer or killers were using the Seminole's reluctance to allow their graves to be disturbed as a way to hide their crimes. He could have been correct on that. But what he did next. That fire still has live embers today."

"What did he do?"

Reading shook his head. "The Sheriff decided that the middens, they were on both properties, were probably housing all kinds of horrible secrets. He didn't ask, he told the Seminoles he was going to bull-dozer the mounds. When they got a court order prohibiting him from destroying them, he went to the press. Adkins told any media person that would listen that the Seminoles were impeding his investigation. Nothing could have been farther from the truth. Terrie Tall Pine and the rest wanted the crime solved as bad as anyone…maybe more. It got hot. Pride versus ego. Adkins escalated it to a peek. He asked the reporters why the Seminoles were blocking his investigation. Was it because they were involved? Were they using their violent past to cover their violence today? We damn near had a mini war touch off. He had his scapegoat and Adkins wanted no part of the twenty-seven names on the list. Things boiled for a couple weeks then gradually cooled. It became such a political hot-potato, no one wanted anything to do with it…except we at the bottom of the pile. We knew the Seminoles had nothing to do with the killings. Adkins just used prejudice as a weapon. I apologized to Terrie and told her the cops doing the work knew her people had nothing to do with the case. I won't say we became friends, but we have lots of respect for each other."

"I'm surprised Terrie will have anything to do with law enforcement or government."

"She doesn't have any more or less choice than the rest of us." Reading shrugged his shoulders. "No more than we had in finding the killers. Adkins gathered up all the files and notes we had and made them disappear. We were told to forget the Burress and Talmadge killings. Other than memory, there's nothing to start from. I remember a few names…that's about it. What I'm sure of is that some type of cult is involved. It's a cult with members in the colleges and universities in this area." He hesitated and remarked painfully slow, "Probably…someone… you…have…met."

I sighed, "Short of becoming somebody's lunch, what do you want me to do?"

Chapter   27

Reading's request sounded simple: Nose around. Find out who belonged to cults or organizations like them. And, if I could, what the main interest of each group devoted its effort. He told me three things I couldn't do. First, I was not to join any of them or attend any meetings. Second, I was not to go anywhere, alone or with their friends, with any person I identified as belonging to such an organization. Third, I was not to divulge anything about the case or what I was doing…even to Mark. I balked at Mark, but Reading's axiom that two can keep a secret if one is dead and his suggestion that I might make a splendid main course, convinced me to agree.

I told him I'd play Mata Hari, but I'd do it my way…with no interference from him. Being someone's entre definitely wasn't an option. My tactic varied from his suggestion. What had happened at Buehl's ranch wasn't a secret…at least the deaths weren't. The details were concealed. I decided my strategy would reverse his. Instead of nosing around others, I'd offer some bait to get them nosing around me. What better way of finding out those with a vital interest in what the sheriff was finding at the ranch. I'd make an issue of not sharing 'the large amount that I knew' and wait for the vultures to pick at my bones.

My challenge? Separate the potentially guilty from the morbidly curious.

With that in mind, I placed a call to Carol Shubert. Carol is vice-chair of the literature department at East Florida. Carol has been at the University since its founding, knows everyone on campus, is filled with curiosity, and has to be among the world's outstanding gossips. A plus was that she was at East Florida with Lisa Talmadge. Since Mark and my participation in the Dillon Development project was well known, the recent discoveries would have her mind stuffed with questions. I needed a pretext to call, if not a brilliant one. Carol is an expert in 19th century American Literature but has few clues on anything else.

I used that knowledge and a bit of trivia I possessed to concoct an excuse to call her. And flatter her. The call I used to plant the seed started with my asking, "Is it true John Fenimore Cooper was thrown out of Yale for a prank and ended up joining the Navy because of that? One of the people on the Buehl dig told me that. I know that if anyone in this world would know the correct answer, it would be you."

"Oh, yes! That's correct, though it is only part of the story. Cooper had a record of misbehavior; he'd brought a donkey into the study room, for example. He was only thirteen at the time. Cooper is one of my favorites of that period." Carol paused after displaying her knowledge. "*Who* is working with you that has that depth of knowledge of Cooper?"

The fish took the bait…I set the hook. "Carol, the whole dig is a hush-hush thing. Mark and I were told we can't discuss what we're learning about the horrible things…well, I've already said too much. I can't give you a name, but I can tell you it was one of the sheriff's deputies." I knew telling Carol I had access to secrets would quadruple her efforts to pump them from me.

The phone remained silent as Carol digested my comments. Then she asked, "I wouldn't want you to break any confidences, but can't you give me some idea of what's going on out there. I promise not to tell a soul. The whole town is talking about that poor Mr. Carson. And, there are rumors that other stuff has been found."

I asked, "Where did you hear other *bodies* might have been found?"

"More bodies!? Really! Sheila's sister said there was more happening out there than just the Wilbur Carson thing. She works for the Sheriff." I imagined Carol drooling.

I acted as if I wanted to 'cover a mistake.' I stammered, "I didn't say bodies, did I? If I did, I misspoke."

Carol laughed. "A card laid is a card played…I told you I won't say anything. You said bodies. How many?"

"I can't say."

"Who are you looking for? Do you have any leads?" Carol's voice rose an octave.

"No individual, yet. In fact, it might be a group."

Carol gasp. "A group? Like who?"

"They haven't said. It's just conjecture. Maybe some type of ritualistic thing." I spelled it without saying the word.

"Like a cult?"

"I can't say." I paused then added something I knew Carol would resist. "Can we change the subject. How are you doing?"

"Fine. When you've taught for as long as I have, it's like being a plow horse. You can pull the darned thing without a lot of thought. How are you? I guess it is miserable out in the field. It's been so hot. Sweaty, yuk! I bet that makes the sand stick to you. How are conditions at Buehl's?" She led me back to where I wanted to go.

"It isn't comfortable out there, but that comes with the job. We talk about all kinds of things to pass the time between discoveries. Sports. What our next site is going to be. What's happening at the University. People we work with or used to work with." I paused to be sure what I would say next would register. "One of the detectives assigned to the Carson case said a woman that used to work at East Florida was murdered. I can't remember her name, but evidently she was dumped in a field…forget you heard that."

"Oh! Lisa Talmadge! That was years before you even were a student here. Was there a discussion about her? Some type of a relationship to the Dillon Development?" Carol asked.

"No. Not at all. The detectives talked about old cases of all types."

"Did you know—"

I cut the conversation off saying, "Carol, I'm sorry. Somebody is at my door. Thanks for the information about Cooper."

My seed was planted. In the proper field. I wondered how long it would take to sprout.

Chapter   28

Dr. Mark Card looked perplexed. His choice for the *spot most likely* turned out to be a bust. The location he had been sure was a midden, *was* a huge pile of sand. Nothing more. Our Ground Penetrating Radar showed a goose egg. Nothing that would hint at being an archaeological find appeared, even after doing two thorough roll-overs. Our Jeep ran over the only evidence we found near the site, a hoe with a still readable manufacturer's tag that proclaimed, "Ajax tools, May 2003, Made in China."

Four of us were making the preliminary radar samplings. Mark and I were joined by Bobby and Sheila, Mark's student assistants. We began folding up the radar unit when Bobby suggested, "Hey Mark, I saw another location marked on the same aerial this place is on. It isn't but a few hundred yards. Why not run the radar over it while we're here? We won't have to break down the unit. Sheila and I can make room for it."

"That's a great idea," Mark agreed. We were soon easing through a marsh that stood between the place we had examined and Bobby's suggested spot. The oak hammock we were on the way to visit formed an island six feet higher than the marsh surrounding it. The oaks on the sandy knoll were huge, many with four-foot diameters or greater. In the center of these trees, an opening devoid of any oaks or underbrush is what drew Mark's attention to that spot on the photo. As the Jeep produced a wake in the six-inch-deep water we plowed through, a wall of dense weeds, custard apple bushes, and scrub swamp maples veiled the area under the huge trees. The curtain formed a thick enough barrier that Mark began circling the island to find a less formidable place to break through.

When he found it, the location had obviously been hacked out by humans. Though not apparently used recently, stumps created by chain saws stood like sentinels guarding the hammock's interior. A hint of tire ruts remained, and Mark steered the jeep into them.

The dense barrier ended abruptly at the fringes of the canopy the oak trees made. It shaded out almost all vegetation leaving the surface of the hammock a vast expanse of loose sand scattered with dead oak branches. The density of the shade took a few seconds for our eyes to adjust. When they did what we saw shocked us.

A theater, much like the one where we'd discovered the headless skeletons, lay under the trees. A much more elaborate one. Logs cut to act as seats surrounded the opening. I guessed the circle created stretched fifty or more feet in diameter. A huge stump from an oak, cut flat on top, lay within the circle. I heard Mark hiss emotionally, "Shit, not another one."

"Should I call my brother?" I asked.

Mark thought for several seconds. He shook his head. "Not until we do our radar scan."

~ ~ ~ ~ ~ ~

"Stop, Bobby," an object appeared on the top of the radar screen. It looked familiar. "Go ahead real slow," I prompted. He crawled the radar forward a half inch at a time. It was another one. "Okay, move forward until I tell you…" Bobby pushed the unit at a slow steady speed. "Stop," I commanded. "Sheila, put a marker here." I pointed to a place on the ground. Sheila stuck a wire stake with a small plastic flag attached into the ground to locate another one.

"Same thing?" Mark looked up from the chart he drew of the clearing.

"Yes."

"How many is that?" Mark asked.

I looked at my notes, "That would be thirty-one. We still have more than half the area to scan."

"Damn! Whoever they are…they like their wine," Mark concluded.

"My only question is why did they bother to bury the bottles?" I quipped.

"So we'd have something to find," wise-cracking Bobby suggested.

"Have you found anything except wine bottles?" Mark inquired.

"Three tin cans, a pair of pliers, and an object that I can't ID that's four-or-five-inches square." I shook my head. "So far, I don't believe there is anything here that predates the twentieth century. As far as things connected to the sheriff's business, he ought to have a great bottle collection when he finishes with this spot." I pointed to the clip board Mark carried. "How is the map going?"

"I'll finish soon."

"Learn anything?" I asked.

"Yes. All twenty logs that frame the circle are exactly cut to three feet and are spaced equally from the center and each other. In the center of the circle there is an iron surveyors rod driven into the ground." Mark pursed his lips, shook his head, and said, "I hate guessing, but I think I'm right on this."

"Right about what?" I asked.

"I don't want to say until I do more research." Mark paused, smiled and asked, "Unless you're an expert on Norse Mythology. Know anything about a God named Vidar?"

"No." I admitted. "Speaking of knowing a little about Norse myths, I know as little as anyone."

"I do," Sheila volunteered. "I have relatives in Norway, and I read a couple books on that when I visited them in Oslo." She shrugged her shoulders. "Ask me something. I might know it."

Mark walked to us, moving a sheet of paper from the bottom of the clip board to the top. He held the sheet up for us to see. It was an irregular shaped outline with a square drawn inside. Each side of the square's drawing underlined a word. Those four words were: Vidar, Gridr, Odin, and Fenrir. He asked Sheila, "The square and the names are carved on the top of the tree stump. Do those names mean anything to you?"

"Yes, they certainly do. I'm sure you know who Odin is. Gridr is one of his wives. Fenrir is the wolf who killed Odin. Vidar is Odin's and Gridr's son. He killed Fenrir in revenge. Vidar is known as the God of revenge."

Mark smiled, nodded, and pointed to the center of the square. "See all the random lines I've drawn there? They represent what I believe are broadaxe marks driven into the wood. Notice that Vidar is 90° from Fenrir. That would be the proper position to behead someone. I think the sheriff is chasing a cult that takes revenge on people who wrong a member of the group."

Chapter   28

"How many bottles did you end up with?" Mark asked.

"Seventy-four," I answered and added, "And, judging from the shape, there are an additional half-dozen Crown Royal bottles in there. I pointed to the 'field of flags.' "Notice they're buried in an order. It isn't as perfectly laid out as the theater, but it definitely has a pattern to it. I took pictures of them. They're three to four feet apart." I held up my electronic tablet.

Mark examined the layout, while Bobby and Sheila loaded the radar unit and other equipment into the Jeep. The two argued like magpies though they were best friends.

"You probably should call Reading." Mark looked up from my I-pad. "This is definitely connected to the other crime scene. He might want to get someone out here to babysit it." Mark rolled his drawings and placed them in his briefcase.

"Why? There isn't going to be anyone around here. Buehl and the Sheriff have all the gates it's practical to drive through guarded or made impassible. I'll see him in a few hours. I can tell him at home."

Mark shrugged his shoulders, blinked his eyes, and crawled into the Jeep's driver seat.

While Mark and I talked, we didn't notice that our bickering students had suddenly become quiet. I saw Bobby silently reach out and touch Mark's elbow.

"We're being watched," Bobby nodded at the opening that we'd driven the Jeep through to gain access to the clearing. "They're dressed in camouflage and kneeling behind tall weeds at the edge of the marsh."

It took me several seconds to find human outline. It was real. I watched as the 'whomever' slipped down below the heavy vegetation.

"What are we going to do?" Sheila asked.

"Wait here and give them plenty of time to get out," Mark said firmly.

"I'll call Reading. He probably will get someone here," I said as I pulled out my cell phone.

Bobby suggested, "Why don't we go after them?"

"Do you have a gun?" Mark asked.

"No."

"They probably do."

There was no reason for further discussion.

Chapter   29

"There's no way Buehl didn't know what those people were doing on his property, Chessie. I agree. Proving that in a court won't be easy. Remember common sense doesn't always rule in legal matters." Reading looked at the big piece of cherry pie sitting in front of him. "You have any whip cream for that?"

I pointed to the refrigerator. "I'm not mother. Help yourself." I watched Reading wrestle with the decision: to get his rear out of his chair and get the whip cream…or not…that is the question. The whip cream won. As he returned from the refrigerator, I asked, "What's next. You have an active murder in Carson. You have a multiple homicide screaming for a solution. I hate to think this will end up like the Lisa Talmadge killing did." I knew I was goading him about something he only had limited control over, but I didn't care.

Reading ignored me. He pushed the nozzle to one side, and white foam piled on his pie. "You know better," he finally answered, his words measured and unemotional. "We have to be able to *prove* what I believe we know."

"Based on what we found this afternoon; I know we have a bunch of nuts out there killing and *eating* people! There were twenty log seats. Twenty! We know they've committed horrible crimes. Hell, Reading, what if the bottles we found represent murders? That's seventy-four human beings! Are you trying for a hundred?"

"Don't' go fe—" Reading stopped and started over. "Sorry. Look, the worst thing law enforcement can do is take some rash action and screw up catching all that are involved, or worse, give the guilty a loophole to escape old sparky. That's where they need to end up."

"Reading, I can't agree with the last part more. But what concerns me is that these folks are running around…free! They could be capturing their next victim as we sit here gabbing. We don't know how many there are much less who. I did some scary math. There were twenty seats in the circle we found today. Where the headless bodies were buried…that little theater had room for eight butts. Why would you have two places like that? Seems we may have multiple groups using Buehl's ranch as a dining room!" I let my last brutal words sink in, then I asked the crucial question. "There are eleven square miles out there. What haven't we found?"

"That's what you, Mark, and the rest of your team will find out for us. Meanwhile," Reading put down his fork and leaned toward me, "we'll have to believe that the individuals in the group or cult or whatever are interested in their self-preservation. The last thing they'll do is commit one of their atrocities while everyone is looking for them. That will buy us time."

"Insane people don't act rationally. These people are insane." I tapped my fist on the table. "It is obvious that Carl Buehl is like an egg over a skillet. He's ready to crack. Why not bring him in? Grill his ass? He could spill the beans. All you need is a few names and you can chain the next ones."

"What if he doesn't? He's worried, now. I'm afraid the old boy will blow his brains out. Maybe in a week or two. We're waiting for lab reports on the skeletons you found, and we exhumed. Bill Worthington has a lead on the Carson killing." Reading leaned back. "Have you done any nosing around? I know you haven't been on campus…"

"Some. I talked to the biggest gossip in the school. She'll get the word out. I told her how I knew important things I couldn't tell her. She swore secrecy. That means half the University will know by now. I figure I'll start getting calls at any time."

Reading looked at me critically. "How are you going to separate the guilty from the nosey?"

"I'm not. You are."

~ ~ ~ ~ ~ ~

"Hi, Chessie. It's Alvin Peed. I'm not sure if you remember me. I teach social science classes at East Florida. We have met several times." The voice coming through my cell phone came from a tall, thin fellow whose most prominent contributions to the University were his impersonations of Icabod Crane at Halloween parties and in a theatrical production of 'Sleepy Hollow.'

"Sure, Alvin. Or is it, Dr. Peed? I know you were working on that." It was a perennial question with same answer.

"Not quite yet. But soon." Peed paused, then spoke in what I perceived as a rehearsed voice, "I'm sure you're wondering why I'm calling."

I lied, "I haven't a clue."

"Dr. Clemmons has asked me to call you to do an interview for the Red Raider. The newspaper hasn't done a feature on the archaeology department in some time. With your work on the Dillon Development dig, she thought it would be a great time for an interview, but she had concerns about letting a student do it. So…here I am."

I had two names! But, I decided to play a game. "You need to interview Dr. Card. Mark's the proper one to speak for department issues. About the only thing I can address is projects I've been involved with."

There was a short delay, then Alvin said, "We will be talking to Dr. Mark also, but what you've said is exactly what we'd like from you." He hesitated a couple seconds then said, "Tell us what you do when you're in the field. What are the interesting things? You're at a dig now, correct?"

"Correct." One-word answers demand more elaborate questions.

Uhhhhh…Let's see…what is the most interesting thing you've discovered since you started your current project?" Peed's fishing pole was in action.

"Alvin, you are aware there has been the death at the property. I can't discuss that. It's in the sheriff's control and we can't say a word. There have been some highly unusual finds. But we are in the early stages, so I won't have anything exciting as far as archaeological items…yet." Reading wandered into the living room to eavesdrop. I continued, "Alvin, I'm going to put you on speaker. I'm doing dishes and I don't want to drop my phone in the water. Okay, so where were we? Oh, I remember. The dig progress is slower than we hoped. Maybe we should talk later when we learn more." I paused to be sure Alvin concentrated on my next sentence. "Our search for artifacts has had interruptions due to finds that aren't what I'd call historical."

"Oh? What are they?"

"I'm sorry, I can't discuss them. I know that sounds silly, but the sheriff is keeping a tight lid on the *investigations*."

"Investigations? More than one?" There was more nervous than interest in his voice.

"Alvin, I can't say."

The cell remained silent for a few seconds before Alvin asked, "How about some type of hint?"

"Hmmmm. The problems we have aren't involved with our assigned task. We will be able to complete it…eventually."

"Does it have to do with the Sheriff?"

"Sorry, I can't say." I thought I heard a gassy whisper in the background.

"Obviously, the sheriff's department is investigating the Carson murder." Alvin sighed, "They must be there for something else…as well. What are they?"

I decided no answer was the best answer.

"Did they find stolen goods?"

I knew that question was a throw away and remained silent.

"Drugs. They find them on the property?" It was another distracting comment.

The question I expected finally was asked, "Did they find more bodies?"

"I can't talk about it." I knew that answer would send electric shocks up some spines. I decided to end the conversation but leave an opening for him to continue. "Alvin, my brother is supposed to be home soon. You probably know he's a Captain in the Sheriff's Department. He'd have a cow if he knew I was talking to you about what's being found out there. Promise to keep our conversation secret. Call me back in a week or ten days."

After I ended the call, Reading smiled and said, "You make a hell of a good Mata Hari."

Chapter   30

"I think we have one," Mark held his hand up and I stopped pushing the GPR forward. "Okay." He scribbled notes in his notepad as he spoke, "Move ahead very slowly."

I pushed the unit through a mixture of weeds and soft sand.

"This one has a skull," Mark commented, "From the way the corpse is laid out, this is an Ais or Seminole, I'd guess Ais." He peered at the screen while I pushed the radar forward as smoothly as I could. After I'd moved the machine another four feet, he said, "Stop!" Mark pushed four stakes into the sand marking the location of the skeleton. He grinned at Bobby and me. "So much for short cuts. We will have to cut all the weeds and finish our radar runs. My guess we'll find more stuff here. There are items that were interred with the body. I recognized a big Welk shell and what could be a stone implement of some type. There were other blurs on the screen. Probably wooden items…items that have deteriorated."

Sheila looked at an exceptionally hot October sun and asked plaintively, "Do you think we should stop until Terrie Tall Pine gives us the go ahead?"

"No. We'll go ahead and remove the surface cover. Chessie and I can chart what's under here with the radar, while you and Bobby cut weeds." Mark's smile held no mercy.

Bobby had little 'dreamer blood.' He walked to the Jeep to retrieve the trimmers and grass whips. In his most Lancelot voice he offered, "Fair Sheila, willst thou have yon Gas Trimmer or Hand Scythe?"

~ ~ ~ ~ ~ ~ ~ ~

"Seven." Mark answered Sheila's question as to the number of skeletons we'd located. Seventy percent of the small glade had been covered by the GPR. We all sat on the ground and sipped on bottled water. The sun had passed its zenith, but not its ability to torture our bodies.

Bobby asked, "Is there any more you want us to cut down?" He pointed to the clearing which had been trimmed to an inch high stubble from tree line to tree line.

Mark surveyed their work and shook his head. "Naw, that's enough. When we come back to excavate, I'll want to go out another ten feet, maybe twenty-five where those young cabbage palms are growing in the open area. No use doing that until I've gone over the site with Terrie."

"Did they all have their skulls?" Sheila shivered as she asked.

"Yes. I don't think any of these are twentieth century." Mark opened his portable drawing board exposing his map of the site. "Come look at this," he said as he motioned for us. Each find located on the paper had notes about its position, items buried with it, and exact geographic location. Mark switched from explorer to explainer. "This has some interesting features; one I've never observed before. Notice how four are laid out in almost parallel position, skulls all at the same end. The fifth one is laid in the same direction, but its skull is pointing toward the others. And it is more or less centered in front of the other four." Mark pointed to his drawing.

"What do you think the significance of that is?" I asked.

"I don't have a clue. My guess is there is some relationship between them, and the layout of their burial signifies that. We might find the explanation when we do our dig. We might find the whole thing is coincidence."

"That's not likely, is it?" Bobby asked.

Mark grinned, "Noooo. But are we likely to be able to prove that?" He shrugged his shoulders. "I tend to be one of our disciplines that takes a dim view of drawing hard conclusions from soft evidence." He pointed to a circle drawn on the map with lines drawn to each of the five skeletons. "There is a cache of items buried next to the single skeleton. I have no idea what's in there, but my theory is that these are items that were buried for a family to use in their after-life. I'm guessing the lines were tree limbs buried that connected the graves to their possessions. I'd also guess we'll find that these people all died at near the same time, maybe from some epidemic."

Sheila said, "That sounds right to me."

Mark laughed, "I have a colleague who uses soft evidence to make hard conclusions. He made a find with a GPR unit. He found what he concluded were four small alligators, wrapped in cloth or some types of wood and vegetation and were set up to mark the four cardinal points of the directions. North. South. East. West. His find was in a corn field on river bottom lands in the low hills of south-eastern Georgia. Claimed it was pre-Mississippian. He wrote a paper on it; about how it wasn't necessary to disturb every find by digging them up. He even got a couple citations and awards for it." Mark chuckled. "Lots of us thought he blew smoke and lots of so-called scientists sniffed it. Some doubting Thomas decided to have a look. When he dug it up, it turned out to be some old tractor tires cut to look like gators. When he ran down the source, he found out some coon hunters did it to pass time while their dogs did their work. Put it in a fire pit to mark the directions all right…but in the mid nineteen thirties."

"It's like evidence in a murder case. Everything isn't always what it seems." My brother had walked up on us unobserved. Reading found a spot that would collect the minimum of sand on his pants and sat down with us. He asked, "Find anything for me today?"

I answered for Mark, "Not today."

"Good." Reading twisted his head around to peer at Mark. "What is your plan for tomorrow?"

"It depends," Mark answered. "I have to call Tall Pine and have her come out, look at this place, and get her permission to dig."

"Do you have to do that right away?" Reading asked.

"No. What's up?"

"Can I talk to you in private?" Reading asked.

Mark looked at Sheila, Bobby and me, "I guess you need to snipe hunt for a few minutes."

Bobby and Sheila got up to walk away. I didn't. "If you want me to do my Mata Hari impersonation, Reading…bro…I need to hear this." I spoke with as much of an authoritarian tone that I could muster.

Reading glared at me, and I glared back. Finally, he said, "Okay, you can stay. You know the rule. Keep your trap shut!"

Mark smiled and said, "One thing we know, Chessie is not a member of the weaker sex."

I snapped back, "There is no weaker sex, just a weaker minded one."

"Touché," Mark said around his chuckle.

Reading looked bored and said, "To get to the point, I'd like you to take a look at something we found today. One of my detectives nosed around the woods behind the ceremonial place you found yesterday. Out about fifty feet away from the clearing he found an old abandoned pickup truck. When he circled around it, he found a bare spot covered with a metal plate for a door, with what looked like a wood handle sticking out of it. He pulled it open a foot and wished he hadn't. It covered a citrus field box…full to the top with skulls. I know what you're going to tell me it is, but if we don't get you involved, and you get the Seminoles to pass on it, I'll get all kinds of grief."

~ ~ ~

"Holy horse manure! Did you make a guess how many are in there?" Mark stammered.

"We peeked inside. Best I can guess there are at least three layers with twenty-five, or so, in a layer. Our killers have been very, very active." Reading exhaled strongly. "Looking at those skulls, figuring how they got there, and what happened to the rest of them…it's horrifying."

"I'll take a look tomorrow morning. I'll have to tell Terrie, but I'll tell her she can't tell anyone, not even the others on her council."

Reading nodded. "Thanks." He hesitated, then added, "Don't eat before you come. Two of those heads haven't been there long."

Chapter   31

"The safest place for all of you is either back on campus or at home," Mark addressed Bobby, Sheila, and I as we stood next to the jeep. "Take a day off."

"Why?" I asked. "There's plenty for us to do out here. Besides, you might need help at the ceremonial site."

"I don't expect to be doing much over there," Mark mumbled as he pointed in the general direction. "Mostly waiting. I'll have to wait on Terrie. She told me she can't get there until at least eleven. Knowing the situation she works under, that means closer to one. Then I have to have a look, assuming she releases me to proceed. That will shoot the day."

Bobby looked disappointed. "Can't you let Chessie, Sheila, and me go to some of the other sites and clear them so we save time when we run the GPR unit."

"Yes. And, if you do need help checking those skulls out, I'd be here to help," I volunteered.

Mark thought the offer over for a few seconds, shook his head, and decided, "I want to do this alone." He saw disappointment on our faces, so he added, "Hey, it isn't that I think you'd screw something up. I know anything you all would do would be perfect." He exhaled in a gush. "The less you're involved, the safer you'll be. When Reading made the call to the station to tell them Terrie would come out tomorrow, and I'd sign off on the skulls, they told him one of the officers at the gates was shot at. It was on the other side of the ranch. The officer believes they shot to miss. But……. The bigger distance you keep between what the sheriff is doing and what our purpose for being here is, the safer you will all be."

I shook my head, "Mark you're dreaming. What they don't want is for anyone to discover what they did. That's not what we're here for but that's what we're going to do as a by-product of what our job is. We are all involved. The door is closed on that *not* happening."

Mark stared at his feet.

"Hey, you won't have to worry. Ask them to assign that Dobbs guy to protect us. They aren't going to do anything with a deputy standing over us, You said they shot to miss this morning. They know if they hit a cop their asses are grass." Bobby added, "I'll feel safer here than sitting alone at home."

"I won't," Sheila exclaimed. "I'd like the next couple days off, if you decide we all should work." She was frightened and didn't care we knew it.

Mark scratched a bicep that a mosquito sampled. After a minute of weighing pros and cons, he pronounced. "If you want to work, I'll have a work plan. If you want to stay home, that's fine. That's for the next week. But I'm setting up this rule whether you work or not. If anyone asks, you don't know anything about the sheriff's investigation past reporting the find. Refer any questions about what is happening to the sheriff's office or to me." He took a deep breath and rolled his eyes. "Reading doesn't know who or how, but the press knows about the sheriff's people finding the skulls. Be ready!"

Chapter   32

Retreating to our duplex didn't provide the seclusion we normally enjoyed there. When we arrived that evening, several reporters and two TV camera crews were stationed in our front yard sulking around like a flock of vultures. They were primarily interested in prying information from Reading, but were equal opportunity offenders. Many quickly abandoned Reading as his steadfast "No comment," was all they got. I had an unwanted coat of columnists and TV field reporters shouting questions. The thirty-seconds to get from our vehicle to inside our home never seemed so long.

Ignoring the doorbell and knocking, we headed for our rooms, changed clothes, and met in the kitchen. Reading slumped into a chair at the kitchen table.

"We shouldn't have come home. If I thought for just a second, I'd have known we'd have a bunch of media around the house." Reading rested his elbows on the table, cupped his hands and buried his face in them. I rarely see my brother let a case he's working, depress him. This one obviously did. He hadn't stopped at the refrigerator for a Coors as he passed. That earthquake maker meant he'd been overwhelmed. I corrected his tactical error, popped the top, and set the can in front of him. I said, "That will make it better."

His features emerged long enough to smile and inhale a third of the can. "I'm glad we changed our number and left it unlisted, or the phone would be going crazy." He guzzled what remained of his beer. His eyes implored me; I nodded. As I set number two down in front of him, he said, "Thanks."

A particularly insistent individual began ringing the doorbell non-stop. "I'll get it," I said and headed for the front door. When I opened it, I was shocked to see twenty or more bodies crammed on our five-foot-wide porch. All screamed questions; the resulting noise none-separable, and unintelligible.

I screamed back, "Go away. We can't answer any questions." I tried slamming the door, but all manner of body parts wedged in between the jam and the panel. Though a few "ouches" were expressed, I couldn't get the door closed. One young lady thrust a microphone through the crack, "Is it true that you've found two hundred bodies on the Buehl ranch?"

"No," I blustered.

"How many have you found?" the reporter tried to trap me in a question-and-answer exchange. I recovered my wits before being sucked in, "No comment." I pushed the microphone out only to have another slip in beneath the first.

A surly reporter demanded, "How close are they to catching the serial killer?"

"No comment!" I screamed and slammed the door on one foot and the wrist holding the mic. Both retracted enough for me to get the door latched.

The wrist delivered his opinion of me, "Shit, that hurt you damned bitch."

Reading tapped me on the shoulder, saying "I'll handle this." He opened the door and screamed, "Shut the fuck up!" He didn't need to repeat his obscenity. The mob of carrion collectors became silent. Then he addressed them. "If you're looking for Captain Reading Partin of the Indian River Sheriff's Department, you've found him. Yes, I'm investigating an active crime scene on the Buehl Ranch. Because of that I cannot discuss anything with you. My answer to any question you ask is, no comment. So go away and leave us alone." Reading can look vicious if he chooses.

One reporter yelled, "Can we talk to your sister? We understand she is on the archaeology team that discovered some of the bodies."

"No, you can't," Reading bellowed. "Listen. I'll say this once. You are on private property. You're trespassing. Get out of my yard and stay out. If you don't, I'll have all of you hauled to jail. Anyone doubt I can have a half-dozen cars here in ten minutes?"

The crowd of reporters evaporated like water on a campfire rock.

~ ~ ~ ~ ~ ~

"I've seen things as gruesome." Reading swished his fork through the spaghetti I'd served him without disposing of much. He normally inhaled pasta. "I think it's the sheer volume. These people have to be among the most prolific murderers of all time."

I added a reason for him to be upset, "You never have encountered a cannibal before, much less a whole raft of them."

"You could have skipped saying that." Reading frowned at the marinara sauce and meatballs. He abruptly dropped his fork on the plate.

"Sorry. I didn't mean to ruin your me—" My cell phone interrupted my sentence.

Reading scowled. "If it's one of those damned news people, tell them never to call back here, and hang up."

It *was* probably the press. Mark and the University paid for a special record function for our phones…protection against the miss-quote. I punched the record icon and said, "Hello."

There was a brief pause, then a deep voice said, "This Professor Partin?"

"This is Instructor Chessie Partin," I corrected.

Silence.

"Who is this?" I asked.

Reading pointed to the speaker icon on my phone. I turned it on.

Silence. Reading wrote the phone number showing on my screen on the tablecloth.

"If you're selling something, I'm not buying. If this is a political call, I'm an independent and don't believe in the party system. If you're some type of pervert, go do yourself." I hung up.

"That call probably came from Orlando. It's from the 407 area co—" The cell rang again; the number on the screen was the same. I asked Reading, "Should I?"

"Yes, put it on speaker right away."

"Hello, who is this?" I asked.

"Someone you don't know."

Reading rolled his hands indicating to keep the man on the phone. I said, "Why do I want to talk to someone I don't know?"

"To learn something," the voice responded.

"Like what?" I prolonged the conversation. Reading frantically dialed his office, hoping to get the call traced.

The caller ignored my question. "What are you doing?" he inquired.

"Eating."

"Oh? That is interesting. What are you having for super?" the voice asked.

"Spaghetti and meat balls."

"Hmmmmm. Sounds good." He laughed. "Don't bother your brother with trying to trace this call. It won't do any good."

"I wouldn't interrupt his meal," I said. At that second, Reading made a circle with his thumb and index finger. He had the trace going. Reading rolled his hands again.

I tried to shock the caller with a brash statement. "If you're in the area, I have plenty spaghetti cooked…if you like marinara and spicy meat balls."

The man laughed. "Sorry. But, I will have you for dinner sometime in the future." The click told me the man hung up and that the call came from a land line.

Reading immediately asked, "Did you recognize the voice?"

"No."

"You know what we just received," Reading stated.

"We just were warned," I answered.

"More than that. You just got a death threat. Have you for dinner?" Reading shook his head. "These people, whoever they are, they're true psychos. There is no logical reason to call us. They know they aren't going to scare us off. They did it because they enjoy what they're doing. Those folks want to terrorize their victims."

"Victims my ass! I don't intend to be one."

"You won't be. I'll see to that." Reading relaxed a little, chuckling as he told me. "And you don't have to worry about the cannibal thing. You're too tough to chew."

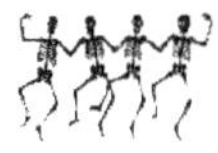

Chapter   33

Reading spoke with the detective who traced the call. He responded to what the detective told him by saying, "Disappointing, but not unexpected. Do you have a location?" Reading grinned and wrote in his notebook. "Given what we know from down here, he gave us more information than he thought." Reading looked surprised. "They have the capability of doing that? By all means. Get the two before and the two after and be sure to get the times." He nodded to an unseeing person and said, "No, tomorrow's fine. Put it on my desk. I'm going to stop at the station before I go to Buehl's ranch."

After Reading ended the call, I asked, "Learn anything?"

"Yes and no, no first. Our caller placed his call from a pay phone in a bar in Orlando. No smoking gun there." Reading grinned. "The old boy did leave a bread crumb or two to follow. First, the bar is in the general vicinity of UCF. That heightens the probability these nuts have a connection to the university system. Second, the Orlando PD has the ability to request the phone numbers of calls made from the pay station before and after the one we identified. And the times they were made. If our boy called right before or right after he called you, we'll have a thread to pick at. If we get a connection…that's a giant step forward."

"Reading, finding out if someone is connected at East Florida is involved will be great." I hesitated, stared at him for a few seconds, then said, "Brother, somebody at the ranch, Buehl or one of his people, has to be in this up to their nose. Why haven't you processed search warrants on everything connected to him and everything he owns?"

Reading made a disgusted grunt. "That's why I have to go into the office before I go to the ranch tomorrow. My boss has run into all kinds of complications trying to get those warrants. First, Buehl doesn't own anything. Everything is in his wife's name. The only thing we got a valid paper on was his pickup truck. Our legal folks had to start over to get the correct wording. Now, the judge is dragging his feet. I'm going into the office to meet the Sheriff and go with him to try and persuade the judge tomorrow."

"What can you do that your boss can't?"

"Tell the judge how time critical it is, from the investigator's viewpoint, to get into where we want to look before any evidence is destroyed. Tell him I believe these people are looking for their next victim now." Reading punched icons on his cell phone. "And show him these." Pictures of the skulls filled the screen with horror movie scenes.

# # # # #

Chapter   34

"Eight more," I told Bobby. He'd asked how many sites we had left to check. Our day hadn't been a good one. The Florida sun beat us up mercilessly. We cleared three of the sites. Bobby and I did thorough radar explorations. The sum of our findings: a group of buried 55-gallon drums with an assortment of other trash mingled in, a buried steer with exceptionally large horns, and a space with absolutely nothing beneath the surface. "This goes in the book as a wasted day."

Bobby looked at the sun. "Do we have time to look at one more?"

I looked at my watch. "It's 2:47. That's too late to start." What I didn't say was that we'd checked the three sites Mark had approved. He hadn't joined us as he thought he might. He'd told me he'd tell us what we should do next. The clouds had rainy dark bottoms. We only had a few bottles of water. The dog probably ate my homework. There were more excuses, but I didn't want to expend the energy to think of them. I could have called Mark, but my muscles protested. I'd had enough for the day. Still, Bobby and the two students in the back of the Jeep looked terribly disappointed. I decided on an alternate strategy. "Bobby, hand me the aerials."

"Coming right up," Bobby said as he removed the map case from the rear seat and handed it to me.

I thumbed through several until I found one that showed the terrain from where we were to the ranch road that led to the gate. It wouldn't be difficult to go 'across country' and ignore the roads we normally used. I picked a spot between where we sat in the Jeep and the gate road. No pines and few palmettoes covered the sand. It could be because humans had cleared it; I doubted that, but it allowed me to say, "There's a place I think we should look at as we go back. It might be something. Bobby, drive us toward those oak woods." I pointed. Bobby smiled and drove.

$\sim \sim \sim \sim \sim \sim$

"It does look like humans cleared it," I spoke more to myself than the other three occupants of the Jeep. From the photo, I'd thought the area would be a depression. Instead, the area's elevation was higher than the surrounding pine and palmetto flat. Surprisingly, there were few weeds growing over the forty-foot square area. The sparse clumps of wire grass and assorted weeds were spaced in a pattern, or at least it seemed that way to me.

Bobby carefully examined the aerial as I pondered whether to do a little poking around and even run the GPR over a portion of the exposed sand. "Hey, Chessie, I think there's an old set of ruts from this place to the main gate."

He laid the photo on my lap and traced his discovery with his finger. I agreed, he'd probably discovered a trail into where we sat. Based on our experience on the Buehl ranch, we'd probably find something. That something would interest my brother more than Mark. I decided to clear some weeds and run the radar over a portion of it.

Bobby read my mind. "Where should we start?"

I picked the spot with the fewest weeds on it. "There," I said and pointed.

"You heard the lady, slaves. Grab a grass-whip and get to work." Bobby's comments to the two students in the Jeep's rear weren't well received. The girls looked at each other, folded their arms, and one asked, "Who died and left you, boss…asshole."

I ended the discussion. "We'll all do this." I climbed out of the Jeep.

"What about setting up the GPR?" Bobby looked for a get-out-of-jail-free card. He looked at me questioningly.

"Haven't you heard of women's lib?" I laughed and the two girls high fived.

We soon were cutting down weeds and tufts of grass. Within a minute of clearing the vegetation, one of the girls, Simone, yelled, "I hit something here." She bent over, then kneeled next to her finding. "It's a handle, a long one. I think it's plastic or metal."

We gathered around the object. What was exposed stuck above the ground an inch, curved at an angle of more than eighty degrees and disappeared back into the ground ten inches from the curve. It appeared to have a silver coating at one time. I quickly got control. "Bobby, this isn't something of archaeological value, but I want to check it out. Go set up the GPR. Simone, get a shovel and a trowel. We'll do a little exploring while Bobby gets set up."

~ ~ ~ ~ ~ ~

"It's metal and it's white!" Simone took one very shallow scope of dirt next to the 'handle' and immediately hit a flat surface. Within a couple of minutes, the mystery was solved. Bobby announced what the rest of us recognized., "It's a refrigerator. It's buried with the door face up."

"Get a camera, Simone. We need to take some pictures." I removed my cell phone to call Reading. Bobby interrupted me.

"Where should we start with the radar?" he asked.

After a moment's consideration, I said, "Just get it out of the Jeep, but I don't want it on yet."

"Why?"

I answered with a smile and resumed making the call to my brother. When he answered, I asked, "Hey, Reading, we found a refrigerator buried out in the middle of the palmettoes. It's probably someone just disposing of an old appliance. I'm going to check inside, before I ask you to drive over here. That okay?"

Reading asked if we found it with the radar.

"No," I answered. "It isn't in one of the spots we thought were suspicious. I don't want to waste time if someone used this spot as a junkyard."

I nodded as Reading told me to check inside.

"Simone, you take pictures. Bobby, leave the radar where it is until we get the door open on this sucker." I began removing dirt from the refrigerator's door with the shovel. Bobby and the other girl soon were helping me expose enough of the door to open it.

Chapter   35

"Take more dirt out from behind the door and the hinges," I instructed as I pulled upward on the handle. The girls responded with shovel and trowel. After another couple minutes, Simone said, "There's a trough dug six inches behind the door three inches deeper than the refrigerator body. The dirt shouldn't be keeping it shut. Give it another try Professor Partin."

I assumed my best dead weight-lifting position and lifted. To no avail.

"Let me take a shot at it," Bobby decided to try male brute strength. He failed miserably. He dropped to his knees and examined the seal between door and box. His conclusion, "I think someone has super glued it shut." He stood looking at the appliance and wondered out loud, "Why did they not seal the freezer portion."

Simone scoffed, "They sealed the part they didn't want anyone getting in." She shook her head. "We know what's in it."

"If we knew, *for sure*, what was inside, we wouldn't be opening it," I reminded her.

Bobby stared at the door. "What do we do. Get a crowbar?" His voice was as perplexed as his face.

I thought for a few seconds. "Do any of you have a heavy-duty serrated knife?"

Simone reached in her pocket, removed and opened a pocketknife, and handed me the handle with its four-inch saw-toothed blade ready for use. I thanked her and transferred it to Bobby. "I think you have enough space. If you don't, we can widen the trench around the door. Puncture the seal and saw both sides and the front. The back won't keep us from opening it."

Bobby nodded, dropped to his knees at the refrigerator's bottom. He punctured the seal and began sawing. "Piece of cake," Bobby mumbled as he swiftly cut the plastic material. When he finished cutting two thirds of the bottom seal, he scrambled to his feet, cursing and coughing. The reason? Unbelievable stench came from the interior of the refrigerator. We all stepped several strides upwind to put space between us and the vile smell.

I asked Bobby, "Can you handle that?"

His voice said, "Yes," but his eyes said, no!

"If you can't do it, I will," I said with as much false conviction as I could. We locked eyes.

After a brief hesitation, he nodded and declared, "No problem, I got it."

There are times when male ego is a good thing.

~ ~ ~ ~ ~ ~

By the time Bobby cut the seal on the bottom and the front, the worst of the odor dissipated, and his gaging and vomit breaks were less frequent. After he finished cutting the front seal, he asked, "Who's going to hold the freezer door open while I cut the top?"

"I will," Simone volunteered. She pulled the door up to a ninety-degree angle to allow Bobby access to the seal. He quickly cut the top. But, before I opened the refrigerator, Simone directed our attention to something in the freezer. She said, "I wonder what is in the manila envelope?"

I told her, "Pull it out. I'll take a look after we see what's inside."

With those words, I stood at the appliance's front and pulled upward. The door provided no resistance. My hard pull and the arcing motion of the door pulled me in. I managed to get my feet beneath me and not bathe in whatever stunk inside.

I looked down expecting to see a skeleton or a horribly decomposed body. What had been blood and body fluids coated the back and bottom of the refrigerator's interior. Lying toward the bottom were skeletal remains of two hands and two feet. Nothing else. I scrambled from the electric coffin and noted correctly, "My tennis shoes are now trash."

"Gross!" The two girls screamed in unison.

Before using a pliers and sticks to strip my shoes and socks off...and using alcohol from our specimen preservation kit to cleanse my feet, I assigned Bobby and the girls a job. "Run the radar over here. See if there are more of these. If there are, Bobby, make a chart. Digging up one of these is enough."

After finding a pair of white rubber boots in the Jeep, I turned my attention to the manila envelope Simone removed from the freezer. I used her pocket knife to slit the top. What she found made all the misadventures of the day worth enduring. Either the person or persons burying the appliance felt certain no one would find it, or they made a glaring mistake by leaving the purchasing information, and evidence, undestroyed.

A sales receipt from Goodwill Industries, Gainesville, Florida, read:

Sold to: KCW at UF

Date: 9/12/2017

Phone: 386-555-1459 call after 5PM

Hold for pick-up

Item sold: One used refrigerator, as is condition.

Salesperson: Nellie

Assuming the hands and feet in the refrigerator were connected to the other finds on the Buehl ranch, which they almost certainly did, the first real leads that could reveal the monsters perpetrating the crimes had been found. I placed the receipt back in the envelope, folded it, placed it in a plastic bag, and stuck it in my purse. I could hardly wait until I showed it to Reading.

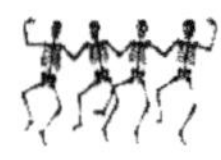

Chapter   36

Reading read the paperwork we'd found in the buried refrigerator. He read it three times. "This was buried with the remains?" It strained his sense of logic that the otherwise meticulously careful criminals left such a damning piece of evidence in existence.

"It wasn't with the remains. It was in the freezer compartment located above the 'frige.' My guess is that's why they missed it."

"It's literally a gift, one we don't want to screw up." Reading pushed the sales receipt aside and slid a legal pad in front of him. "So, I need to think how to get the most out of this." He clicked a ball point pen and wrote as he spoke, "Find everyone that worked at the University of Florida with the initials KCW in September of 2017. Find out whose phone number was 386-555-1459 at that time. Check with the Goodwill store in Gainesville to see if they have additional records...but after I've done the first two. Last, see if 'Nellie' still works there and what she might remember."

"You might want to check to see who picked up the refrigerator from any records they have at the store," I added.

"Very good," Reading remarked, then asked me, "Would you or Mark have a 2017 roster of employees at UF?"

"I know we have a current list of faculties. It would show their employment date, so we'd know if they were around in 2017. I don't know of a list we have on all Florida employees or if there is anything from 2017 that remains in the files. That's electronically or paper. I'll have to ask Mark if there is. Can I tell him why we need it?"

Reading turned my question around in his mind. He shook his head, and said, "No. I know he isn't involved with this, but the less people who know about the sales slip the better. How about this Simone girl? Is she likely to talk about what she saw?"

"She never saw the sales slip. I didn't open it in front of anybody," I grinned. "At this point, only you and I know this exists."

"You told me the radar picked up eight additional refrigerators?"

I nodded, "Freezers and friges. But we have no idea what's in them…if anything. It does bring to light part of their MO. I bet you'll find that murders that happened away from the Buehl ranch got stored in those refrigerators until they could move them."

"Very good deduction, Watson!" Reading quipped. "Now, how do we connect these people with Buehl? There doesn't seem to be a logical connection between campus life and ranching."

I shrugged my shoulders.

"Have you heard anymore from that professor that called you the other night?" Reading asked.

"Not a word. Want me to call him?"

Reading stroked his chin as he often does when he's deep in thought. "No. Not now. First, I want to find out everything we can about the Goodwill connection. Then I want to wait a little longer. Just the fact he calls us first, if he does, tells us something." He changed the subject. "Tell me, how did Mark react to you finding another beehive for him to worry about?

I chuckled, "After he stopped cursing? Not happy. He spent most of the time talking about how we could wash our hands of the whole business. One thing he made clear, I wasn't to go prospecting without his knowledge and approval. It's not like he's mad at me, just upset we're getting drawn into something that's your business, deeper and deeper."

"I can't blame him." Reading snorted, "Can you imagine how Beth Dillon is looking at this? She already has big bucks invested in a property that she still doesn't actually own, has part of it that will be lost to the native American community, and the rest will have the stigma as a burial ground for serial killers. I can see the sales pitch. '*Buy a home in Ghastly Oaks where you may find a body in your backyard.*' That will appeal to a very limited customer base."

I nodded and asked, "What's next?"

Reading picked up the sales receipt and said, "Let's make a phone call."

Chapter   37

Reading turned the speaker on my cell phone. He punched the phone number into it, but hesitated. "Let me get a prop," he said as he walked to the refrigerator, removed a beer, and returned to the kitchen table. As he sat, he announced, "There's nothing like the pop of a beer can in the background to convince someone the call isn't part of an investigation. I learned that from Captain Wahoo Latrell. He might have been pure redneck, but he was a foxy one."

Reading readied his writing materials, then he punched the call icon. The phone rang five times before a deep bass voice answered, "You've reached, Hector Bertram McCall, Alachua County Clerk of Courts. My office hours are 10 AM to 5 PM. If you would like to leave a message, wait for the signal, then leave your name, phone number, and the subject you're calling about. I'll return your call as soon as possible." Reading hung up before the recording activated.

We stared at each other from opposite sides of the table. Reading sighed and said, "This isn't getting easier. Having the college set involved is complication enough. Having county officials in this shit, ones that have close connections to law enforcement, that really could gum things up!"

"It might have been someone else's number. By coincidence it ended being transferred to the Clerk."

"You think? Chessie, there's as much chance of that happening as me winning the lottery three weeks in a row." Reading scribbled, *check to be sure who had number in 2017.*

"You know we're assuming that this guy McCall is part of the thing. He may not be. Maybe he just picked up the refrigerator." My body shook along with my head. "Damn, Reading, I can't believe we have law enforcement officials killing and eating people."

"Chessie, can you see the folk you've sat with in the cafeteria at East Florida chowing down on their neighbor for their previous meal? We can't exclude anyone from any level of society." Reading slapped the table. "Either way it makes it harder." He pointed to the phone number on the sales receipt. "When I ask for the court for a call list for John Doe there's not much of a stir. Ask for one that has celebrity or influence involved, the machinery grinds. This one…" Reading simulated the sound of cars crashing.

"Are you going to skip asking for it?" I asked.

"Hell no! I'll probably get it. The thing I'm most concerned about is putting a mask on the request. When you pull paper on someone that high in the pecking order, they tend to be told about it. My paperwork isn't going to read on the line stating why I want the report, *suspicion of murder and cannibalism.*" My brother rubbed his forehead. "Even if I don't get the order, I can ask for phone reports for the people that are connected to the Buehl ranch. And when you finish your Mata Hari impersonation, I can do the same for the names you come up with. Then we start comparing. We find names in common, and we do the same for them. It's a lot of work, but if there are the same folks exchanging calls, we can be pretty sure we're on the track."

"What if they use email?" I asked.

"I'd say they're too smart to have used email. The jails are filling up with criminals who used email to communicate. Seize their computer and they're toast." Reading rubbed the top of the Coors. "Anything you can do to speed up prospecting for the cult?"

I thought for several seconds. "There might be a way. I'm not sure you'd want me to expose what I'd have to…to make it work. I could call Alvin Peed back. The pretense would be to ask for help. I'd ask him to find someone familiar with the word Vidar. It could shake them up enough to call us to try and find out what we know."

"It could work," Reading said and added, "Let me think for a few seconds." After massaging the beer can for a half minute, he decided, "Not right now. Let's be patient for a couple more days. If it remains quiet, we'll try prodding them with your suggestion." He finally popped open his beer. "Anything else come to mind?"

I shook my head. "Are you done with Mark?"

"Yes. He'll be back running your dig tomorrow." Reading chuckled. "Your boss has a sense of humor. He said he's renaming the dig. Mark says it's now the Forrest Gump site; it's like a box of chocolates…you never know what you'll dig up."

Chapter   38

"I've made a decision." Mark waited for the chatter to die. He spoke to all the dig site team assembled under an oak next to the five middens. "Safety is a concern. You know that much of what we're finding isn't what this project was originated to do. Until we can all work together, I'm sending everyone home except for Bobby and Sheila. We have an officer assigned to us by the Sheriff's Department. He can only protect so many, and all have to be in one place. Right now, that isn't where we're at. Do I think the risk to you is high? No. Do I think there is some? Yes. Don't make plans for next week. I'm sure you'll all be back by then."

"Dr. Card, everyone has heard about the ranch foreman being killed, and we know that you've found evidence of other murders. Is it safe for us to come back?" One of the girls sounded like she'd prefer not to return.

"Anyone who does not want to return on this dig, is excused. Just let me know so I can replace you." Mark nodded. "I understand your reluctance. A piece of advice. You may have lots of questions asked by the press, friends, and so on. If you start answering them people will assume you know more than you do. That could put you in danger when you shouldn't be. Tell all that ask you don't know anything about the police business out here." Mark let his comments register. "Any questions?"

"No." and shaken heads answered. Within ten minutes the group faded away in pickups that bounced their way to the ranch gate.

As they left, I asked Mark, "What are we going to do and where will we start?"

"Have you had enough of playing in the dirt?" he asked.

I shrugged my shoulders. "In this place? This isn't one of my ten favorite places to hang out, but it beats getting callouses on my butt, playing with computer printouts."

Mark shook his head in disbelief. "Well, I want out of here as quick as I can…and still do what we contracted to do for Beth Dillon." He picked up the aerial photos, sorted through them, and waved the ones remaining in his hand. "These photos have the eight places that we thought have the highest probability of finding something. Two look like they're something from the Twentieth Century. I'm not going to look at them unless Tall Pine and Mitchell insist. I know Beth will be happy if we don't. That leaves six. We should be able to clear them and do radar scans in two, three days at most. That's next. I'll evaluate what follows after that."

~ ~ ~ ~ ~ ~ ~

Bobby and Sheila finished clearing the area Mark selected to examine first. Mark and I carefully studied the aerial that rested on the Jeep's hood. "Why this spot? I asked.

"I think it's the highest probability site left to find something of archaeological importance." Mark pointed to the area where we stood. "See this. That lighter area is sand that I think formed a midden at one time. If I'm correct, the vegetation growing on it tells me it's from long before the 20th century. A few of those pines are twelve inches in diameter. The palmettoes that are growing on it have been there a long time. It's only four feet higher than the surroundings and maybe thirty feet in diameter. I'm thinking burial site for a small village or a family."

"Ais?" I asked.

"Very probably. I'd say 90%. As soon as—" Mark's remark was interrupted by a squeal from Sheila.

"Ooooohhh, another snake!" She dropped the bush hook she used to cut palmettoes and brush from the site and took four quick steps back from where she'd been working. A large yellow rat snake slithered away, at least as frightened of Sheila as she was of it.

"Shit, Sheila! If it doesn't rattle ignore it. You scared the crap out of me!" Bobby tripped over a palmetto when he reacted to Sheila's scream. He tumbled to the ground and lay in the palmetto patch. As he looked around to get up, he mumbled, "I'm not believing this." Bobby peered at something under the palmettoes. He pointed at an object under a frond. Mark and I went to investigate.

White sand acted as an apron to a large gopher tortoise burrow. The entrance to the turtle's home was large, very large. The descent angle, the steepest I'd seen, hid anything inside in empty darkness. But what caught Bobby's attention, and ours, a skull, wedged into the corner of the opening.

~ ~ ~ ~ ~

"Nine," I answered to Sheila's question as to how many skeletons we found. Our radar survey covered most of what Mark Card had designated as the likely midden area. Parts of the mound where large pine trees and cabbage palms grew weren't disturbed.

Dr. Card elaborated on our find. "I'd say these are Ais burials. A number of items are buried with them. Some look to be intact. An unusual aspect is that the individuals buried here are small. Two are infants. Four of the rest I'd guess to be juveniles. My guess is six to ten years. The remaining three look to be adults, but small. I'm guessing women on these. No men. Of course, there are parts of the site we haven't looked at, but that's unusual." Mark nodded. "This will be worth excavating. It will be interesting, and we should learn something."

"How about the skull Bobby found?" Sheila asked.

"It came from one of the juveniles. The turtle pushed it to the top when it dug its burrow," I suggested, and Mark nodded.

"I think we have company," Bobby pointed 200 yards across the pine flat. The Gator four-wheeler made its way to us. The person driving the vehicle wore a large straw hat, was on the small side, and wore no clothes! All four stared at the visitor as it approached. I removed a set of binoculars from the case on my belt.

"It's a woman." I verified.

"You sure?" Mark asked.

"If it's a he, the man's been to the plastic surgeon to add a set of "C" cups," I confidently opined.

Sheila wanted confirmation on what she thought she saw. "Nothing on her?"

"Nothing, Nada. She's as naked as a newborn." I took a last look and corrected myself. "She has that straw hat on, and I think I see cowboy boots."

Chapter   39

I watched, as fascinated by our approaching visitor as my three companions. The woman had long peroxided hair streaming from under a white straw cowboy hat. Her body, not a young one, was thin to skinny, brown all over, its only covering a pair of boots. My conversations with Wilbur Carson prepared me for the naked lady's appearance. Based on what he'd told me, the women driving the Gator all-terrain had to be Buehl's wife. When she got close enough to see, the lines and wrinkles in her face spoke to her age. A combination of her leather textured skin, deep-set eyes, and sharp features gave her a fierce, wild look.

My three partners wore astonished looks on their faces. I wondered if Mrs. Buehl enjoyed the shock value her nakedness had on those who happened on her as much as any perceived therapeutic benefit derived. When she stopped her ATV fifteen feet from us, she obviously enjoyed our surprise.

"Are you having any luck?" she asked.

"Matter of fact, we are," I answered. Mark, Bobby, and Sheila's mouths hung open and they hadn't regained their ability to speak. "Mrs. Buehl, correct?" I inquired.

"Laurie Buehl." She climbed out of the Gator and walked up to us. For a lady I guessed to be in her mid-fifties, her body was toned and tight. She extended her hand to me. Her firm grip and handshake had a bit of challenge to it. She made a concerted effort to engage me in eye contact. "You would be Chessie."

"Guilty," I confirmed.

She looked at the others serially, shifting her eyes and attention to each as she addressed them. "You would be Dr. Mark Card, you would be Bobby, I don't know your last name, and you would be Sheila Portner."

Knowing their names added to my companion's astonishment. She smiled, seeing her knowledge had the effect she desired. I decided to be sure I knew how she obtained them. "Did you find out who we are from your husband or from Wilbur Carson?"

She looked at me with a strange emotion on her features. It took her several seconds for her to answer, "Both." Laurie looked at the GPR and asked, "Is that a radar unit? I've read about them but never seen one."

"Yes," Mark answered. "Would you like to see it operate?" He'd regained control of his vocal cords, though control of his eyes focus still remained a problem. Mark solved his problem by purposely looking away from her.

"I certainly would." Laurie tromped over to the unit. Mark walked with her, looking for clouds in the sky. His attempt to avoid seeing her nude body, caused her to laugh. "Professor, I can't believe you haven't seen a woman naked before. If it doesn't embarrass me to show it, it shouldn't bother you to look at it."

Mark smiled but he remained uncomfortable. "I've seen lady's naked bodies, but not in such a public environment."

"This isn't a public place. It's my home and I do as I please in it. I'm not a conventional person, surely you guessed that. I live by my rules and the rest of society be damned." Laurie made her statement without any emotion. It was clear, what she said was cold, hard, fact.

Mark flipped the switch on the GPR, and their attention focused on the screen. He rolled the unit over one of the areas marked with miniature flags, explaining what they saw on the unit. I decided to distract Bobby and Sheila's attention from our visitor's bare butt and boobs. "Come on, crew, let's get our tools packed in the Jeep. I want to go home."

We loaded brush hooks, axes, machetes, edgers, coolers, and a toolbox into the Jeep's rear. Sheila quickly turned her focus to work. Bobby remained distracted until he pinched his finger between the Jeep's steel seat and a heavy cooler. Then Laurie's private parts were less interesting. By the time we had the Jeep loaded, Mark completed his demonstration.

"Nice to have met you. I'm sure we'll see each other as you finish your project," Laurie Buehl said as she climbed into her ATV. She drove away, bouncing along ruts and through palmetto bushes, without ever looking back.

Mark wheeled the GPR unit to the Jeep and began breaking it down to place it in its carrying case. The 'shit-eating' grin on his face prompted me to comment. "You got a close up look. So?"

Dr. Card shook his head. "That is one different lady." He lifted his eyebrows. "She's smart. Very smart. She talks like she has a doctorate, then says something that blows you away."

"Did she proposition you?" I asked.

"Not exactly," Mark closed his eyes. "Let's just close out today, and hope we aren't visited by her many times."

I hesitated then asked, "You think we'll see her again?"

"Oh yeah, oh yeah!"

Chapter   40

Reading listened to me. I didn't expect that. Normally, anything I expressed as a 'gut feeling' got less attention than a road sign advertising a lawyer's service. I told him, "We had a visitor on the site we were exploring this afternoon. I have this feeling she knows about what went on out there or is directly involved." I paused then asked. "Have you met or questioned Buehl's wife, Laurie?"

"Not me. Bill Worthington did two days after your group found Carson's body." Reading focused on me and the conversation.

"What did he think about her?"

"He thought she was a nut-job. She asked more questions about him personally than she answered that he asked." Reading, grinned, nodded, and said, "She had clothes on. Everybody involved with the case learned that early. We asked her for an interview. She agreed. That surprised us. We'd asked to search Carl's house. Wilbur Carson lived in the bunk house. He gave us permission to search the bunk house, not his ranch house. Worthington strategized that if we asked to speak to Buehl's wife…a…a…"

"Laurie," I reminded.

"Yes. Anyway, Bill thought that would get us into the house. Instead, she volunteered to come in. I saw her. She dressed for a high society cocktail party, not a visit to your local police station. Worthington told me she didn't show anything a guilty person would. No sign of hiding anything. Not anxious for the session to end. She was at ease, confident, answered what he asked…openly. He told me the woman *is* preoccupied with sex."

"Really, Mark told me something similar. Do you know what she asked?" I inquired.

"Not really, but you can guess. She asked about his private parts. He didn't elaborate." Reading took a breath. "Bill told me she asked about what Mark and you found. When he told her, she responded with, 'fascinating.' The woman asked some ghoulish questions. Bill said she is very intelligent, but weird."

"Did he tell her about the cannibalism?" I asked.

Reading shook his head violently, "Hell, no! We're keeping that secret." Reading left his chair and went to the fridge for a beer. When he returned, he brought a question with him. "That tingling in your gut. What about your meeting with Laurie Buehl caused it?"

I looked at him as I tried to invent a reason. A gut feel is a gut feel. Being creative put substance in my apprehension. "Why seek us out? Is she concerned with what more we might find? The whole naked thing makes me think Buehl's wife likes to flaunt social standards. Eating people is about the biggest flaunt I can think of. She doesn't fit. What I mean is she isn't the rancher's wife type and certainly doesn't fit as Carl Buehl's partner. Can you think of two more diametrically opposed personalities?"

Reading nodded and said, "Anything else?"

"Yes. I'd like to know when Laurie married Carl and if the date the first bodies were buried coincides with it. Plus…" I hesitated then added, "There was a message in her handshake. I felt it. She challenged me…us…to do anything. I think she's the center part of what went on out there."

Reading wasn't smiling, a sign he seriously considered my theory as possible fact. "I'll check it. Finding out what the date of Carl and Laurie's marriage is won't be hard. I'm supposed to have information on how long the first skeletons you found have been in the ground later this week. It's a starting place. Unfortunately, it is one of the few we have."

"I thought you'd find something when you dug up the rest of the radar signatures. And, you have that County Clerk lead. Nothing has worked out?"

"Zilch, nada, zero. Lashann Hargrove supervised every shovel full of dirt taken out of the graves and the area around them. Screened every grain of sand. Nothing. He even took samples of earth where the organs were and sent it to a high-powered lab to see if any chemical traces of poison were present. We haven't gotten that back, but… As far as *modus operandi*, take your pick. Stabbing. Shooting. Beaten severely with a blunt instrument. Strangulation. Since the skulls aren't there, I'm sure some died of smashed craniums. Lashann thinks he matched a couple of the skulls from the field box we found at the theater site to two of the skeletons. We'll have to wait for the samples he sent to FDLA's crime lab to do DNA matches, before we're sure." Reading scratched his temple and he looked discouraged. "The skulls, many of them, had some or all the teeth removed. That takes away using dental records to ID the victims for the most part. We hope we'll luck out, get some unusual surgeries or implants to trace. But even if we get that…it helps but not that much. Knowing who our victims are narrows the suspect base from many millions to millions. We still have to figure out if there were associations with the killers or if the victims were random. I don't think so, but we haven't completely ruled that out."

I asked, "What about the invoice we found buried in one of those refrigerators? Did any of that go anywhere?"

"So far no luck. The Alachua County Clerk of Courts seems to be an upright guy. He's involved in all types of do-gooder organizations. He uses his influence to get discounts, donations and the like for groups he has connections. I talked to him about the refrigerator you found. He said he didn't remember the purchase, but he said either he or his secretary might have done it. They buy and pick up all kinds of things for charitables, 501Cs, and the like. He said he'd ask his secretary and look at his records and call back. That did bother me. Who in hell keeps records on those kinds of things? But… Worthington did a background check. It was clean."

"Did you find out who Nellie is?"

Reading chuckled. "It's like everything else connected to the case. Would you believe there were two Nellies that worked at the Gainesville Goodwill during that time? I have both last names and the addresses that Goodwill had in their employment records. Jones and Williams. Neither has worked for Goodwill for three or more years, neither lives at the address in their record, and neither has a forwarding address."

"What about additional paperwork?" I asked.

"The manager, who didn't work there when the ladies did, told me there could be in their archives. I was welcome to try to find something. The archives he talked about are file boxes with all the paperwork for each year; twenty-seven for the year I'm interested in. They are in no order. Finding anything would be like finding fly shit in pepper. As a last straw, I might send somebody up there." He looked like a beggar and asked, "Have you heard from Alvin Peed?" knowing that I hadn't.

"I'll swing by his office the next time I'm on campus." I added, "You owe me big time!" Alvin...not one of my favorite associates.

"When is the next time?" my brother nagged.

"Probably in the next couple days." I had no idea but half-lied.

"Oh, it will be in the next few days. I have a notice Buehl is trying some legal maneuver to stop what you are doing out there. Everybody involved, that includes Dr. Mark Card, meets at the courthouse day after tomorrow."

"How does he think he can make that happen?" I asked.

Reading squinted his eyes and tilted his head, "Billie Mulhee."

"Ohhh, shit!"

Chapter   41

I expected a bolt of lightning to flash down from the cloud of tension floating under the ceiling. The huge meeting room where those having interest in the Dillon Development of Carl Buehl's ranch had gathered, had the characteristics of an ammunition dump guarded by a pyromaniac. It would explode! The stated reason for the meeting…to avoid a bitter, long term court battle. Looking at the individuals gathered in the room, I suspected a mud wrestling match. Kumbaya around a campfire? Out of the question!

The two sides were drawn into battle lines. Clearly drawn battle lines. Beth Dillon and those siding with the development of the Buehl ranch into a retirement city, swelled one side of the room. The anti-everything community activists had a healthy group assembled. In the minority in numbers, the vocal and aggressive nature of those present would more than offset their deficiency in body count.

The pro-development group sat in circles around Beth Dillion. It reminded me of an army protecting a queen in her castle. I knew many of the 'soldiers.' Millie Lane sat next to Beth, her other flank girded by Chamber of Commerce president Phil Malloy. Three additional business owners sat in the same row of seats. All were active in the Chamber. Isaac Steinman, Beth's administrative assistant sat behind her as did Stanton Griggs, Bill Wheeler, and Lois Levine…all financial partners of Buehl's who desperately wanted to see the property sold and development progress. Two members of the local newspaper and a TV crew sat behind Beth. I recognized a few bodies from civic activities who came to lend moral support. Four of the people seated in Beth's stable were lawyers. They had the rich, arrogant, useless look that I associate as a mark of the profession. There were more but I assigned them the roll of curious spectators.

Carl Buehl's cheerleaders sat on the other side of the aisle and provided a defense force. Buehl and his wife were seated on the front row on the walkway. Laurie's clothes, yes, she wore them, were what a rancher's wife of the depression years would have worn. The obvious message they intended to send, poverty and hard times, were lessened severely by the fact they were brand new…and the bag and shoes she wore easily cost more than a grand.

The army of good-doers, or activists, or bunny huggers, or community eco-terrorists, depending on your viewpoint, sat in the rows behind her. It was plain this army took its orders from Billie Mulhee. The woman dressed for the occasion, her attire selected by an LSD victim from the 70s. She swaggered around her soldiers preparing her troops for battle. Wendall O'Dell, local Audubon Society president, and a lady I didn't know sat immediately behind Carl and Laurie. Next to Wendall sat Cathy Olinsky and five identically tee shirted individuals proclaiming the Nature Conservancy would protect the 'Natural World.' The row behind them started with Willow Able and Johnathan Frakes, president and vice president of the Knights of Nature who represented a group that wanted electricity outlawed. Tom Wynn sat next to them. He fought any encroachment of land not covered with concrete. He didn't represent a group, but his money and social position made him more effective than most. There were three individuals I didn't recognize. The two men seated with the Buehl supporters looked out of place in the group of activists. They were 'suits.' The woman siting between them looked to be the female equivalent. I decided they represented…money. Completing Buehl's battalion were Joni Maddox, leader of the Socialists for a Green World, and Miller Anthony, editor for an anti-everything local magazine whose audience didn't exceed four times the numbers gathered in the room.

I viewed the two warring factions from the rear of the room. Dr. Mark Card and I were invited to the meeting and chose to put as much distance between us and the combatants as possible. Our intent was to stay neutral; we sat against the back wall one on each side of the entrance.

Two of the last to arrive were Jim McMillan and Terrie Tall Pine. Seeing us, they split, Terrie sitting next to me and Jim taking the seat next to Mark. It was obvious. They didn't want to be part of the upcoming bloodletting.

I nodded and smiled at Terrie. She nodded in return. I asked, "You here because you're supporting one side?"

"No. I was requested to be here." Terrie thrust her head toward me. "And you?"

"Same thing. We got a note from Buehl's people saying they needed us here as potential witnesses. Dr. Card wanted to skip it, but the University board wanted us here. So…"

"Ummm," Terrie pointed to a desk at the front of the room. Three lecterns and microphones sat on top. Another lectern positioned facing and centered to the audience would accommodate those who wished to address the throng. In the background a screen stood, and projector hummed, both ready for use. "I thought there would only be one judge running the meeting." She pointed at the setup.

"That's what I heard. Judge Wilma Westinghouse is going to run this thing. My brother told me. He's going to be here with the Sheriff. They are attending to be sure nothing interferes with their homicide investigations."

"Your brother is Reading?"

"Yes."

Terrie nodded. "Why is a judge involved? I understand this is just a meeting set up by the sow."

"Sow?" I asked.

"The Mulhee woman. I am sorry I insulted pigs." Terrie eyes flashed.

I chuckled, then said, "I see we agree on that. I—" The opening of the door interrupted our discussion.

Sheriff Travis, Reading, and Bill Worthington accompanied Judge Westinghouse entering the room. All walked to the table at the front and took seats at or next to it. The hum of conversation and glares back and forth between the enemies ceased.

Judge Westinghouse cleared her throat to get the crowds attention. When they quieted, she spoke, "Good morning. Before we start, I want to be sure that everyone here understands this is not a court proceeding. I'm here at the request of an individual who wishes to avoid a long, expensive litigation regarding an issue of property ownership. Mr. Carl Buehl is the historic owner of the land in question and retains a significant interest in his ranch. He does not want to sell the property. He wishes to sever a contract which he was forced to accept. Through an intermediary he wishes to offer an alternative. I'm here strictly in an advisory capacity and to maintain order in what has already proved to be an incendiary circumstance. To be sure all interested parties have an opportunity to be in the know, I've insisted they be invited, not commanded, to attend. In light of a recent murder and other possible discoveries on the property, that includes law enforcement." The Judge looked to either side where the Sheriff and Captain Worthington were seated. "As you see they accepted." She paused, looked at Carl Buehl, then asked, "Mr. Buehl, is it correct that you've asked Miss Mulhee to speak for and represent your interests?"

Carl said, "Yes," as he nodded.

The Judge motioned to Billie Mulhee, "Are you prepared to make your offer?" At the word offer, the people in the Dillon contingent showed surprise.

Mulhee already stomped her way toward the speaker's lectern. She answered the Judge as she positioned herself behind the oak lectern and opened a file folder on the polished surface. "Yes, your honor."

"Proceed."

Mulhee smiled…actually, smiled…and began in a most conciliatory manner. "I know the whole prospect of developing the Buehl ranch is a divisive issue. I have a proposal that I hope can satisfy everyone's interest. Those interested in developing the property are primarily interested in protecting their investment and benefiting from the development of the land. Those interested in preventing an ecological treasure from being totally destroyed want the property to remain completely undisturbed. If this goes to court, I don't think either side will get their wish. The compromise we will present is the best action to answer our collective needs."

I sat stunned at Mulhee's opening statement. There were no four-letter expletives in her speech. I didn't believe it possible; my heart reached the verge of inaction.

She nodded to one of the 'suits' from her side of the aisle. "Would you please provide everyone a copy of the handout." The man nodded, rose to his feet with a thick stack of stapled papers, and gave them to all that wished one on both sides of the aisle.

"While Mr. Tragmeyer distributes copies of the proposal, I'll describe what's in it." Mulhee shuffled the papers on the lectern. "A number of donors have come together to offer to purchase the Buehl ranch with the sole purpose of creating a wildlife haven. This will be a completely undisturbed wilderness. It has Mr. Buehl's blessing. Everyone will benefit from this proposal. Mr. Buehl's partners will each get the amount they were promised by Dillon Development. *Plus, ten percent.* Mr. Buehl will receive the amount prescribed for in the original sale. *Plus, ten percent.* Dillon will receive a contract severance payment equal to *twice* what was offered to purchase the land plus *all the expenses* associated with the transaction. That makes all parties better off financially than positioned under the original transaction." Her proposal left everyone in the room looking at each other with surprised faces. Unexpected anger appeared on a few. Hands flapped above a few of the people seated on Dillon's side of the aisle. Mine, Terrie Tall Pine, Mark's, and Sheriff Charles Travis were among those that rose.

Mulhee placed her palms up and in front of her requesting patience. "Let me finish. Then I'll answer questions." Billie removed a different document from the stack in front of her and placed it on top. "The questions of the Native American artifacts that have been discovered, as a result of an invasive archaeology program, and the resultant uncovering of unexplained more recent burials, must be considered. This is what we propose to satisfy those two issues. First the Native American artifacts. Those that have been disturbed will be handled in accordance with the directions of the Seminole Nation's representative. All expenses will be paid. Those unexcavated sites will be marked, fenced, and left undisturbed. Permanently." Mulhee glanced over her shoulder at an unsmiling Sheriff Travis before reading, "The discovery of recent burials is a valid concern. We propose that the East Florida University archaeological team take time away, we recommend a week, from the site to reorganize their efforts to find additional modern burial sites. We would allow for a two-week period. These expenses will be paid for at the rate currently being paid for by Dillon Development. Any sites discovered will be open to exhumation and recovery for an additional period of thirty days. This is at the discretion of the Sheriff and at his expense. Of course, the immediate area, that's a 500' radius, of the Carson murder, will be available to the Sheriff for the duration of his investigation." Mulhee smiled. "We believe this satisfies all concerns about our proposal to save this pivotable piece of Florida's wilderness."

The hands waving in the air told Billie Mulhee, there were questions or objections. She kept her cool, but a trace of annoyance entered her countenance. My hand waved with a dozen others. I could see her evaluating the hand's owners; her selection of a calling order would be the ones least difficult first. That would put me near the end.

She pointed to one of her group, first, "Wendall, what would you like to know?"

"What provisions will be made to see no one can sneak on the property? This has obviously been done in the past."

"Two-tiered fencing will be installed completely around the perimeter of the property. This will stretch eight feet high, with barbed or razor wire on top. A security system that informs an office of attempts to cut or scale the fence will be provided. The thirty-four gates currently providing access will be reduced to two. Two fulltime wildlife ranger, security guards will be employed to prevent any disturbance. It will be very secure." When Billie concluded, O'Dell nodded his satisfaction with her words. Two hands dropped, their concerns answered.

Terrie Tall Pine waved her hand vigorously, but Mulhee ignored her. Mulhee recognized one of the Chamber of Commerce representatives. The woman asked, "I'd like to know how the proposal recognizes the loss to the local economy. The planned development would add jobs, continuing growth, and income to the surrounding area."

"You see that growth as a positive. We see it as a bigger negative. Our area is becoming crowded enough without this development adding to the land that is turning Indian River County into a concrete desert. Everything isn't measured by the money you can grub from nature."

Another hand disappeared in addition to the speaker's. A half-dozen palms remained.

Mulhee evaluated the remaining individuals wanting answers. She turned to Sheriff Travis. "What would you like to ask, Sheriff?"

The Sheriff stood, looked at Mulhee with a jaundiced eye. "Thank you, Ms. Mulhee. My problem is that your proposal doesn't adequately allow us to acquire evidence by putting a time limit and area restrictions on what is a crime scene. The way it stands, I'll be forced to challenge it in court. I'd like to ask Judge Westinghouse about access to the land. Where would the court stand on issuing warrants to do additional searches?"

"I can't answer for every judge that might review a request. I can only respond to the way I might look at giving you a warrant. First, you would have to show me a reason you believed there were additional evidential sites that you did not discover during the discovery period provided by the agreement. I would look at the diligence and thoroughness of that search. Second, I would ask for specific areas where you intended to look. There would be no fishing trips by asking to look at very large sections." Westinghouse smiled. "Does that answer your question, Sheriff Travis?"

"Judge, may I suggest a hypothetical case?" the Sheriff asked.

"Sure."

"If we were to find a part of a body, but not all of it, would that be sufficient to grant a warrant?"

"As long as you defined a prospective search area, yes." The Judge's tone was positive.

"Does that answer your question?" Billie asked.

"I'll have to think about it," Travis answered.

Mulhee quickly moved along. She pointed to Terrie. "Ms. Tall Pine, you have a question?"

"No. I have a statement." Terrie pointed to Beth Dillon as Terrie stood. "The Owner of Dillon Development has agreed to deed part of the property to the Seminole Nation. We will demand those promised areas are either provided to us with the provision we may access them, or we be paid for the property…again stolen from us."

Mulhee and Tall Pine exchanged visual punches as they stared at each other. Realizing her opponent had the higher ground, Billie avoided a battle by saying, "I can't give you an answer now. I'll have to get the donors to agree."

"Understand, if you do not agree to one of those stipulations, the Seminole Nation will not accept. We will challenge it in court." Terrie sat down while she and Mulhee continued their eye contact war. After several seconds, she progressed to the next more difficult on her mental list, "Stanton Griggs, would you like more information on our offer to you?"

Her answer came in a belligerent burst. "Where do you and your nut case friends come off putting a value on our investments? You have no idea of the informal aspects of the deal we have with Dillon. Your offer is chicken feed. *Chicken feed*! I won't dream of settling for less than seven times the value of what I'd get out of this." Stanton held the papers high in the air, dropped the offer, and stomped on it after the papers finished fluttering to the ground. Stanton Griggs marched out of the room. He was followed by a number of those surrounding Beth Dillon. Wheeler and Levine, Griggs partners, were the first to leave, followed quickly by Phil Malloy and a number of Chamber of Commerce members. After their exit, my hand was the only one that remained raised.

"Miss Partin, you have a question? Are you part of the deal I don't know about?" The snark in her voice pissed me off!

"I'm here because I'm part of the archaeological team. I was told to be here and participate by the University. So…I am. I've got a couple questions. Okay?"

Mulhee smirked as she told me, "Go ahead."

"One. Why is your group willing to pay such a premium to purchase this particular piece of land? I'm familiar with land costs. If you maximized the land you could protect, you could get between three and five times the land for what you're spending in this proposal."

Billie's eyes flashed. "That's our business." After a few seconds she thought better of what she said, "The property is unique. Blue Cypress Lake is a one-of-a-kind ecological setting. So, in one respect, the Buehl ranch is priceless."

"That's a reasonable explanation," I replied. "Just one more thing. Given the generous nature of your donors and the need for many humanitarian improvements isn't it reasonable for you to provide the Sheriff's office a complete list of those contributing? I'm sure Sheriff Travis would keep the list confidential and only contact them in cases of urgent need."

"Hell no!" Billie Mulhee went ballistic. "These people want to stay anonymous, so they aren't bothered by such requests."

I replied, "I'm glad to hear that. I'd hate to think they wanted to gain control of the land so no one could find what might be buried there."

Mulhee began her tirade with, "You fucking bitch…" and followed it with her normal speech pattern including more than her normal vulgarity. The meeting disintegrated immediately, the participants leaving with strings of four-letter words screeched by Mulhee in their ears.

As they left my friends and associates had comments and suggestions. Mark shook his head and mumbled, "You just put a target on yourself." Terrie Tall Pine put her hand on my shoulder and said in a loud voice, "Well said, sister!" Beth Dillon passed, looked concerned, and said, "I hope you're wrong." The doubt in her voice was palpable. Finally, Reading stopped by me and told me, "Chessie, you walk out in front of me. You're going to need someone covering your back constantly after that little speech. You always tell me not to punch a hornet's nest without protective clothing. Sister, you just did that in the nude."

Chapter   42

"Wait for me in the truck," Reading pointed to his F-150. "The Sheriff wants to talk." He looked around, saw Billie Mulhee's angry face staring at me, and modified what he said, "Maybe I better walk you to the truck, then see the Sheriff."

He put his hand on my arm and I jerked away, growling, "I can take care of myself. If she tries anything, I'll whip her ass."

Reading growled back, "That's what I'm afraid of…I don't want to arrest you for manslaughter, even if it would be justifiable." After signaling to Sheriff Travis, he escorted me to the truck. Slamming the door after I got in, he warned, "Keep the truck locked, keep your temper under control, and don't talk to the Mulhee woman if she comes over here. You got that?"

"Uh-huh," I nodded knowing if Mulhee got close to the car, I'd attack her at the slightest provocation. When angry, my brain loses control of my fists and fingernails…at times. I watched him leave me and the truck and join Sheriff Travis, Judge Westinghouse, and Bill Worthington. They began an earnest and serious conversation.

Others passed the truck as they went to their vehicles. The way they stared at me, I wondered if my makeup went awry but knew better. A commotion on the sidewalk captured my attention. In a split second, I determined its cause. Me.

Billie Mulhee wrestled with five people I did not know. She stared at me, angrily, her mouth moved, I'm sure her words were derogatory and obscene. Her effort to break away from them, I'm sure, was to rush at me and do what damage she could. The people surrounding her had complete control, so I decided to send a missile her way. I smiled, waved, and blew her a kiss. This infuriated her further and she lashed about trying to break free of those restraining her. Billie almost succeeded. A very large man finally got his arm around her neck in a choke hold. After several seconds her mania cooled, and her supplicating look at the man told me any thoughts of harming me were put aside…for now. The group controlling her whisked her from the sidewalk and into a car when Reading left the conversation with the Sheriff and returned to our truck.

~ ~ ~ ~ ~ ~

"What did he want?" I asked as Reading climbed into the seat next to me.

"I can't tell you everything, but he thinks we should zero in on Mulhee and Buehl. And I do mean zero in. When Travis says spend what you need, he is convinced." Reading started the F-150. As he drove us out of the parking lot, he added, "Mulhee's performance certainly helped, I'm sure. He told me that what she screamed at you had to be considered a death threat."

"I didn't hear her."

Reading didn't smile when he said, "Billie yelled, you should keep out of others business affairs, or somebody would end up digging your bones up a hundred years from now."

Chapter   43

It didn't take long for my phone to become active that evening. It rang as Reading removed super dishes from the table.

I answered, and the voice on the other end responded, "Is this Miss Partin?"

"Yes."

"My name is Celeste Anders. I'm a freelance writer. I'd like to get an interview with you to discuss the Dalton Development project on the Buehl ranch. Would you grant me some time?"

"I don't have anything to do with the development. You need to talk to Beth Dillon." I'm sure I sounded annoyed and defensive when I added, "I won't give you, her number. I'm sure she doesn't like being hassled any more than I do."

"Miss Partin, I'm not interested in the business portion of the story. My articles all center on archaeology. I've got many articles in '*Archaeology Today*,' '*Gateway to the Past*,' '*Trowel and Brush*,' and several more publications. You can look them up." Anders hesitated, waiting for me to respond. She clarified, "I'm legit, not someone from the *National Inquirer*."

She got my suspicious attention. "What type of information are you looking for?"

"Honestly, I want your take on a scientist's view of becoming involved in something that you had no intent of becoming a part of and how it affects you and your partners."

I shook my head at the unseeing phone. "You are speaking to the wrong person. Dr. Mark Card is in charge of the team. You should speak to him."

"Pardon me, but a friend of mine works at your local TV station. She was at the meeting this afternoon. She explained what happened. It was you that was emotionally involved with what's happening there. That's where the info I'm looking for is centered. Your boss doesn't have the part of the story I want. You are the right person."

The lady sounded sincere. I tried to put her off the trail, telling her, "Look, you'll have to get approval from my boss, Dr. Card, as long as this is active and in process."

Anders hesitated, then asked, "All I want is a brief discussion. I'm not interested in the political and crime stuff. I promise the first word on that, and you can get up and leave. The people I sell my articles to won't buy that shit. If you're worried about compromising your work, I won't sell the article until you're done with the project. Put that in writing if you want. We can meet at a very private place…keep it secret, again, if that's what you want."

"Let me think about it," I said.

"You can go on the net, look up the magazines, and find my articles to check me out," she volunteered. "I'll call you back tomorrow evening." She hung up without saying goodbye.

"Are you going to do it?" Reading asked.

"You do realize the fact we share our home doesn't mean we share everything in our lives." Eavesdropping is a continuing subject.

"You mentioned Dillon. It must have something to do with the Buehl ranch. That's my business too." No smile on Reading's face or voice. He was serious.

Before I could answer, the phone rang again. I looked at the name and number on the LED screen. "You'll want to hear this," I said as I answered with the speaker on. "Hi Alvin, how are you?" I pointed to Alvin Peed's name on the screen and his phone number. Reading nodded and searched for something to take notes.

"Good evening Chessie. I'm sure you know why I'm calling. Everybody on the faculty is talking about your performance on the five o'clock news. You are now East Florida's celebrity of the month!"

"TV? That meeting at the courthouse was on TV?" I was incredulous at first. Daaa…Why else would there be cameras in place? "I didn't think doing an archaeological dig is big news. So…how much of that food-fight did they put on the evening broadcast?"

"Not the whole thing. But the exchange between you and that lawyer…that made it. Don't worry, you didn't come across as the bad guy. The station had to bleep out a third of what she said." Alvin sounded like a sorority sister tattling on a friend. "When can we meet? I have to get this in the Red Raider."

"Do you really want to put something in the University paper about this? I wonder if Dr. Andrews would welcome you shining a spotlight on the problems we've encountered there."

"I checked with him. He doesn't care as long as we don't name names." Peed repeated, "When can we meet?"

I looked at Reading and he nodded, but held his finger up and wrote something for me to read. I babbled a little to let him finish his instruction to me, "Gee, I don't know. I probably should talk to Mark. Let me think…" Reading slid the note in front of me. It read, *Meet him in a public place*. "Well, I guess it will be okay. But not on campus. How about at the *Party Hardy*?"

I paused, as I peeked at Reading, he wrote, *3:30 tomorrow?* on the pad. As I read the time, we heard someone whispering to Alvin before he cackled, "That would be fine! That's a great place."

"How about 3:30 tomorrow?" I suggested.

After a brief pause, he answered, "My calendar is open. I'll see you then."

After goodbyes, Reading began his instructions. "I'll call Mark and clear everything with him. You supposed to be at the dig tomorrow? Are you going?"

"Yes."

"Alright, you tell me when you'll have to leave Buehl's to get to the *Party Hardy* at 3:30. I'll have a green and white shadow you."

"Two-thirty. Why do I need a patrol car escort?"

Reading didn't smile. "If someone wants to harm you, you are an easier target coming and going than when you're there." He waved his hand in front of his face. "I'll have three detectives in the bar an hour before you're going to show. Don't give him any details, but let it slip that you've found suspicious remains there. Drop hints, not facts, He will pump you…don't divulge anything else. He'll probably want to meet you again. Tell him you'll have to think about it. Whatever you do, don't go anywhere with him or agree to a place to meet until you've talked with me." He stood up to leave the table.

I nodded and asked, "Where are you headed?"

"Make two phone calls." Reading pointed to his bedroom. "My cell's in there."

"Who to?"

"Mark, to get you excused and keep him informed…and to Judge Westinghouse to get a cell phone tap. I want to find out who Alvin talks to before and after your meeting him." My brother disappeared into his room several seconds before the phone rang again.

I answered and a deep voice asked, "This Chessie?"

"Yes," I answered.

"Partin?" The voice was ominous.

"Yes."

"From East Florida?" I figured out the sequence he used was to instill fear with the veiled threat.

"Yes, I'm an archaeology instructor. But you know that." I hoped that crushed him.

It didn't. "Just wanted to be sure I had the right number." He hung up.

As I ended the call, I knew I'd heard the voice before…I just couldn't remember where.

Chapter   44

I watched Mark swing the ranch gate open as I drove toward it. Bobby and Sheila sat in the back of his CJ-5 ready to explore one of the last five sites on the aerials. His smile looked forced as I drove past.

When I climbed into the Jeep, I told Mark, "Let's go."

"Can't," was his one-word answer.

I screwed my face into asking, *what's up*, without verbalizing.

"We have to wait for Al Dobbs, your brother reassigned him to baby sit us because of your sermon at the meeting." My boss' tone…humorless. His upset wouldn't go away with an apology and clever words.

I said them anyway, "Sorry, Mark. I let my emotions get away."

He stared at me for a few seconds before saying. "It's one thing to endanger yourself. It's another to put all of us under threat with your big mouth." That was the harshest Mark had ever spoken to me. It shocked me. We sat in silence as we waited for Dobbs. Bobby and Sheila's shocked countenances echoed mine. Had I unknowingly gone a bridge too far? I had a chilly ten minutes to think about it.

When Officer Dobbs arrived, Mark popped the clutch on his Jeep, jerking us into motion. He piloted our two-vehicle convoy into the ranch, the sheriff's cruiser following close behind. A day I hadn't expected to be easy, started worse than I dreamed.

We bounced along the ranch trail ruts in utter silence. Mark's eyes and scowl were fixed on the trail. If they varied at all their last destination was me. While his reaction didn't surprise me, the severity certainly did!

I glanced at Bobby and Sheila's uncomfortable faces in the back seat. Sheila raised her eyebrows and made a face, silently asking what's wrong. I shrugged my shoulders in response though I knew. My comments at the meeting had evidently created a firestorm in the one place Dr. Mark Card was hyper-sensitive, his…and my…place of employment. Who had chewed him to get the reaction I saw?

The more I thought about the situation, the more my psyche changed from upset tinged with guilt to unadulterated anger! If I'd been out-of-line, why didn't the administration discuss their problem directly with me? Was it because they considered me an 'underling?' Was it because they didn't consider me capable of taking criticism? Or worse, did they avoid engaging me because of my sex? This possibility made me furious. I counted to myself trying to control my rage. Evidently, Bobby read my expressions and leaned toward me, asking as he did, "Chessie, you okay?"

I smiled at Bobby, nodded, and mentioned, "I'll be fine. I have a couple of rats I need to corner and spank with a machete."

Both Mark and I realized we'd over-reacted by gigantic proportions. We looked at each other, laughed, and postponed explanations until we reached the base at the five middens, our relieved student assistants finally relaxing in the Jeep's rear.

Chapter   45

Mark made an excuse to send Bobby and Sheila out of hearing distance, they gladly complied. When they reached a place where a rabbit couldn't hear a gunshot, Mark grinned sheepishly. "I don't like getting my ass chewed. Particularly, when I didn't do a damned thing and I didn't think the issue that had the powers to be upset and screaming their guts at me meant much."

"Sorry you had to take shit that should have been shoveled on me." I bowed up, pouted, and did my best impression of a seven-year-old. "Why didn't they talk directly to me?" I demanded.

Mark considered that possibility for the first time. It showed clearly in his expression. "I don't know. I guess because I'm your boss."

"Did they threaten your job? If they are that pissed, tell them to fire me." I felt like fighting.

"No Chessie. Look, I had three calls. None wanted me…or you fired. They want us quiet! I told them that Dr. Andrews insisted we show up at the meeting and participate. That calmed them down a bit." Mark shook his head as he mumbled, "Two of them were insane until I explained we were there because we were told to."

I made an assumption. "What did Dr. Andrews say?"

"Nothing. Not until I asked why he wasn't upset. That was after I called him." Mark became at ease the first time that morning. "He said he saw the TV clip. It was what he expected. Andy tells you what he thinks. The only thing he told me…to tell you, and I quote, "Remember to tell Ms. Partin to use more restraint when dealing with arrogance and inferior intelligence.""

I stiffened, "That's all?"

Mark nodded.

"Who called? If Andrews isn't mad, who gives a Russian rat's rump about the rest?" I suddenly saw the mountain ahead as a sand dune, a small one at that.

"Colin DeFarge." Mark's mention of the name told me there were legitimate concerns. Vice Chancellor DeFarge remained a CPA at heart. The University's finances were his venue. I saw the connection and his valid concerns. Accusing a group, though anonymous and veiled, as mass murders wouldn't grease the zippers on their coin purses. I mumbled, "Oh, shit," as I inspected the top of my boots. The sand dune grew to a foothill. "Who were the other two?"

"Vernon Admunsen and Norma Keller."

I recognized Admunsen's name but not Keller's. "Who is the Keller woman?" I asked.

"Norma lives in Jacksonville. She taught at North Florida for a short time, married money. She came from Charlestown University. Norma has contributed to a couple of my projects a few years back. I'd lost track. She buys art from want-to-be artists and lays on the beach mostly now, or so I've heard."

My ears perked at the mention of Charlestown. "Charlestown? That's the one in South Carolina?"

"Yes. Why?" Dr. Card looked too inquisitive.

I moved the conversation onward. "What got Vern Admunsen's underwear twisted? He's not the type. I've always thought of Admunsen as someone to wait for the room to clear if a fire alarm went off before he'd decide to move."

"So did I," Mark shook his head. "Boy, were we wrong! He went ballistic as soon as I answered my cell. He ranted about his friends having nothing to do with the Buehl's or what went on out there. Vernon actually cried. I heard him sobbing." Mark hesitated, rubbing his chin with one hand. That meant he was deciding to tell me something he hadn't intended. "Chessie, he was losing it! He started screaming things that didn't make sense. For some reason he has the notion you know the identities of the bodies we discovered. Vernon thinks you're going to make up theories and accuse those ecologists of the murders because you don't like them. I tried to convince him we didn't know who the bodies were and that you didn't know who the donors were." Mark hesitated. "You don't, do you?"

"No."

"Good. I had to promise him I'd have you call him and confirm that. He said if you'd do that, he could call his friends and tell them they were upset for nothing. That seemed to be the only thing I could use to calm him down."

I stopped listening halfway through his last sentence. My answer, "Sure, I'll phone him this evening."

Mark said, "Thanks, hopefully this thing will go away. Wait here. I'll go rescue Sheila and Bobby," and walked away.

I removed my cell phone immediately to make an important call. When my brother answered, I said, "Reading, I think you need to get with Judge Westinghouse and get warrants for some more phone taps. Quick. It's vital, take my word for it. I'll give you the names now. We might have caught the spider in the web."

Chapter   46

I saw a familiar face in the passenger seat of the green and white sheriff's cruiser parked at Buehl's ranch gate. Reading's huge bicep rested on the open window. I stopped next to him and yelled, "You my security motorcade?"

"Yep."

"Did you get those warrants for phone taps?" I asked.

Reading smiled, nodded vigorously, and said, "I sure and shit did! You were right! I've already asked for additional ones. I've listened to some of the strangest calls I've ever heard today. Complex code…like they used in France before D-day. I'll tell you about it this evening." He waved me on.

The trip to the *Party Hardy* proved to be pure anti-climax. No ominous vehicle appeared to trail us or monitor our progress. I was disappointed, Reading relieved.

~ ~ ~ ~ ~ ~

Alvin Peed sat at a table in the rear of the *Party Hardy,* a campus hangout that acted as an unofficial spare meeting facility for East Florida University's students and faculty. The fair-sized crowd, a third of the tables and booths were occupied, arranged itself in a manner to provide privacy for those gathered.

He waved for me to join him. I had to swallow a laugh. Despite his likeness to the Disney created cartoon character of Irving's *Ichabod Crane,* he did his best to break the stereotype. Alvin convinced himself that he'd look interesting dressed as a French bistro customer. Below a maroon beret, he wore a black and white horizontally striped shirt, partly covered by a plum-colored vest. Royal blue pants with a large gold belt buckle covered the rest of him. His white tennis shoes were an afterthought. I couldn't help wondering where the red ball to cover his nose had been discarded.

It was hard for me to view the man I approached as potentially sinister. I'd considered Peed one of humanity's, harmless. The only potent thing near him was a Long Island Iced Tea clutched in one boney claw. Would he turn out to be something shocking? His welcoming smile said no.

"Hello, Chessie!" He stood up and pulled a chair from under the table for me to sit in. I perceived it as overdone, and in a way, condescending. It increased my suspicion level. I smiled, repositioned the chair a bit, and sat, consciously making the effort not to speak first.

He obliged, "How did your day at the dig go?"

"Very routine." The first rule in responding to interrogation…volunteer nothing.

Peed's smile remained, though I could see resentment flit under it. He tried a different approach. "Is Dr. Card happy with the way things are going out at the Buehl place? I know that excludes the problems that are involved with the question of possible modern homicides. Have you found more of those?"

"Modern homicides? I really can't say," I said, as I parried his thrust.

Alvin leaned away and folded his arms, his smile two-thirds faded. "You aren't going to be uncooperative, are you?" He hesitated, then leaned toward me. "I know things are complicated with your brother working for the Sheriff. But there has to be some things you can share. I promise anything you tell me that is confidential will never see print." I had the vision of Harrison Ford saying, *trust me*, in the first Indiana Jones movie.

I folded my arms presenting defensive body language to convince him he would be dragging information out of me I didn't want him to have. I baited him by stretching my response time out. I decided to let him ask me about the information, draw me out, thereby allowing me to find out what he wanted to know. "Alvin, I can't volunteer anything. I can answer questions about the archaeological portion freely. Tell me what you're interested in, and I'll answer questions about what the Sheriff is investigating, if I can." I'd find out his primary interest in seconds.

His first question was immediate. "Have you found out what's buried there? I mean you said you were concerned there might be things buried on the Buehl place. Is it actually something that might be considered…criminal?"

After a few seconds hesitation, I said in a low voice, "You know about the Carson murder. That's criminal!" I gave Peed a chance to tip the direction of his interest.

"He wasn't buried, was he? The news media accounts are available on that. They all alluded to the fact his body was found in the palmettoes. I'm sure I know all you can tell me about that." Alvin leaned close to me, and half whispered, "Were there actually other things buried out there? Things that could be considered, say, criminal?"

"Uummm," came from between my clenched teeth. "Why would anybody who reads our school newspaper be interested in that?"

"Oh, come on, Chessie. That's juicy stuff. It's a real-life mystery. A who-done-it. Who wouldn't want to know that…particular with East Florida people in the middle?"

Though I doubted it, Peed's interest could simply be National Enquireresk. I pushed a little. "Prurient. Creating an urban legend isn't enough."

I could see the wheels that made his mind function, spinning at a phenomenal rate. His probing question carefully protected what he really wanted to know. "There is a remote possibility that some things you found might solve mysterious events connected to East Florida. Materials that were part of the space-engineering program were stolen from the campus in the early 70s. Much of it was large, too large to hide in a garage. The theory that law enforcement had…someone buried it." His first statement's intent? A misdirect. "And, over the years, we've had students, faculty, and others associated with the university just disappear." He feigned innocence. "Maybe you found a body buried out there?" He winked at me. "That is the rumor that's circulating."

I remained silent. Let him stew. If I could alarm him enough with my next couple of sentences, then clam up, I felt sure he'd be making phone calls as soon as we parted company. Phone calls that my brother would be waiting to intercept. I tried to look and act as if I was reluctant to tell him anything else. Tension built in his face. I swung my head from side to side as though looking for an eavesdropper. Leaning close to him and speaking in low tones, I said, "Alvin, you or no one at East Florida wants any connection with what happened out at the Buehl place."

Peed's countenance replaced tension with fear tinged with panic. After a few seconds to do composure recovery, he asked, "Is it really that bad?"

I nodded vigorously. "And then some!"

"Like, what did you find out there?" His words were a breathless whisper.

I pretended to be battling my desire to tell him and let the pressure build. "I can't tell you," I said.

"Tell me. I won't tell another soul." Peed twitched in his chair.

"Sorry, Alvin." After waiting for several seconds, I added. "What's buried on Buehl's ranch is out of a Hollywood horror movie. Discovering those things." I shook my head and looked at the ceiling as I cut my sentence off. "I've said too much." I sighed deeply. "I can't tell you anything else. When this thing is over..." I paused to add impact to my next words... "And they round up the people responsible, I'll tell you what happened out there."

"People? They know who did the killings?" Peed was in full panic mode.

"Killings? I didn't say anything about killings," my words made him wriggle in his chair.

"What else could it be?" Alvin finished his drink in three gulps. His breathing came in snatches.

"I didn't mean to upset you. Don't worry about there being any connection to the University." I paused to be sure he got the full impact of my next few words. "There are too many to be connected to the school." The sentence slapped him as directly as if I used my hand. Changing the subject, I offered, "There are a few things I can tell you about the archaeology part of our dig. It would be better to wait for us to complete it to really discuss, but if you want something for the paper?"

"It would be better to wait for that," Alvin agreed. He looked like a sprinter at the start line. Peed waved to the waitress and indicated he wanted his check.

"Before you go, there is one unusual thing I can tell you about. Someone planted artifacts in one of the middens. Would you believe Navaho pottery and parts of a skeleton stolen from a local collection?" Watching Peed's face told me his surprise was genuine. He knew nothing about it. That surprised me.

His puzzled look accompanied his comment, "Why in earth would anybody do that? Navaho pottery?" He shook his head in disbelief. Alvin said, "Chessie, I am sorry. I didn't think our meeting would be quite so premature. Would you mind terribly if we postponed this to a later time?" He reached for his wallet as he spoke.

"Not at all. I've got things I have to do tonight and getting a head start will be a good thing." I watched Peed remove a credit card from his wallet to hand to the approaching waitress. He smiled at her and dropped his billfold to the table. I stared at the embossing on the leather. The best connection and clue Alvin had a part in the mystery had been presented to me. A square with the four sides being depicted by bones had been engraved with Nordic symbols at each corner. Odin, Gridr, Fenrir were written on three sides and on the fourth in larger print Vidar was inscribed.

Alvin chatted with the waitress when my eyes lifted from his wallet to his face. I hoped he hadn't seen the recognition in my face when I saw the symbol. His full attention centered on the girl, and I hoped it had always been there. I'd reconsidered. Peed definitely wasn't harmless.

Chapter   47

Reading's eyes narrowed to slits as I relayed the last part of my meeting with Alvin Peed. The engraving on the leather sealed the connection between Peed and the cult. He said, "When you put that piece with what we're learning from the phone taps, it certainly locks a lot together. We have a great start on *knowing* who. Our problem is going to be *proving* who." He removed his vest pocket notebook and opened an electronic tablet sitting on our kitchen table.

"You still keep notes on that little pad," I stated, then asked, "When are you putting your second foot into the 21st century?"

"I'm a Sinatra kind of guy…I do it my way." Reading flipped through the notebook until he found the info he wanted. "Okay, right now the number of wiretaps I've requested is up to fifty-six. Your spider web analogy wasn't far-fetched." He brought up some information on his tablet and spun it around. "Look at the area codes."

Column and row listings illuminated my brother's I-pad. They were sorted for each individual phone number on his tap list. It only took reviewing the first ten to realize the same phone numbers and area codes appeared repeatedly. *But in blocks!* There were associations within separate groups. As I moved my finger over the screen, I had the impression there were four groups centered in four different area codes. The 772 code, our local area, was the most prevalent. The 904 code, the Jacksonville region, represented the second largest grouping. The third largest code regions were from 843 and 854, both representing coastal South Carolina. The last area featured code numbers 352, 386, and 407, all from north central Florida. Within each 'grouping' the list showed calls interlocked to each other. I remarked, "This is four separate games of connect the dots." Reading's broad grin told me he had a large head start. "What have you learned?" I asked.

"First, I'm sure you've seen there four separate and distinct groups. There is lots of interaction within each group. But little to none that we've seen so far between the groups. Each time an event tied to what's transpired recently at the Buehl place has occurred, a flurry of phone activity follows it within these groupings of numbers." Reading looked at me; I assumed he wanted a question or observation from me.

"So, that's good. You can begin checking out each person. It shouldn't take long for you to fill a few jails with these people," I concluded.

"Numbers don't always mean people. All the numbers we're looking at are from burner phones, all purchased from the same place, at one time, for cash. That fact cements these four groups together. As far as I'm concerned, it proves all have some part in this bloody mess." Reading drew in air like a vacuum. "But…it also proves these are some shrewd folks. Catching them won't be easy. I also have a gut feeling. My gut asks me, how do you keep a secret like that, when so many know about it? You make the consequences of betrayal so horrific the fear keeps everyone involved petrified."

I shuddered, "Like if you do anything that might compromise the group, you become the next lunch?"

Reading nodded grimly.

Something occurred to me. If that were the case, if those that broke the covenant in some way became a victim, it would be logical for those in the group the guilty one belonged to not execute sentence. It would be difficult for those who knew the individual well to perform their gruesome work on the victim. Consciences could drive others to some desperate act. Others, from one of the other three groups, would do it. Retribution against an unknown, and self-preservation avoiding exposure were monumental motives.

We said it together. "The groups enforce the cults dictates on each other!" That explained a lot. If a person offended an individual in one of the sects, it was the members of another that gained vengeance. There wasn't a connection to the person who desired another's murder. That member had no part in the act...there could be no evidence of committing the deed! If four groups remained anonymous the chance of discovery was remote.

But there had to be some way in which they were connected. How were victims identified if they weren't?

Someone, or maybe a few ran things; they had too. "There has to be a head of the snake," I said.

Reading nodded. "Finding it isn't going to be easy. I have a hunch that besides being plenty smart, they are powerful people. Individuals with clout, that's political, financial, and more."

I nodded. I thought for a few more seconds. Then I added my opinion. "Reading, I think eating people will trump influence." Something else occurred to me. "How far back can you get those records?"

"I'm not sure. One of my administrative people asked me how far I wanted to go back. I told him six months. He said, *'that's all?'* That implies he could go farther." Reading cocked his head to the side and inquired, "Why?"

"Just a thought. Reading if you could correlate the activity of one of those groups in one time period to unsolved missing persons cases in the three areas you might get a victim's name to match a skeleton from Buehl's ranch. It would be a lot of digging, but…" I raised my eyebrows asking the question, *why not?*

Reading scowled. "I hate it when you're right." He tapped his fingers on the table before saying, "That's if all the victims are buried there. The South Carolina thing bothers me. As careful as these people are, I can't believe they haul corpses 500 miles or so to depose of them. I see the South Carolina group having their own dump site."

That shocked me! Multiple graveyards, as a possibility, boggled my mind. I nodded and said, "That is logical.

And…very scary. Is there any way to tie the groups together? A common phone number perhaps?"

"Actually, we have six of those. There is one number from each group that calls one of two other numbers. I'm theorizing those are four group leaders communicating with the two heads of the group." Reading made a face and exhaled in disgust. "All the numbers are from the burner lot purchase I told you about, so they are no help."

I thought for several seconds until I remembered Reading told me he'd listened to some taped conversations. "I know you said that you monitored some of the calls and that they were in code, but you at least get something. Gender? Age? Accent?"

"No, no, and no. I told you these people are careful. All the conversations are electronically generated. They are disguised to all sound the same. Remember, I told you how strange the exchanges were? They all ask and answer using the same phrases…plus yes and no. Just a second." Reading found a recording on his tablet. "Listen to this." He started the recording.

"Viking."

"Oslo."

"Wolf."

"Yes."

"Ale at the table."

"Yes."

"AA."

"Yes."

"AG."

"Yes."

"Table…A, H, C, J."

"Yes."

The clicking noise ended the conversation. Reading shook his head. "Outside of the first two words where they are identifying each other, what can you get out of that?"

"Actually, maybe, a lot," I replied. "Was there any individual letter above J?"

"Not that I remember."

"Okay, here's what I think it's saying. Wolf means there's danger of some kind. Ale at the table probably means meet at a particular spot. The letters, if I'm right, is a code my girlfriends used in high school. A equal's one, and so on, up to J equaling zero. If I'm right, I'd say they are meeting on AA, 11 month, November, on the AG, 17th day. They will be at the table, wherever that is…at 6:30 PM. The AHCJ is 1930 in military time or 7:30 PM."

Reading stared at me before saying, "That's pretty good. I never learned that in high school, in or out of class."

I laughed, "I didn't either. The cryptology class I took in the Marines helped. What's next?"

"Keep collecting information on the phone numbers and deciphering it. The big thing would be if we can connect any familiar names to the burner phone numbers. The Buehls, Mulhee, Peed, people like that."

"How are you planning to do that?"

"Just keep watching those cell numbers and hope we get a break. I'm planning to explore your suggestion about matching missing persons to phone activity within a group. And, of course, we'll put as much pressure as possible on anyone that we think is a suspect, with a couple exceptions where pressure would do more harm than good."

I nodded, "Anything else?"

"Yes. Keep you alive."

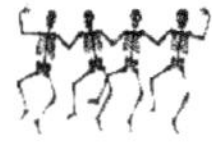

Chapter   48

"Hey, Mark, we have company," Bobby said while pointing at a HUMV lurching along the ruts of the ranch road.

Our group looked at the vehicle several seconds before Mark inquired, "Anybody recognize that truck?"

"It belongs to Beth Dillon." Al Dobbs looked guilty. "The officer at the gate told me she was coming back here. Sorry, I should have told you when he called."

"I wonder what she wants?" I thought aloud.

Mark shrugged his shoulders. "I wouldn't doubt she wishes she never heard of Buehl's property. Who knows? She may be looking for a way out."

Sheila remarked, "She has people with her. Two at least." As the HUMV came closer, the silhouettes of one person in the front passenger seat and another seated in the rear were visible.

Mark looked at me and grumbled, "I wouldn't be pissed if she shut the whole thing down today." He exhaled a gust of frustration. "Chessie, will you get everything packed into the Jeep. Take Sheila and Bobby and keep them busy. I'll see what Beth wants. I want to finish prospecting the sites we haven't looked at by the end of the day. We start excavating on site #4 tomorrow…no matter what! I want to finish this project and be out of here. I can't wait to be done with this shit."

I watched Mark approach the HUMV which stopped a hundred feet from us. What would be important enough for her to make an unscheduled visit? Maybe it would be something simple…like a progress review. Though I hoped that would be true, I doubted it. Nothing connected to the Buehl dig happened without complications and problems. At that second, I wished I'd never pushed my nose into the business. The computer printouts and my desk at the University were less odious every day.

~ ~ ~ ~ ~ ~

"You won't believe this!" Those were the first four words Mark Card spoke when he climbed into the driver's seat of his Jeep. He slumped over the wheel, turned his head toward me, and closed his eyes. "Beth had two of Buehl's partners with her, the ones that want the deal to go through. Stanton Griggs and Bill Wheeler. They wanted to know what the probability is that there are more bodies buried out here. The Wheeler guy is concerned there are. Griggs don't care. He wants this deal to go through. I don't think Beth knows what to do."

"What did you tell them?" I asked.

"The truth. I don't know. They asked what my best guess was. I thought about lying to them and say I didn't think there are more buried out here. I didn't." Mark made a disgusted face. "I shouldn't have answered. Beth asked what it would take to find out. She has a map of what her company wants to develop. Beth showed it to me; it amounts to about 60% of the land. They wanted to have us look for spots that could have graves on the portion where they want to put houses. I told her in time and money, but I also explained the only way to be sure was to run the GPR over suspect places. If I did that and found something, ethically, I'd have to tell the sheriff. That didn't go well."

"Didn't go well?" I repeated. "What happened?"

"Griggs went ballistic. He got so mad he became incoherent. Stuff about no one would keep him from getting rich because of dead Indians or dead bodies. He kept screaming 'no one could help them now.' Griggs leaned his head out the window and pointed to his cheek. 'She did this,' he growled, 'that eco-nut Mulhee. I'll kill the bitch if she does this again. I'll kill her if she gets close to me!' Beth warned him about talking that way. From what was said next I gather that Billie threatened to kill Griggs already. Evidently, Mulhee met with him to convince him to take the deal she offered. It didn't end well."

Mark opened his eyes. The look in them combined the emotions one would see in the eyes of a child stealing cookies with a college senior being told their exemption from final exams was cancelled. I probed, saying, "So…where does that leave us?"

"In the area Beth wants to develop, she's paying me to spend another week to search for possible graves. I mark the areas on her map, do no radar check, and I do not volunteer what I found to anybody." Mark closed his eyes again. "I agreed to do it myself. She knows your brother is in the sheriff's office. You're out of this one."

I stared at him. "You don't think I'll tell him that?"

"I'm asking you not to tell him, unless I find more graves. I'll tell you either way."

I wished Mark's eyes were open and I could assess the truthfulness of his words. What he said didn't make much sense. It only postponed the result if more bodies were discovered. Then I decided he lied to me. If he found bodies, I'd never know about it. I tried to keep a straight face but failed. His closed eyes protected him and for now, me. I took a breath, "What do I do when you're doing…nothing?"

"You've wanted to run a dig. You have your chance. Use Bobby and Sheila as your assistants and pick six of the best student volunteers and finish the five middens site. You can do it." His comment's intent was an indorsement to pep me up. I didn't need that.

"Oh, I know I can do it." I purposely placed an edge in my tone.

Mark's eyes opened. He knew he screwed up and that fact blinked on and off like a neon sign.

I gave him a way out. "Let's get Bobby and Sheila and do what you originally planned for the day. I'll talk to them about who they think would be our best six choices for *my* dig. We can both get started on *our* projects tomorrow."

Chapter   49

It wasn't Dr. Mark Card's best work. The normally meticulous scientist I knew had a replacement invade his body. This person's modus operandi translated to a pragmatic quick and dirty. Mark's stated objective of finishing the three remaining sites that showed evidence of human disturbance would have been a very hard, long day or impossible employing his normal procedures. When we reached the first location, it was apparent this would not be the case.

Mark glanced at the aerial photo, walked around the area quickly, and issued a self-fulfilling prophecy, "This place doesn't have a high chance of having anything under it. We'll do a sample run with the GPR…to be sure." Sheila, Bobby and I exchanged disbelieving glances. Some alien being had to have invaded our boss' body.

The one-third of the area he selected for the sample wasn't the area I would have picked. It was selected to be cleared quickly, not as the place that would most likely yield results. A depressed area ten feet from the selected spot would have been my choice. Never-the-less, we attacked the weeds covering the area with energy. Within a half hour, we had the rectangle cleared. Normally, Mark's decerning eyes made a close examination of the terrain looking for anything that would awaken his 'artifact instincts.' This time he looked for the radar unit and said, "Let's get this started."

Bobby pushed the GPR back and forth over the ground without the usual constant banter and instructions from Mark. I stood with a notebook to record observations Mark made as he peered at the screen. He did so with what I perceived as disinterest. There were few comments to record, most of those being…"nothing of interest." Within two hours we were packing up to go to the next spot. Bobby and Sheila mumbled their conversations low enough neither Mark, nor I, could hear. I knew what they were about anyway. All discussions ceased when we climbed into the Jeep to drive to the next site.

Driving between sites he remained uncharacteristically quiet. My years of association with the man told me things were more complicated…and threatening…than he had shared with me. The tension stretching grim casts to his features reinforced my intuition.

Our visit to the second site transpired identically to our first. It was a large area; three times as large. Mark instructed us to clear a smaller percentage sample area than the previous one. His selection told me *he didn't want to find anything*! He selected the area least likely to have anything buried beneath it. Our examination of the site was a football replay of the first. We were done and on the way in two hours.

As Bobby, Sheila, and I finished putting the tools into the Jeep, I said, "On to number three."

Sheila raised her eyebrows and grumbled, "Why bother?"

I'm sure Mark heard. Normally, the Dr. Card part of his persona would have snapped back, admonishing her. The stranger leaning over the Jeep's hood, viewing the last aerial, showed no reaction though I know the words burned in him.

The last stop was the same as the first two. Instead of the long arduous day I'd imagined, we were done two hours before quitting time on a normal day. Mark drove the Jeep back to our base at the five middens in complete silence while Bobby, Sheila, and I discussed the selection of the six students to form my "dig team." His silence during that process underlined that something had him tied into knots. Mark would have usually been affirming or objecting to our selections.

I purposely leaned against my truck and delayed leaving until after Bobby and Sheila. Something serious gnawed at my boss and friend. The man handled pressure well, but he wasn't handling whatever he'd been saddled with at all. You can't help if you don't know the problem. I waited for him to speak.

"You ready to go, Chessie? I want to get to the gate before Al Dobbs leaves. I'd like him to drive back with us to 60 and back to town," Mark said. Nervous concern smothered him with a dark blanket.

"Okay, Mark. Cut the crap. What is going on? Ever since Beth Dillon was here this morning you've acted like a kitten in a cage with a pit bull." I tried sounding as forceful as possible. I expected a smoke screen of disinformation from him. That didn't happen.

"I guess you should know." Mark walked to me, put a hand on my shoulder, and said, "I'm sorry. When I talked to Beth, we discussed a lot more than I told you. When she left, she was going straight to the sheriff's office." Mark dropped his arm to his side, his shoulders slumping as he said, "Billie Mulhee, tried to kill Beth early this morning, that's after having the fight with Stanton Griggs the afternoon before."

"Are you serious?"

Mark nodded. "About four in the morning, Beth woke up when her dog growled. She turned the light on and there stood Mulhee…three steps from the bed…an ax held over her head. Before she could swing it down on Beth, Dillon's Doberman attacked. That allowed Beth to get a revolver from her nightstand. She took a couple shots at Billie but missed. Billie didn't miss the dog, it's at the vet."

"Since you're acting this way, evidently the Sheriff couldn't find her."

"You're wrong. Beth didn't call the sheriff right away. She should have. She didn't. Beth took her dog to the vet immediately. The vet is doing her best but…the Doberman is in bad shape."

"Had she called the sheriff before she came here this morning?" I asked.

"Yes. She called from the vet's office, but the delay allowed Mulhee to escape. They sent cars to Mulhee's house. The woman was gone." Mark took a breath. "That's far from all. When Beth returned home to meet with the Sheriff's people, Mulhee called her. The woman told Beth, she'd die and gave her a list of others that would die also. Griggs, Wheeler, Millie Lane, and a bunch more. I was on it." He paused. "You are on it. She claims if we catch her, we'll all die anyway. That's probably true."

"Shit!"

"I came up with a wild idea to trap Mulhee. If she knew I was wandering around out here, by myself, looking for more graves, and am on her list, I'd be bait. I could catch her or kill her if I had to." He shook his head. "I don't know if I could kill someone."

"That's the worst idea ever! Mark, you make a great archaeologist. You make a piss poor Rambo."

"The more I thought about it, the more I realized that is true."

"Besides, you know Mulhee is only part of this. About the only thing different is that we know she's part of whatever the evil is that infects this place." I thought for a second. "Should we cancel the dig for tomorrow and tell Bobby and Sheila to stay home?"

"Yes. I'll make the calls." He pointed at my car. "We need to get to the road before Al leaves. Just you and I tomorrow?"

"Sure," I said, but I wasn't.

"I want to start site four. You have a gun and I'll bring my shotgun. I think we'll be alright with Dobbs here. We're probably safer here than at home with him here to protect us."

I wasn't sure of that either. "I can ask Reading to assign another officer."

Mark considered my offer for several seconds before rejecting it. "No, we'll be fine with Al. I'll tell everyone we won't be here. Fewer folks that know we're here the better."

I looked at him, reticent, to voice my opinion and to have to defend it. One of the lessons *I* hadn't fully learned is sexual equality requires us to face conflict. That's with our male friends as well as antagonists. My failure to do so almost cost me my life.

Chapter   50

"Seems like the earth swallowed her." Reading told me as we walked to our vehicles. Our discussion over breakfast continued as we prepared to leave for work. The subject of the majority of our conversations remained the progress he and the sheriff's department were making on the Buehl investigation. Three days had passed since the attempt on Beth Dillon's life. Reading's reveal of his department's progress wasn't uplifting. Billie Mulhee had disappeared. Leads continued to be uncovered by researching data provided by phone taps and the call history related to the numbers. The problem remained. Volumes of info gathered by phone number remained valueless unless names could be attached. One or two connections, that would be all it would take. Reading's positive attitude and his belief they'd find a slip-up, reassured me.

Since no sign of aggression toward any of the individuals threatened by Mulhee had occurred, tension within the potential victims lessen. I looked over my shoulder less frequently. One or two individuals openly expressed contempt for the now publicized threats. Stanton Griggs taunted Mulhee with a challenge, "The woman can pick her time of death. That's whenever she shows her face to me." He and a few others scoffed at the 'danger' stating that the threats were ravings of an unbalanced kook. I wasn't sure that had a sniff of truth to it.

Since I was on Billie's short list of those to exterminate, I asked, "What are you doing to find her?"

"Twenty-four seven surveillance on her home, taps on all three of her phones, there's a bulletin out on her car, plates, and license, we're monitoring all her credit cards and bank account, and we've got all transportation hubs surveilled within 150 miles."

"Rental cars too?"

Reading nodded. "Even the ones in hotels."

"Nothing?"

"Nada, zilch, no hits at all." Reading frowned. "Most of the detectives thinks she got away. I don't. First, it isn't her style. She's not a runner and she's irrational enough to ignore reality. Second, we are sure there is a cell here. I'm sure they'll shelter her. Sitting around someone's lanai keeps her away from discovery."

"If one of them doesn't decide to eat the evidence," I interjected.

Reading scowled and added sarcastically, "That's lady-like. I guess that's the Marine in you. Or, maybe not." He knew better than to hint anything negative about my Corp in my presence.

"Semper fi. The Marines taught me I didn't need lace on my panties. I taught myself to be realistic."

He waved his hand in surrender and continued, "Third, those weren't idle threats she made. That woman is grave serious. I know how she is about her commitment to ecology. She's around here. Somewhere. Watching." Reading paused and his 'listen close' look appeared on his face. "Don't get careless or sloppy about watching for her. My gut says you're number one on her list or close to it. I don't want to make your funeral arrangements."

"You won't. I check behind me frequently."

"Make sure you stick close to Dobbs. He's a good man."

I nodded. Al was, but our previous relationship made me avoid him in one-on-one situations. Al took note, tried to keep a comfortable distance, and this resulted in compromising my safety to a small degree. I was happy for the bargain. "Anything else?" I asked.

Reading detected a little cockiness in my voice, "Just because it's been quiet, don't think this is over. The group is large, and it will take time for them to react. When they do…it could be bad.

Chapter   51

"Where are you headed?" I asked.

Reading avoided details, "On a date."

"With who?" My brother seldom wore a tie. That required a special occasion or person. The rest of his clothes confirmed his 'date' exceeded the 'casual' definition.

"Damn, Chessie, get a life!" Reading didn't like me, his *big* sister, invading his love life.

"Mine's just fine, thank you. Who is she?"

"I don't ask you who you're going out with." The master of defensive banter hunkered down in a trench.

"You don't have to, I volunteer it." My smug answer? Only partially true.

Reading answered with an emotionless stare.

I smiled and asked a question I knew would get the answer I wanted. "Is she so ugly you are afraid to tell me who it is?"

The stare continued for several seconds before he said, "Millie Lane."

"You finally getting around to taking her out again? It's about time." I knew they'd had a date at the beginning of the Buehl mess but didn't know if they kept in contact afterwards.

"We've been out a few times." Reading scowled and folded his arms. "Sis, I don't need your nose in my business or dating advice from you. Your credentials aren't great."

When you know someone intimately, you know their tender mental vulnerabilities. He certainly hit one of mine. I'm sure my face clouded immediately. "I go on dates when *I* want to." I saw his unasked for retort and beat the words from his mouth. "I get plenty of invitations. I'm just particular about who I date." His half-smile told me the 'who' portion of our conversation had finished. "Where are you going?" opened the 'where' part.

Reluctantly, my brother mumbled, "To West Palm…for a string quartet recital."

I grinned as wide as my mouth allowed. "Why, Reading, I'm glad to hear you're adopting culture in your life. The only string musicians I ever knew you listened to were, Earl Scruggs, Chet Atkins, and Charlie Daniels. *Rocky Mountain Breakdown* and the *Devil Went Down to Georgia* are a lot different from the *Minute Waltz* and *Polonaise*. Seems as though Millie is having a positive impact on you."

Reading tilted his head and stared coldly at me. "Yes, Chessie she is." His voice and countenance told me the conversation was through.

~ ~ ~ ~ ~ ~

Television is so terrible! I lamented my failure to stop at my local bookstore to pick up a new read. Turn it off! I wandered into my room and perused the shelves of my bookcase looking for a favorite rerun. My fingers found Norman Maclean's *A River Runs Through It*; it's my go to reading entertainment whose masterful writing never gets old.

Before I could revisit my old friend, my cell phone played, *Wild Thing*. I shook my head as I hurried into the living room and snatched the noisy cell from the coffee table. Reading's familiar number lit up the LED. Why would he be calling me while on a date?

I spewed a few flippant comments, "Flat tire? Forget something? Need Instruction? I'm here to serve, bro."

"I need your help, Chessie. Listen, This is serious. I'm at the Hospital and—"

"What's wrong? Are you hurt? Is Millie, okay? Have you been in a wreck?" I frantically interrupted.

"Calm down. Hear me?" He waited for me to respond.

"Yes." I bit my tongue to restrain it from producing a stream of questions.

"You know Millie's parents from when you hung around with her in high school. I need you to call them. Someone assaulted her. Don't alarm them any more than possible. They need to come to the hospital. Tell them I'll meet them in the emergency room. They're going to ask what's wrong and how bad Mille is injured. Don't answer that. Tell them you don't know, and I'll have all the answers."

"What in the hell happened?" I shouted.

I heard Reading take a deep breath. "When I went to pick Millie up, her front door was open, and I could hear her screaming. I didn't have time to go to the truck and get a gun. When I yelled to her, her attacker tried to flee. We met in the hallway to her bedroom. The man had a knife and knew how to use it. He got past me, but he left me three remembrances. Nothing that three or four stitches hasn't fixed. I let him go. I didn't know how serious Mille was. She'd been stabbed twice. Initially, he tried to slit her throat, but Mille saw him in the mirror. She got away with a surface cut on the side of her throat. The stab wounds are serious, but no vital organs were hurt. She's in surgery to repair damage to her intestines."

"Are you telling the truth?"

Reading exploded, "Shit, Chessie, I need help, not the third degree! Call Millie's parents then get your ass over here!"

"Right away." After a second's thought I asked, "Can I tell them she's not in danger of dying?"

Reading hesitated, then answered, "Yes, she isn't that serious."

His answer concerned me. "Are you telling me everything?"

"Damn, Chessie!"

"Okay, okay." I couldn't resist asking, "Did you get a good look at his face?"

"No. He wore a mask."

"That's a bad break," I grumbled, "That could have put an end to this."

"It may anyway. I think I know who it was." He forestalled any further talk. "Make your call and get over here. I'm not saying another word until you do."

Chapter   52

Reading lied. Kind of. After making my call and racing to the hospital, Reading stonewalled questions about his encounter with the intruder and the man's identity. I did get him to commit to providing all the details when we returned home. His agreement to that accompanied a question he asked me: "Chessie, do you still record your phone calls?"

"Sometimes," His question mystified me. "Why?"

"Obviously, I want to listen to one I know you received." That was all I could pry from him. His full attention centered on Millie. Her doctor assured him and her parents she'd be fine in a few weeks. I saw something in Reading I'd never observed before. His concern level reached that of ones reserved for a parent, a son or daughter, or a spouse.

~ ~ ~ ~ ~ ~ ~

"What am I looking for?" I asked Reading. His visible intensity pounded through the veins in his neck, flushed cheeks, and pupil sharpness. He believed he'd discovered a break-through clue.

"Remember the day you and Mulhee had the confrontation in the courtroom? We had a phone call that night. Remember?"

"Sure, you traced it to a pay phone in Orlando. No help so you told me…other than it was close to UCF." I spun the cell screen backward, looking for the call. "So, is it now the answer?"

"A piece of it. The clue has four parts. A license plate, some keys, the sound of a voice, a knife cut…all that can equal a name. I'll explain it if I'm correct." He smiled. "Actually, I know I'm right, I just want to confirm it."

The date I looked for indicated I had recorded two calls. I glanced at Reading and asked, "Got them…at least I have two recorded on the date. Are you ready?"

He nodded.

I played them both. Before the first one finished, he smiled. When the second ended, Reading's smile broadened, and he added a vehement head nod. "I've got the bastard." He slapped the table and added, "And a way to prove it."

"Explain!" I was as excited as Reading.

"Beyond a reasonable doubt. I'll go over it in sequence." Reading held one finger up. "When I arrived, I noticed a black Ford sedan parked in front of Millie's house. Two things. It had Alachua County license plates and a small dent in the trunk. I didn't get all the number, but I remember TQ7 were the first three. We can identify from that." The second finger came up. "When he and I wrestled and grabbed each other, he had a big set of keys in his one hand. I'm guessing he held his car key. My hand grabbed the dangling keys and I yanked…hard. One of the rings broke and a dozen keys fell to the floor. They fit something. We just have to find what.”

“That’s a close second to mission impossible,” I groaned.

“There’s more. We have the keys in the evidence room. Two of them have security numbers on them. You can’t duplicate them unless you are on an approved list. It will take a little tracking but…those keys were assigned to somebody. I know who. It was the person who is on the phone call you recorded. He and I exchanged a few threats in the hall. There was a third time I heard that voice. Remember our phone call to the County Clerk of Courts in Alachua County and the recording on his voice mail? They *are* all the same!”

“You got him!” I yelled to our couch.

“Even more.” Reading pursed his lips in a confident smirk. “When I pulled those keys, Hector Bertram McCoy took a swipe at me with his knife and the jerking pulled his hand under the knife. He cut himself…bad. Our crime lab will sort out blood from the scene. We’ll get DNA, the works. Plus, the wound will be his scarlet letter. It isn’t going away quickly.” His smile broadened. “I have his ass.”

I remained silent for a few seconds before observing, “Yes you do. But…with him being connected to law enforcement, won’t he realize that. He’ll be leaving for parts unknown.”

Reading looked like I'd slapped him across his face with a dead fish. His editorial comment, "Shit."

"You'd better go after him now," I suggested.

Reading ran out of the room.

Chapter   53

I returned to reading *A River Runs Through It* after my brother left so fast smoke rose from his footsteps. My intention to stay awake for Reading's promised call was foiled by heavy eyelids. The visit to 'Black Jack's Bar' ended my trip on Maclean's literary train. The sound of *Wild One* jolted me awake, the book dropping from my hand as awareness struck. At 2:30 in the morning, it had to be Reading and he had to know if he got to McCoy before he escaped.

There wasn't any sleep in my hello. I checked the cell screen. It wasn't Reading's number.

"Hello," I repeated.

After a brief silence, the call disconnected. I quickly found paper and pen and scribbled the number for future use. Then I tried redialing the number. It rang…and rang…and rang…and rang. No one answered. My apprehension rose to a state of alarm. I went to my bedroom and retrieved my security blanket. I removed my 9mm Glock from my dresser drawer. I felt compelled to stealthily ease the curtain at my front window aside so I could peer out to see if a potential danger lurked there. I could see nothing. But with the darkness of deep night blanketing the exterior, I experienced little relief.

Adrenalin made sleep impossible. I picked up my book from the floor, placed my automatic in my lap, and prepared to find my place in the novel, when the phone rang again.

Electricity shot through me. I could feel the hair on my neck stiffen. I deliberately set my book down, picked up my cell, and read the number on the screen.

I relaxed. Reading's familiar number had appeared. "Hello, Reading," I answered.

"Hey, Chessie." I could tell from the sound of his voice things hadn't gone well.

"He got away, didn't he?"

"No."

"No? You don't sound very happy. I'd think you'd be popping a cork on a champagne bottle."

Reading hesitated for several seconds. "We have him. Unfortunately, it won't do us one damned bit of good. McCoy held a double barrel shotgun under his chin and pulled both triggers at once. Apparently. What we have is a corpse with half a head."

"Did you find him? Or someone else?"

"Someone else. We knew he'd be at one of two places…at his house or at his office. When we contacted the Alachua Sheriff to ask them to authorize us entering his jurisdiction and to help us, he said for us to go to his home. He and his people would go to McCoy's office. The Alachua Sheriff was the first person to get there. He heard the blast. We rerouted when they called to tell us what happened."

I thought for several seconds before asking, "Are you going to be able to do a search? Or do it in joint with the Alachua people? To look for evidence…like one of those burner phones?"

"I don't see why not. At the very least, we can observe." Reading cleared his throat. "I'd thought of that." Reading told me he had questions with that comment.

That prompted me to ask additional questions. "Is McCoy a tall guy?"

"Not particularly. Maybe five-ten. Not over that."

"Was the damage to his head straight up through his chin or off to one side or the other?"

"Straight up. What are you getting at?" Reading sounded curious.

"Well, if McCoy's arms weren't really long, it would be very difficult to pull the trigger and keep the line of fire straight up through the chin. And, that's particularly true pulling both triggers simultaneously. I don't see how that gets done. From the data I know from anatomy I learned for archaeology; I think it's impossible. Measure the arm length, the distance triggers to barrel end, and see if that works with the dead man's shoulders square. The shoulders would have to be square to keep the axis of fire straight up." I hesitated before stating the obvious, "You may have a murder there, not a suicide."

Chapter   54

We passed each other. A red-eyed Reading drove toward our duplex for some sleep as I steered my truck to the Buehl ranch. We honked an acknowledgement. I would have to wait for the evening to learn if the Alachua Sheriff's department cooperated fully, letting Reading and his detectives be involved in the crime scene investigation.

My less than full night's sleep showed when I pulled up to the Buehl ranch gate. I yawned, "Good morning," to Al Dobbs. He yawned in sympathy.

Al nodded to me and said, "Mornin' Chessie. Dr. Mark is already back there." He held up his hand as I prepared to drive through the gate. "I thought you should know that Sheriff Travis has ordered me to stay within a hundred feet of you and Dr. Mark and you all's student assistants. Sorry, but I don't have an option."

Al was more aware of my uncomfortableness due to his close proximity than I was aware. The problem? It was mine, not his. Al Dobbs had been the complete gentleman in my presence. The past was past...I decided to bury it.

"Al, you're not the one who should be handling this. You don't have to worry about your bothering me. I showed my rear and should not have. Our relationship in the past shouldn't affect us today. You've been great. I haven't treated you like a friend. I should have."

"I am your friend," Dobbs said as he extended his hand.

We shared a warm handshake and I added, "Friends!"

He nodded. "That's good." Al pointed toward the archaeological camp. "As soon as my replacement gets here, I'll be back there. Would you tell Dr. Mark to keep everyone tight until I can watch the herd?"

I laughed, said, "sure," and pointed my truck down the ruts that led to the five middens.

~ ~ ~ ~ ~ ~

Mark didn't receive the news we were going to have to stay together until our 'baby-sitter' arrived, well. Mark's words…not mine.

"That's BS. Whoever takes his place may not show for hours. What are we supposed to do except stare at each other?" Dr. Mark Card's fondness of efficiency showed.

Bobby, Sheila, and Ruthie, another student, smiled, content to sit in the sand and gossip. For my part, my lack of sleep made the idle time welcome.

I knew the increase in safety precautions had to do with the happenings of last night. If I told Mark about the attempt on Millie Lane's life and the pursuit and death of her attacker, he'd be comfortable with the delay. Reading always cautioned me to never divulge any sheriff's department information unless he told me I could. I wouldn't break my word. Four of us sat and relaxed while the 'boss' sat and stewed.

Mark began his tirade about lost time for the third repeat, when Bobby pointed and interrupted the replayed gripe, "Dr. Card, here comes the deputy." Al's cruiser became visible as it emerged from behind a stand of cypress. Mark's, "About time," lacked justification. It had been less than a half-hour since I delivered the news.

After Al parked in the shade of one of the oaks, he yelled, "Hey, Dr. Mark, I need to speak to you over here." Mark walked the twenty steps to the cruiser. The transition on Mark's face was a serious one; the conversation was one he did not like. It closed with Al mouthing, *I'm sorry* and Mark nodding reluctantly. They walked to the four of us in silence.

"Listen up," Mark made sure we were all focused on him. "There's been a serious number of events that happened overnight. Because of that, I've been instructed to send all of you students, home. Before you ask, I can't share *any* details. You are being sent home for your safety. The less you know the safer you'll be. Don't discuss being out here with anyone. You all understand…this is serious stuff."

All nodded.

"That include me?" Bobby asked.

"Afraid so, buddy."

"What about me?" I asked.

"The two of us can finish up the two excavations we've started. Then the Sheriff said we have to clear out. I don't know for how long. Honestly, after what I've been told…" Mark didn't finish his thought. "Okay, Bobby…Sheila…Ruthie, you take off…now."

~ ~ ~ ~ ~ ~ ~

We watched the college students trace the ranch ruts to the gate in Bobby's old Land Rover. As they disappeared behind the cypress head, Mark said, "I need to bring you up-to-date on what's happened."

I nodded, thinking it better to allow him to 'enlighten' me on things I already knew, than confess it was old news.

"Overnight, we had two separate events that are certainly a result of what we discovered here."

I nodded again feigning no knowledge of what he would tell me.

"An attempt to kill Millie Lane occurred last evening and the person that attacked her has died. He was murdered."

I hoped my attempt to look shocked and surprised succeeded.

"The second thing is the murder of Stanton Griggs. His head was discovered in one of the canals over by Feldsmere by some fishermen."

The shock and surprise on my face required no acting.

Chapter   55

"No loose ends," Reading summarized what he thought before he went into the details I wanted. "What happened last night is also a graphic warning to anyone who tries to interfere with what this group does. There will be consequences. Terrible ones. That includes law enforcement, anyone. If you cross them, they'll get their revenge. That's what they're all about."

My brother and I leaned against a wooden railing on a ramp leading to the beach. Breezes fanned off the blue Atlantic, its color darkening as the sun raced to the horizon behind us. The scene and salt air didn't provide the relaxing tonic it normally did; we were both too tense. I knew the aesthetics lacked the influence over us it usually exerted. A beautiful, bikini clad young woman eyed Reading as she passed without his notice. The fact I didn't comment about that underlined our preoccupation with the deadly mystery surrounding us. Neither of us spoke the words. We knew our lives were in danger as well as many others.

"What happened to Griggs," I asked. An involuntary shiver ran through my body as my mind conjured possibilities.

"Other than we're sure he's dead, we know nothing." Reading sighed. "The detectives that responded to the call were careful to preserve everything they found for a hundred feet on either side of where the fishermen found his head. They made impressions of some tire tracks and collected three boxes of trash that could be evidence, each isolated in its own plastic baggie. The lab will check it all, but we'll have a better chance winning the Lotto than getting anything useful from it. One thing I can tell you, Lashann, went to the canal. He examined Griggs head. Lashann assured us that the head had been severed from the body, hours, not even a day ago. There were absolutely no marks on it and the neck showed a clean single cut. There wasn't as much blood in the bag as Lashann said he would expect to find. He theorized that Griggs died maybe a day before decapitation occurred."

"Have you found the rest of him?" I shivered again. Thoughts of the headless skeletons and gnawed on bones we'd discovered, flitted through my brain.

"Not a trace. The Sheriff had cruisers surveilling his house. He hadn't returned in a few days. That's concerning, but since he's a bachelor and in the habit of being away for days at a time they never went further before his head ended up in the canal. Of course, as soon as that happened, we got our warrant and went inside. Nothing out of the ordinary, no signs of violence. The dirty dishes in the sink will tell us when he was there last. The lab is working that also. Since you and Mark found those refrigerators buried at Buehl's place, the lab is checking the tissue to determine if the head was refrigerated. Lashann said he could tell it hadn't been frozen."

I asked, "Do you know anything else?"

"Not much. We contacted his business assistant. She sent us a copy of his schedule since the last time she saw him. That was three days ago. He was supposed to have lunch with Beth Dillon yesterday. We called her. She told us she had to cancel the meeting and called him that morning. She never spoke to him; she got his voicemail and left a message." Reading grimaced. "We thought we'd gotten a break. Grigg's car turned up in the high school parking lot. It has security cameras. Guess what? They aren't working. The school claims they forgot to do the daily check…for the last month!"

"You don't think he'll end up buried at Buehl's, do you?"

"No, that's too brazen even for this group. There's too great a chance of a slipup and them getting caught." He paused, then added, "As far as Griggs, that is all I know."

"How is Millie?" I asked.

"Physically, she had serious stab wounds. They repaired everything…she'll be sore and in bed for a week, but she'll be back to normal in the end. Mentally, that's more of a problem. She's frightened out of her wits. Her nurses told me anytime strangers walk by her room's door, she panics. They've tried to assure her she's protected by the hospital. Millie told them she has seen movies where people were attacked in their rooms like in the Godfather. I've been in to see her three times and she begs me not to go when I have to leave. She's terrified to be alone."

"I'll visit her."

"That's good. She'll be happy you're there but expect a rough time when you leave." Reading managed a wry smile. "We did turn up something at McCoy's office. They found a burner phone stashed in a file cabinet. The Alachua Sheriff's people and ours are going over it together. Hopefully, that will net something."

"Have you learned anything more from the phone tap information?" Self-discipline is an art few master. With so many individuals involved, I believed one or more of them broke the 'rules' and that slip would expose them. Someone called a number outside the cult…or from a place that could be identified…or used words other than in their established code…something.

"Our tech folks will update us tomorrow morning." The approaching darkness had begun to obscure Reading's features, but I could see well enough to know he'd spotted something that concerned him in a large clump of sea oats growing on the sand ridge at the ramp's end. He asked, "Do you have your gun?"

"No," I answered."

"Someone is hiding in the bushes." He removed his automatic from a holster located at the small of his back. "When I run down the ramp, whoever is there will take off or shoot. You hit the deck."

"That's no good. They'll shoot alright. You!"

"No. When they move, I'll shoot first."

"Bull shit!" I said in as strong of a whisper as I dared.

Reading didn't give me time for further argument. He ran past me, raising and pointing the .45 as he sprinted the fifteen yards to the ramp's end. No one moved. No one fired. Reading stopped, stared at what was behind the sea oats, and lowered his gun. Two small children emerged. Our nerves almost created a disaster in addition to the one which we were already immersed.

Chapter   56

"Yes, it's on the list of burner phones we've compiled from the phone taps." Reading examined his taco critically. "This thing is as skinny as one of those…well, it's just damned anemic." He saturated the soft cornmeal shell with hot sauce. Reading leaned back in the booth seat. Jose's Mexican Bistro is one of our regular haunts. His grumbling escaped the ear of the waitress who had delivered his plate. Rather, I believed she ignored him and left.

"Send it back," I challenged. My brother is one of those people that likes to complain but avoids the unpleasantness required to correct his gripes.

Reading shrugged his shoulders. "I'd rather tell you about the Buehl case phone taps."

"So…tell me."

"The number for McCoy's cell is on the list. It is one of the more active ones. That's the good news. The problem is we don't know who has the phones with which he was in contact." Reading squinted at the mush he'd made of his taco. "How am I going to eat this without bathing in hot sauce?"

"You should have thought of that before you emptied half of a bottle Tijuana Fire on it," I said. "Eat it with the knife and fork or ask the waitress for a tarp to cover your clothes." I returned to the information from the burner phone investigation. "McCoy's burner, were you able to isolate numbers dealing with him?"

"Yes. There were fourteen of the phone numbers that were in regular contact with him. That's out of forty-two that we think is the total. Absolutely none from others on the list. The real depressing thing is these people stay within their rules. Our techs haven't found a single call to any number outside the parameter created by the group. No incoming calls to them, either." Reading took a breath and rolled his eyes. "Maybe that's understandable when you think of what happened to McCoy."

I thought about watching 'who-done-its' on TV. "What about checking where the phone calls originated? Check the towers they bounced off…that kind of thing."

Reading nodded. "We thought of that. Is the information in existence? Yes. Can we get it? That's dicey. Feds have access to that type of technology. We are in the process of seeing what it will take us to get access."

I thought for several seconds before asking. "You told me you looked for patterns and relationships between the numbers. You still doing that?"

"Yes."

"What about looking at the time period right after Mulhee put on her show in the courthouse?" I hesitated as I fleshed out my idea. "Mulhee had to be in contact with someone from the groups and they probably were in contact with her. Your theory is that the identity of the group members is shielded from the other groups. It's logical, to me, that the leaders would be the ones that contacted Billie. One could be McCoy. See where I'm going?"

Reading thought for several seconds. Nodding, he agreed, "Yes, that is likely. It's also a good chance those same people were in contact with her a couple of days before. I'll get our techs to check it out. That should give us Mulher's number. The problem is we still won't have names." Reading thought for several seconds. "There is a chance that these folks had contact in person with each other. Checking on Mulhee's social contacts might give us a lead."

"Do you think she's still in the area?" I asked.

"Yes, for two reasons. "The net we have over the area isn't easy to get through. I don't think she's the type to run. Billie is a fanatic. She's more likely to die trying than give up. You need to remember that."

"Who do you think killed Griggs?" I asked.

Reading slowly shook his head. "Think killed him…we have all kind of clues but no where to stick them. I guess I can tell you who we think, *didn't*. Stanton was a big guy and strong. Billie Mulhee couldn't have overpowered him, and he wouldn't have trusted her to have had a drink where she could drug him. Lashann believes the killer is left-handed and the weapon used to sever his head was a commercial grade meat-clever." Reading hesitated, then theorized, "As far as I'm concerned, that last info isn't worth much. Lashann also said the man was dead for a while, prior to being decapitated. That means we could have two different people involved."

"So, what you're telling me is you don't have squat?" I observed.

"Yes."

"What's next?"

Reading rubbed the stubble on his chin. "Work with what we have and hope we get access to phone tower records…and get plain lucky. What we have is Billie. Catching her is our number one priority. We know she's involved. Number two. Stay on the Buehls like stink on manure. They have to be involved. I hope we can hassle them enough that one of them breaks."

"Don't count on getting anything from Mrs. Buehl. She's diamond hard." I compared what I knew of her to bunkmates I'd had in the Marines and judged her as tough as any.

"I know that. You remember that when you're wandering around her ranch."

"Don't worry about—" My cell phone interrupted our conversation. I didn't recognize the number on the screen. "Hello." I answered.

"Hi, Chessie. This is Celeste Anders. We spoke a week or so ago. I'm a reporter writing for *Archaeology Today*. At least, they've offered to buy my article on an interview with you if you'll grant it."

Reading pointed to my phone and mouthed *put it on speaker* three times before I understood. I complied.

"Are you there?" she asked.

"I'm here, just thinking." I looked at Reading and asked a question so he would know what was going on. "You are the reporter that called the night of the courthouse meeting with Billie Mulhee, right? You aren't interested in the Buehl case…just the excavation."

"Uh-huh." We both detected wiggle-room in the tone.

I watched Reading search for a napkin and pen.

"I haven't had time to check you out," I stalled.

"I'll text you the name of the editor at *Archaeology Today* and her phone number as soon as we are done talking." Celeste didn't hesitate a second in providing the information.

"Right now, I don't see how I can provide you with enough to interest your magazine or its customers. Not on the dig. We aren't close to completion." I added emphasis on my last sentence. "You know I can't give you any information regarding what the sheriff is doing."

Reading smiled and wrote, *Grant the interview*, on the paper he found.

Anders suggested, "Would you let me be the judge of that? I promise I won't pressure you for information about anything involving the criminal aspect of what you are doing."

"I don't know about that," I said, talking to Anders and my brother at the same time.

My brother grimaced and tapped his finger on the words, *Grant the interview*.

"I promise I won't take more than a half hour of your time," the reporter begged.

I stared at Reading giving him a last chance to change his mind. He pointed to the paper again.

"Okay, Celeste. Give me a time and place on the weekend." I saw Reading's broad smile in response.

"How is Saturday, ten in the morning, at the Marriott's lobby, in Vero?" Anders suggested.

"As far as I know, that's okay. Can you text me a phone number where I can reach you if I have to change that?"

"Sure. I'll add that to the *Archaeology Today* info."

After goodbyes and hang-up, Reading asked, "Do you believe she really is only interested in the dig information?"

"No! She's a free-lancer. My experience is they capitalize on every opportunity that happens by. She'll try to squeeze everything she can out of me…and sell it to whomever, for the highest bid."

Reading smiled and raised his voice, "Good!"

I stared in disbelief.

"What's wrong sister? Haven't you ever heard of smoking bees so they'll leave the hive?"

"Yes, but you aren't the one who is likely to get stung."

Chapter   57

I didn't like Reading's plan. Would it work? It had better than a 90% chance of success. Would someone become endangered as the result? That would be better than ninety. Who would likely get clobbered? Me!

To date, the sheriff had insisted on absolute secrecy…at least as much as could be mustered in a situation that so many knew of its bits and pieces. The fact multiple bodies not of an archaeological nature had been found on the Buehl property was widely known. The murder of Wilbur Carson had extensive coverage by local news media as had the wrangling of ecologists versus developers over the Dillon development. Billie Mulhees' explosion at her own meeting in the courthouse cast suspicion on her and the fact all occurred on the Buehl's land made the public's jaundiced look at them, understandable. What wasn't known to the public, the sensational nature of the discoveries, the huge number of bodies, and the fact that so many perpetrators were involved.

Sheriff Charlie Travis reflected the attitudes of Florida "Cracker" country folk. He kept important information as closely held as possible. Serious, critical information? Distribution constituted a mortal sin. But his department continued to be bogged in a swamp with no solid ground…leads…and the increasing elapse of time gave the culprits the opportunity to slip away and possibly commit more heinous crimes. Within that framework, Reading approached Travis with a simple plan, and one that had a high probability of breaking the stalemate the case had become.

Smoke them out. Reading reasoned if the public knew of the scope and gruesomeness of the deaths, public reaction would be so fierce that one to several of the cult would try trading the names of those involved for escape from punishment and relocation in a "witness protection program." Travis, reluctant at first, eventually realized the time element made Reading's trap the most feasible way to proceed. If they could get their hands on just one of the burner phones and one name, the cards would fall! Since I, not the Sheriff's department, would be the source of the leak, he saw less risk. By Thursday, everything had been approved. Travis assembled every resource he could to monitor all those suspicioned, even to the slightest degree.

Reading laid out a tale for me to relay to the reporter that stirred the pot. No. Boiled the pot. That isn't strong enough. The pot would probably explode.

According to the plan, I would allow Celeste Anders to ferret information from me regarding the Buehl ranch murders. No specifics were to be shared but what was dribbled out to her were to be spectacular enough to ensure she immediately auctioned off what she knew to the highest bidder. The teasers I would use were journalistic steak. One liners Reading invented as bait were sensational.

"One of the largest serial killings in US history." "Might be the largest number of perpetrators tried for a civilian crime ever." "The details of these murderers are the things novels are written about."

Reading spent a lot of time crafting plans for my survival. Part of the plan…an electronic tracking bracelet for me. Most of his effort centered on keeping me within the parameter he constructed. I tend to freelance, particularly if I feel there's a tinge of sexism involved. Yes, I do over-react, occasionally. Most of the time. However, he continued to school me on the details, using a rhyme, until I became so annoyed, I shouted at him. Still, I continued repeating… "Go nowhere alone, or without a phone, your GPS tracking, must never be lacking, carry your '9' and a knife, to ensure your life, keep a 360 view in whatever you do, and always report, any type of a threat…Quickly!" The nursery rhyme redundancy stuck in my mind and my craw. Exasperated, I finally asked, "Where did you get the idea for this?"

"Old movies."

"Really?"

"Really. You watch *Sleepless in Seattle* and *Steel Magnolias*. I watch *The Dirty Dozen*." Reading added, "Three more times, please. I want to be sure that saying is branded on your mind as surely as if it was placed there by a red-hot iron."

I remembered the movie and the scene. "I'm not, Telly Savalas."

"You're not Lee Marvin, or Charles Bronson, or Jim Brown, or Clint Walker, either. Any of those people might survive being attacked by a big and strong killer…if they decided to do their own thing." Reading pointed his finger at me. "I don't want to arrange your funeral. Repeat *it* once more!"

~ ~ ~ ~ ~ ~ ~

I saw him peeking out our front window. Reading pulled the curtain aside enough to view the street, but in a manner focused on one area. Alarm bells rang. My face flushed as I asked, "Is someone out there?"

Reading said, "No," but continued to peer to intently not to be focused on one thing.

"Liar," I snapped.

He shot a bird at me without even a momentary glance in my direction.

"What are you watching?"

Reading's mouth moved but nothing audible passed his lips.

"Louder," I prompted.

"ATP 8236"

"License plate?" I asked.

He nodded. Finally, he looked away. "It's leaving. Three people in a pickup. I'll check out the number tomorrow."

I wouldn't sleep soundly that night.

Chapter 58

I wanted to kick myself. Short cuts are the bane of my existence. As I scanned the Hilton's lobby, the small additional effort it would have taken to search the net for a picture of Celeste Anders would have been advantageous as I tried to pick a face to match the image I had of the freelance reporter.

In addition, I neglected to call the references she provided. My logic, she wouldn't furnish sources unless she knew they would avidly support her. That logic might be built on sand. A couple of short cuts put me at a disadvantage before we met for the interview.

Viewing the lobby, I didn't see a face that matched the voice or the profession. The collection of people was predominantly male. Sisters that were scattered about the lobby, weren't candidates for my stereotype. The registration area, modest in size, meant we were sure to hook up. I just wanted an opportunity to size Anders up before we met. How would I know who she was? Since I searched faces for her, logically, she'd be doing the same thing. I looked for a female searching for a stereotype, mine being an archaeologist. My jeans, tee shirt, and camo long-sleeve, worn as a jacket, fit the expected dress code. I picked a chair close to the entrance and began looking for a person looking for me.

Disappointment came after fifteen minutes. My cell phone showed no missed calls, or messages, but did tell me the reporter was ten minutes late. The only person who had any interest in me? The desk clerk. He spoke to someone on the phone while staring at me. When the clerk finished his conversation, he stepped away from his counter and straight to my chair. I expected him to deliver bad news, that Anders had cancelled, or for him to run me off as a vagrant.

"You're Miss Partin, correct?" he asked.

"Yes," I answered plaintively.

"Miss Anders is waiting in the dining room. She asked me to send you in."

"What does she look like?" I peered through the glass partition that separated the dining room from the lobby. For the first time, I thought about its existence.

"I'll point her out for you." He pointed to a thirtyish woman who met all my stereotype check points. She smiled and had her eyes fixed on me. Anders had been able to do what I hadn't, check the opposition before meeting. That told me I'd better up my level of respect and caution in dealing with her. I approached her table with that in mind.

~ ~ ~ ~ ~ ~

I liked Celeste Anders. She was someone I could go to the mall with or meet after work for a beer. It didn't take long for me to discover her high level of intelligence and perceptiveness. Combined with a sharp sense of humor, my thoughts made me hope to add her to my list of friends. It also brought some guilt since I would be using her in a way. After pleasantries and the process of getting a feel for each other, it was Celeste who got to the reason for our meeting. "How are you fixed for time? I could spend a couple more hours just chatting."

"I don't have a tight schedule, but we should get to the dig. That's why we're here." I smiled forlornly. "There isn't going to be much we can talk about."

Celeste nodded. She removed a small recorder from her purse. "Do you mind if I record?"

I could respond immediately. "No and yes. No, I don't mind if you record what we say about archaeology. I will mind if we get into anything I might tell you that is off the record."

"Off the record being about?" She knew but verified.

"Anything I might say that even remotely impacts the criminal investigation going on at the Buehl ranch."

Anders leaned away; a knowing expression accompanied her silence. The possibility I'd made a mistake before the interview even began, washed over me. I tried my best not to exhibit any visual signs. After a long delay, Anders suggested, "I'll only take notes. I do that whether I record or not. Turning the recorder on and off will be a hassle."

I nodded, "I don't know what you want. Ask me questions, and I'll answer the best I can."

Anders removed a steno pad. "Okay, lets start by discussing how you became involved in the project."

"It is different than most of the sites we do. Usually, a road crew or the like, digs up something that's a surprise, or there is a historical background which makes us want to initiate a dig. In this case, neither of those occurred. A development company was responding to concerns of local activists. The company requested we look to be sure no rich source of relics and artifacts got destroyed by them." I watched her use shorthand to record my words. "Gregg?" I asked.

She nodded, "Best elective class I ever took." She hesitated, then asked. "The development company is Dillon, right?"

"Yes."

"Do you know why they decided to get you involved? They could have told the people I understand are fighting it, to pound salt. I don't think any of them would have standing in a court of law." Clearly, Anders had done her research. "I don't see anything they could do except fight rezoning. That would be mission impossible."

"That's not entirely true. There is a known set of middens on the property. The Seminole nation has control of all native American historic sites where possible burials are involved. They could restrain activity in the immediate vicinity."

"How large of an area has mounds on it?"

"Less than ten acres."

She laughed, "With a piece of property as large as the Buehl ranch, who cares? Fence it off and go on."

"Buehl doesn't want to sell the property. His partners own more than a 50% interest. They want to sell and make a killing. Buehl used the fact the mounds are on the land to squelch the deal. He let the ecology activists and historical preservation people know he thought there are lots more historical sites than just the one. He wants to keep it in his family. Or so he says." I emphasized my last sentence. I saw a way to 'leak' what I wanted her to know.

Celeste's eyebrows rose. "You think something else is involved?"

I acted reluctant and spoke that way. "Off the record," I paused waiting for her to nod. When she did, I continued, "Yes, I'm positive there is."

Anders stopped writing. After several seconds she asked, "Have you found archaeological evidence on the property in addition to the middens you told me about?"

Her failure to follow-up on the tidbit I threw her surprised me, but I answered her question. "Yes, we've found several places that sampling, and ground penetrating radar, disclosed the existence of artifacts." After a few purposely added seconds, I added, "And some other things."

"Other things?" Anders laid her pen next to the steno pad. Suspicions were written all over her face. Celeste Anders was a very astute woman.

We stared at each other in silence for several seconds. Reading's plan wouldn't work. Anders smelled fish. It was shortcut time. I decided to gamble on my gut feel about the woman sitting across the table from me. "Are you willing to put some very bad folks in jail for the rest of their lives?" I asked.

Celeste didn't hesitate, "That's what this is really about. After checking you out, I was very surprised you'd talk to me, your brother being an investigator for the sheriff." After several seconds of hesitation, she continued, "Yes, I'll help, if I know the details. There will have to be a couple conditions. One of them is that I want something out of this." She expected my question or something approximating it.

I thought about that for several seconds before answering her as honestly as I could, "I can tell you enough of what I know to convince you to help, but not all. That's the best I can do."

"What can't you tell me?" Celeste asked.

"Names. Details of how we know some things. I can't tell you exact numbers. Things like that. Telling you what we know happened…After you hear what I have to say, you *will* want to help."

Anders took a deep breath. "I'll listen. If you convince me, I'll help. Either way, I'll volunteer a promise to you, and I have to get one from you. I need that to go further."

"What are the promises?"

"I promise you to keep silent everything you tell me and what you're trying to do until you tell me otherwise." Celeste took another breath. "You promise me the first and exclusive story about what happened at the Buehl ranch. Deal?"

"Deal!" I affirmed. "You staying here?"

"Yes. I have a room. But before we go there, I need to know I can absolutely count on protection from the sheriff. That's a condition!"

"I can guarantee you'll get deputies assigned to you until they trap them. When you deal with the type people these are…no one can guarantee complete safety for any of us."

Celeste stared at me as she weighed the risks. "My great-grandfather landed on Iwo Jima. He faced a better chance of dying than I do, against people that weren't any worse. I can't do less than he did."

"Let's go to your room and get to it." I leaned toward her and said, "I don't want to take any chance that anyone can overhear what we are talking about."

~ ~ ~ ~ ~ ~

Shock spread over Anders' face. "How many?"

"We don't know. We may never know the total. I can tell you that it is more than forty. It could be a lot more. Forensically, there are questions…" I purposely trailed off my sentence.

"The victims were all dismembered?"

"In most cases they were decapitated. That is something that shouldn't go into print." I'd already shared many items with the reporter I knew would get my butt chewed unmercifully. Celeste nodded. I hoped she was as trustworthy as my evaluation. If not, I'd be unemployed, and my brother's job could be gone. I consoled my mind by rationalizing I could stand losing a few pounds. That reality jarred me. I announced, "That's what I can tell you. It's a hell of lot more than I intended. You have enough to write the article to panic them?"

Celeste nodded, grinned, and said, "Chessie, after they read what I'll write, all of them will be looking for the tramp steamer to Antarctica."

"When do you think you can get it in print?" I asked.

"With something like this? Overnight! Is that too quick?"

"Maybe. Give the sheriff at least forty-eight hours to be sure. They need to be in a position to monitor communications between individuals we know have a high probability of involvement with others, see if any take a sudden trip out of town, those kinds of things."

"No problem. I'll make a call to you before I release the article. I know the editor at the two papers where I'll peddle this. You can tell me what provisions have been made to keep me from ending like those buried at the ranch." Anders made a face. "You sure about this? When this comes out, there aren't many people that could have furnished the information. It would have to be someone in the sheriff's office or someone close to the dig. Since you've told me to be sure that I make it clear that the sheriff isn't the source of my story, that makes you and Dr. Card the top two remaining sources. Doesn't that frighten you? You've told me this cult exists to provide revenge on those who have hurt someone in the group. That's you. You said you can count on the group to react. Putting an end to you might be part of what they do."

That made me think. Reading had a plan to safeguard me…not Mark. "I'll see to that." After making the statement, I realized that wouldn't be easy! I'd be involving and endangering one of my closest friends without his knowledge or agreement. Guilt and responsibility weighted me as a I parted company with Celeste Anders.

Chapter   59

I didn't get the reaction from my brother I expected. Instead of his yelling, "What were you thinking!" he calmly told me, "You rolled the dice and did the best you could." Reading's major concern? Finding a way to protect Mark…and to spare my relationship with Mark as much turmoil as possible.

He did so in a way that I couldn't object. Reading asked, "Where do you think Mark will be this afternoon?"

"He'll either be at his house or on his sailboat." I answered.

Reading picked up his cell phone. He placed it on speaker as he had it dial Mark's number. "Hello," Mark answered.

"Hey, Mark. It's Reading Partin. Where are you at?"

"I'm working on my sailboat over at Bailey's Marina. Why? Do you need something?"

"I need to talk to you. Can we meet you somewhere for supper?"

"Sure. We? You and Chessie?" Mark sounded suspicious, "Why do I get the impression, this isn't going to be a purely social meeting."

"Because it's not. Look, I asked my sister to do somethings in relation to the Buehl investigation. You need to be aware of *what I did*. It might involve you and it might put you in danger. Actually, I'm sure it will." Reading stared at the phone waiting for a response.

"Where and at what time?"

Reading looked at me and asked, "His favorite place to eat?"

"Charley's Steakhouse," I answered.

"You're paying," Mark insisted through the cell.

"What time can you make it?" Reading asked.

"Let's say 6:30."

"You're taking this very well," I interjected.

"I can't do anything about what's already done. Besides, you two are buying my drinks, also. I have a feeling to continue to have a positive attitude, I'll need to be a little drunk."

Chapter   60

When Reading finished briefing Mark about the latest status of the Buehl investigation, I learned some things that shocked me. The sheriff had been successful in his efforts to get state and federal assistance. Tracing the network of tower phone calls from the cult's cell phones disclosed areas that many of the calls were made from and received. East Florida University had five numbers associated with it!

Mark received the news stoically. He interrupted sparingly, waiting to tell us his thoughts until Reading completed his update. He said, "With what we've discovered on the ranch, nothing you've said surprises me. The fact you know as much as you do…that does. As far as being in greater danger, I might be. The way I see it, the people involved already view me as a danger to them. And I am. So, I see it as just a straw on what's already there." He took a breath. "Okay Reading, what can we do to stay alive, and what can you do to help?"

"Try not to go anywhere alone or to some place you're isolated easily. That's number one," Reading declared. "It is many times harder to abduct or kill you if you're not by yourself."

Mark frowned. "That will take some doing. You know I live alone. Unless I start using Uber or cabs to get around, I'll be alone when I drive. I guess the safest place I can be is at the dig. You have officer Dobbs protecting us there."

Reading looked at me, not Mark, as he asked, "What would you say to bunking with us until this situation is wound up?"

I nodded my assent.

Mark asked, "How long?"

"It will probably take a couple months until the greatest danger is past. You and Chessie have a good relationship. There's can't be a stronger motive to stay vigilant than to stay alive. Mark, you observe the rules. From a selfish point, I'll feel Chessie will be safer with you around."

"I can take care of myself," I grumbled.

The analytics in 'Dr. Card' came out. "Wouldn't my being here make it easier for them? They could look at us being under the same roof as a two-fer."

"I think the fact that I'm part of the sheriff's department more than cancels that."

Mark considered what Reading said for several seconds before nodding. "If you can put up with me. I'll move in next week."

"Aaaaaa, I think sooner than that." Reading lifted his eyebrows. "I'll arrange for a squad car to meet us at your place. We can leave as soon as I get a green and white here, I don't want Chessie by herself."

"The article isn't out yet. You really concerned that much?"

much?"

Reading nodded solemnly. "Yes, Mark, I am."

Chapter   61

"I asked Dr. Andrews, if we should cancel any further work on the dig. His answer surprised me. He told me, *No! The publicity is actually favorable to us.* I wonder if he'll feel that way after Anders' article hits the newspaper tomorrow morning." Mark Card, though not a serious politician, kept his options open. He loved being the department head at the university and did what he could to protect it…given the manure he'd stepped into.

We sat in the Jeep, waiting for Al Dobbs call. The sheriff instructed his deputy to drive ahead and check for intruders before he allowed us to proceed to where we would work that day. The procedure made me feel less secure. While we waited, we sat a hundred yards inside the gate to the county road. It was in an open field of palmettoes. A person with a rifle wouldn't have to be a crack shot to do us in from a passing vehicle. I kept my eyes focused on the road and became very nervous if any vehicle appeared too slow.

"Did you hear me?" Mark inquired.

"Sorry…Yes, I did." My distraction was a beat-up pickup truck. "I don't feel safe until we get back to the dig." I broke eye contact long enough to comment on

Mark's revelation. "Dr. Andrews sees us as the cavalry. We represent the good guys. So far."

Mark's cell phone rang. I could hear Al's voice but could not distinguish his words. I did notice the conversation exceeded his normal, "It's okay to come on back." Watching Mark's expression confirmed something of concern to Dobbs was discussed. I asked, "What's up?"

Mark hesitated. Then disclosed, "I don't know if there is a problem or not. Al said he found fresh tire tracks around the dig. Nothing on the road, though. He thought that was more alarming than having tracks back to the gate. He's concerned someone has another way in. He told me he hasn't seen anybody, but he told me we should be alert for anything strange as we drive back." Mark stared at me hard enough for me to ask, "What?"

"Could anyone overhear your conversation with Celeste Anders?"

I shook my head emphatically. "Absolutely not!"

"What's it going to be like after the story prints tomorrow?"

~ ~ ~ ~ ~ ~

"Somebody has been around my excavation," I said as I examined the ground around the meter by three-meter trench.

Mark stopped removing tools from the jeep. "What do you see?"

"It's what I don't see. All the footprints that were here yesterday have been brushed away. Someone has been here and didn't want us to find out about it." I followed a trail of obviously smoothed sand for forty feet to tracks made by an ATV. A green palmetto frond with a freshly cut end lay on the ground next to the tracks.

Mark had walked to my side. "I see what you mean. But, why yours and not mine? The area around my work is undisturbed?" He attempted to answer his own question, "Maybe, there is something buried around your dig they don't want us to find."

"What could it be? This isn't one of their body dump sites. Why be concerned about the archaeological artifacts we might find?"

Mark nodded, "You're right it doesn't make sense from that standpoint. But still, they were there for some reason."

"What are you two looking at?" Dobbs asked as he approached.

Mark pointed to the palm frond. "Someone snooped around Chessie's dig since we left yesterday and obliterated footprints with that."

Dobbs asked, "Have you touched it?"

"No," we answered in unison.

"Don't disturb it. The lab might be able to get something off of it. I'll go get a garbage bag to place it in." Dobbs motioned to the tracks. "There were two ATVs out here, Those were made by different tires than one I was following."

I asked, "Al, do you think you can follow them to where they entered the property?"

"I probably could, but Sheriff Travis said no. I'm to stay in your hip pockets. He said he'd send someone else out to do that."

"Is he expecting an attempt to harm us out here?" Mark's tone sharpened.

"I can't say."

Chapter   62

Mark held a copy of the Treasure Coast News in his hand. He'd just finished reading Celeste Anders article. It occupied a place on the top half of the front page. When I read it, though I knew what to expect, electricity went through me. The hair on the back of my neck stood up. The article, written in a way to support the sheriff's work, implied his department closed in on the solution, and that the culprits merited the waving of the cruel and unusual punishment clause. Anders hinted that the sheriff had identified culprits in high social circles from education to governmental officials.

"This will do what it is intended to do. The hornets are out of the nest. My question is will they sting or fly?" Mark folded the paper and handed it back to me. "Have you heard anything from Reading?"

"No. I don't think we will hear from him unless things aren't going the way we thought they would." I looked at the headline as I laid the folded paper down. *'Murder cult discovered in Indian River County.'*

"I'm thinking we should stay here today. There isn't any reason to make it easier for them to get a shot at killing us. If we head to the ranch, we're going to their ground. Possibly to their leader's home." Mark pointed to the front door. "Leaving will just make it multiple times more difficult for Dobbs and his three buddies to protect us."

I thought about what he said for a couple seconds. "If we're going anyplace or want to do anything, I'd say now is the time. This group is closely controlled by its leaders. They'll probably plan a course of action. I think we have a couple days before they come after us."

Mark leaned back into the soft padding of Reading and my sofa. "You could be right. In fact, if they're interested in their own preservation, they should be in the process of trying to disappear."

"If we were talking about normal human beings, I'd agree. We aren't dealing with that type of individual, particularly the leaders. There are probably a lot of them who'd like to flee. But look at what happened to McCoy when he failed to kill Millie Lane. Dead in less than twelve hours." I pointed to the paper. "The people Celeste wrote about in that article aren't normal people. I bet they will react…violently…dramatically. Mark, we aren't dealing with humans, we're dealing with jungle animals. We're playing by their rules if we meet. Kill or be killed."

Chapter 63

The smile on Reading's face told me the answer to my question would be favorable. "We have fourteen of them nailed and think we have three more identified. Travis will put twenty-four-hour surveillance on all of them starting tomorrow. He wants two more days to follow leads and identify more." Reading's face became troubled. "I think we should get the ones we know about in custody. Something could go wrong. I'm for collecting what we have and pressuring them for the rest of their comrade's names. But…the boss is the boss."

Mark, my brother, and I sat around our kitchen table enjoying the first moment in the last forty-eight-hours where the level of tension became bearable. We sipped beer to celebrate. Rather, I sipped, they gulped. I asked, "Who have you ID'd so far?"

"I feel shitty about this. I've been instructed not to tell you two. I can confirm the ones you know about, that's Peed and Mulhee. By the way, Billie is still around. Her cell was located near Wabasso. She hasn't gotten out of Dodge. I think she'll try going down in a blaze of glory."

"What about the Buehl's?" I asked.

"We haven't been able to make a direct connection to the phone chain. That's one reason Travis is holding back."

Reading shook his head. "There has to be a connection to one or both of them but so far, no proof."

"None? That's surprising," Mark said.

"There have been several things we discovered that we didn't expect." Reading pinched his lips tight. "I guess I can share this with you two. It doesn't involve names." He stopped.

"And?" I prompted.

"There have been a couple strange activities. It's like a notification was sent to all the members of the cult at one time from the leaders. The messages were in code, and they were all the same. I have the text message. I'll show it to you both, but I want to tell you the other really strange thing that's happened. We've identified what we believe are the leader's cells. Right after the coded messages were sent. The same four cell numbers sent the same message to the same number of cells that aren't in the group of burners. It has Travis excited out of his gourd. He thinks the group is planning something and the leaders are being sure the message gets to all the group right away. He expects something big! In the next couple days."

"Do you think he's right?" Mark asked.

Reading nodded and added, "Yeh, I do. These nuts will react. How, that's the question."

"What was the message?" I asked.

Reading nodded, removed a folded piece of paper from his shirt pocket, opened it, and laid it on the table. "That's it." The message consisted of an unbroken string of letters and numbers. It read,

3RUOHEHTT7AYA266DIRF8ELPMETSRADIV23.

"Can you make anything of that?" he asked.

Mark quickly shook his head, "You probably need some type of a key to interpret it. By the time you figure it out whatever it says will probably have happened."

"Let me study it for a few minutes," I said as I tried to remember my G2 cryptography training. The few minutes turned into a half-hour, then an hour, then two. I finally realized the numbers had no significance, and they were there to confuse. Without the numbers the code read, RUOHEHTTAYADIRFELPMETSRADIV. I tried dividing the chain into words; that didn't work. The, in, to are words used so commonly, I looked for them. It was when I recognized EHT as 'the' I instantly knew the interpretation key, take out the numbers and reverse the order of the letters. I scratched the letters on the paper, VIDARS TEMPLE FRIDAY AT THE HOUR.

I yelled for Reading and Mark who had long since gone to the living room to find a football game on the tube. "Hey guys, I know what it says!"

They rushed back to the table. I spun the paper around so they could read the words. "Fantastic work, Chessie!" Reading said excitedly. "That's got to be the place on Buehl's ranch!"

"There is a problem," I leaned back in my seat. "Today is Friday." I pointed to the kitchen clock; its hands told us it was eleven-forty. "Friday's almost over."

Chapter   64

Al Dobb's cruiser sped down Florida Highway 60, siren blaring…red and blue lights flashing. Reading, Mark, and I sat inside. After Readings frantic emergency call to Sheriff Travis, we and as many squad cars as the sheriff could redirect were all speeding for the Buehl ranch. As we raced to the scene, Travis was busy rousting the rest of his deputies from bed. Their orders were to form an iron-ring around the Buehl property. To come heavily armed. To shoot anyone who failed to stop on command. To shoot to kill. We sat in silence each wondering what we would find. The sheriff didn't want to take a chance even one would escape. I hoped they would arrive in time to stop whatever the culprits had planned.

Dobbs, who remained our assigned security man, was stationed at our front door. It allowed us to leave for the ranch immediately. We raced through lightly trafficked streets of Vero Beach, Al occasionally having to dodge sleepy motorists after the midnight hour. When we reached the open road, he increased speed to ninety miles-per-hour. The frightening race plastered us back in our seats.

We were still several miles away when Reading exclaimed, "Good, God. Look there!" He pointed toward the northeast. A faint red glow lit the horizon, it had to be coming from somewhere on the Buehl ranch. Reading said,

"Al, call in the station. Tell them there is a possible arson on the ranch, possibly at the scene we are heading to."

I asked, "Do you think they killed the Buehl's and are burning their home?"

"No. it isn't in the right spot."

Mark guessed, "I'd say it is back in the pasture where we found that ritual area."

"They're burning everything. Trying to destroy the evidence." I suggested.

"It's too late for that and they know it." Reading said. "Al, call ahead. See if any cars are there and what's going on."

As we watched the red light grow brighter and more intense, Al spoke to several cars that were at or close to the ranch. The fire, they said, was back at the ruts where we had found the amphitheater-like clearing. In accord with Sheriff Travis' orders, they were blocking every gate and spacing themselves around the property perimeter the best they could. As Al finished his discussion, Reading mumbled, "Too late. We're going to be too late."

~ ~ ~ ~ ~ ~

"It will be a bunch of hours before we can get it under control. Lots more before we can get back to its source. Days, not hours. That's a hell of an inferno. The interior is bright white fire. That's 1400 degrees centigrade. I'm guessing that a hell of a lot of accelerants, of some type, was used. I'll promise you this. You ain't likely to find any evidence. Powdered ash. That's it." The fire chief's face, lighted by the gigantic blaze, showed evidence of his being near to it. Soot covered his face, a face flushed from heat and streaked with perspiration. "I've got every brush truck I can get either here or on the way. Most of what I can do is keep it from spreading too much. We're damned lucky it isn't windy. If it were, every tree and bush from here to sixty would be embers."

"When do you think we'll be able to get in there?" Travis asked hoping for a different answer.

"Damned, Charlie, you don't listen good." The fire chief didn't attempt to hide his disgust. "Want a time. Okay. Three days before you and your crime scene people can stomp around in there. It will be the twelfth of never before anyone finds anything that can help you." He walked back to his fire crews.

Charlie Travis shook his head. He spoke to my brother and Bill Worthington, "Have you done all you can to keep anybody that's in here from getting away."

Bill said, "We've got cars on every road blocking all traffic. Every gate has officers controlling it."

My brother added, "We're got cars at every pasture gate that connects to an adjoining property. I have seven cars patrolling the roads that adjoins the ranch. I have three cars at the Buehl's house. They're there. Scared, I guess. Bob said he only said a few words to Mrs. Buehl, but Carl Buehl told him just before the fire started it sounded like World War III had broken out. Bob asked why he didn't go investigate. He said he didn't want to die tonight. Carl said he heard machine gun fire, but I don't believe that. After they spoke to the deputies, they've locked themselves in their bedroom."

Travis waved to the sky, "I have our chopper and two of mosquito patrols up searching. Melbourne, West Palm and Ft. Pierce are sending theirs. We should be able to spot anybody trying to get out. I'm working out a refuel schedule with them, so we have birds overhead until we catch the bastards."

I looked at my brother. Our exchanged glances said the same words to each other. We were too late. Too late to stop what ever happened. Too late to recover evidence. Too late to keep the guilty from escaping. Too late to catch those who might wish to kill us!

Chapter   65

"Travis believes it's a Jonestown replay." My brother spoke to Mark and my eager ears. He added, "I'm not sure he's right." Reading's face showed the signs of stress that non-stop work and lack of sleep produce. We saw and spoke to him for the first time since Mark and I left the fire, three days ago. What he would tell us would affect our lives, certainly in the short term…possibly for a lot longer.

Reading had just explained they found evidence that at least twenty-seven bodies were burned in the huge funeral pyre the fire on Buehl's ranch turned out to be. Most were unidentified or unidentifiable. Some had remains or items that provided enough to attach a name. Those nine all were suspected members of the 'Vidar Cult,' a name used by Celeste Anders in her newspaper article that stuck. Alvin Peed was one of them.

"Why does he think it's Jonestown?" Mark asked. "Sure, *some* of the suspects are ashes, but there's no proof that *all* are."

"Exactly!" Reading said.

"Particularly the part about burning the bodies," I added. "Why do that? I think it is obvious. It was done to make people believe everyone involved is dead…while some are escaping."

"Travis is buying it. I'm not sure whether he really believes that or not." Reading tapped his fingers on our kitchen table. "It is something he wants desperately to put in the solved case column and move away from."

I asked, "Why is he ready to accept something that looks like it was made to order to provide the killers a way out? Charlie Travis isn't dumb and he's too good of a politician not to see that just accepting a few bodies allows him to pronounce case closed."

"Oh, he definitely has more than some skulls, joint implants, and personal effects. The evidence he's weighing heaviest is the data gathered on the burner phone network. Remember, I told you how the duplicated message was sent to non-burner phones? Well, that allowed us to identify almost everyone by matching a burner to another personal phone number each one had. We couldn't ID the senders…who would be the leaders. Or, at least, it gives that appearance. Forty-two burners, forty-two personal numbers, it balances. I'm betting we end up finding that number or reason to believe somewhere between forty-two and forty-six bodies were cremated." Reading hesitated, taking a deep breath. "But what if some of the people were innocents? You could set them up by simply sending the message to their personal number. The leaders could save anyone they wanted from exposure by incriminating someone entirely innocent. They find and kill the victims. Presto! We have bodies, but maybe not all the ones we want."

"What do you think happened?" Mark asked.

Reading shrugged his shoulders. "How can anyone be sure without continuing to investigate? Thoroughly. I'm guessing the leaders survived. Hell, they could be in Mexico by now. They could have selected some followers to spare. How many? Who knows?"

"Not many," I interjected, "The leaders of this group are meticulously careful. I'm betting few, if any, of the followers survived. I can't help believing that those who ran the cult believed the old saying, 'two can keep a secret if one is dead.' They'll kill off any possible weak links you bet on that."

"Remember, Travis told us about Buehl claiming to hear automatic weapons fire? Maybe he did." Mark blinked. "That brings a terrifying thought to mind. If somebody killed the rest and set the fire, there is at least one of them that survived. What will the person or persons do? The cult's purpose was to seek revenge."

I asked Reading, "How much danger do you think we, Mark and me, are in?"

He answered immediately, "Very little in the short run. Obviously, those who survived are doing their best to avoid capture. The risk is too great. They've lost the supporting structure, their feeling of invincibility. Long term they might plan something. I'd bet eighty percent they don't."

"That twenty percent bothers the hell out of me!" I snapped. "Do you think you'll be able to determine if some did survive?"

"If Travis devotes the resources? Yes, there's a good chance we would," Reading said.

"Will he?" Mark asked.

"I don't know. He won't step completely away from tying up the loose ends. Bill Worthington still has Wilbur Carson's murder which may or may not be part of the mess." Reading saw the heat building in my boiler. "Yes, Sister, I'm sure they are connected. Old Wilbur was silenced. He knew what happened." Reading traced his index finger across his neck. "We have to prove that. Or so Bill and I hope."

"Will Sheriff Travis support that?" Mark asked.

Reading shrugged his shoulders again. "I really haven't any definitive facts. My gut says he'll have to say he will, but…" Reading shook his head.

Mark thought about Reading's answer, then asked. "How long until we can finish the archaeological contract I have with Dillon? I want to get it done, if she insists we finish."

"LaShawn, that's our crime scene tech, tells me it will take four maybe five days before he finishes what he has to do. He doesn't want anyone out there until he determines if anyone walked away from that mess."

"Do you think you can talk the Sheriff into keeping Dobbs assigned to protect us?" Mark clearly believed our problems were not over. "It will only take a week and a half. Maybe less."

"Yes." Reading smiled. "The last thing he'd want is something happening to you on his watch."

"You said us," I looked at my boss. "You answering for me?"

"I figured you'd want to finish—"

"Mark, I'm pulling your leg. I wouldn't think of quitting before the dig is finished."

"Good!" Mark looked relieved. I hoped he didn't realize I wasn't entirely honest about what I just told him.

Chapter   66

I thumbed through the stack of computer printouts, correspondence, and University directives that glutted my desk's incoming mailbox. It would take me an additional week to go through the stack and, for the most part, overburden the waste can. Dr. Mark Card whistled as he entered my office, a courtesy he extended to me. His idea of male chivalry provided for not scaring or creating an imagined feminine embarrassment. Completely unnecessary, ignoring such issues is easier than correcting them. Actually, I wished some of his concern would transfer to my brother. Reading showed no concern for my privacy when engaged in the shower or other personal bathroom activities.

"I'm sure you know this, but I've been given the approval to finish our work at the Buehl ranch." Mark looked resigned and added, "I couldn't talk Beth Dillon out of finishing. I thought she might drop the whole development or at least give up on our completing the survey. No such luck." He sat in the side chair next to my desk.

I nodded. "When do we start?" My brother had already informed me we would be allowed to resume work on the dig. I knew a lot more but waited for Mark to tell me what I already knew. The teeth marks were still fresh from divulging too much information to Celeste Anders. My butt figuratively needed time to heal.

"Day after tomorrow. I want to wait another three days after that before I call Bobby and Sheila back. We can start them back Monday of next week. Dillon says she'll have everything settled with Buehl, but I don't want to take any chances with their safety." Mark realized how that sounded. "Not that I think your and my safety is less important."

"Do you think there is anyone left to come after us?"

"If what your brother told me is near correct, there isn't much chance of that." Mark held up six fingers. "Seven they can't account for out of the forty-four. That's good odds. Reading told me that the fire was so intense there could be ones completely consumed. All that it would leave is dust. Unidentifiable dust. If any survived, they should be in Canada or Mexico by now."

"What about the Buehls?" I asked.

"What about them?" Mark replied.

"Do you trust them?"

"No, but I'm not worried. They're too vulnerable to be blamed for anything that happened to us." Mark sounded very confident.

I spoke my thoughts aloud, "Old Carl, I'm not concerned about. Laurie, his wife, I'm not sure she's certifiable, but damned close if not. Anyone who runs around naked in public isn't exactly normal."

Mark grinned. "She does that for shock value."

"That doesn't make her less crazy. You don't think they had some kind of involvement in what happened on *their* ranch?" I shook my head. "My brother says the sheriff hasn't proved a direct connection. Everyone involved with the case believes they had to know what was going on and one or both of them were part of the cult."

"Al Dobbs is going to provide security. Although, you can bet he keeps busy chasing off the press. Reading told me there were over a hundred hanging around the ranch gate and the sheriff's office building." Mark remained silent for several seconds as he rethought our situation. Then he concluded, "We'll be alright. If any of the cult survived, they did it in a way that keeps them from being identified. Why risk exposure by trying to kill us?"

His logic was sound. Still there were seven individuals not accounted for, maybe more if some of those killed and found were 'stand-ins' for a killer that used them as a corpse proxy. I said, "You are probably correct. I know one thing. I'll be carrying, so don't sneak up behind me. Anything that does will have more 9mm holes than Swiss cheese."

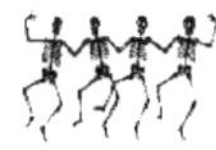

Chapter 67

"Are you bringing Bobby and Sheila out here on Monday?" I asked. We bounced our way down the familiar ranch ruts. A cold early December breeze vibrated the palmetto fronds and made oaks and pines toss their foliage about. The open Jeep made our ride a chilling one. The overcast denied us sunlight and dampened our psyches as well.

"Yes," Mark answered. He'd been very quiet since we met at the gate. Al Dobbs asked if he was okay. Mark said he was. When in one of his "Dr. Card" moods, I'd learned to wait for him to disclose his problem. He always did.

I didn't have long to wait. Mark asked, "Do you ever get up and get a gut feeling you should go back to bed and lock the bedroom door?"

"Yes, every time I have too much to drink."

"I'm serious." Mark scowled in my direction but not at me. "Chessie, since my feet hit the floor this morning, I've had this premonition. Like something bad is going to happen. Like I won't be coming home tonight." He winced as we bounced over a large bump in the road. "Like I'm going to be killed today."

"Did you have a nightmare? They can seem real."

"I might have. I don't remember." He slowed down as we neared our base camp site. "It is so strong, I almost decided to wait for Al to run off those reporters and have him come back with us."

I examined his features. Anxiety! "You are spooked," I said.

"Damned straight, I am!" He stopped the Jeep but made no attempt to get out.

I thought for several seconds then asked, "Do you have a reason for this? Did Reading or someone from the sheriff's department tell you something." I thought of things that might have caused his fear. "Did you see someone trailing you or did you get a threat?"

"No, no! Nothing tangible. I went to sleep last night thinking how well things have been going out here. Good. Really good. When I woke this morning all that evaporated. My gut tells me something terrible will happy…here…today."

I felt my Glock stuck in my waist band. "Did you bring your Colt?" I asked.

"No. That's stupid, isn't it?" Mark shook his head.

I removed my automatic and handed it to him. "Take this. It's trouble repellant. You probably won't need it, but you'll feel a lot better just totting it."

"I don't need it." That's what Mark's mouth said. His eyes said something entirely different.

I shoved the gun closer to him. "Take it. We'll be together. Peace of mind is a lot."

Without another word he accepted the weapon.

~ ~ ~ ~ ~ ~

Our instructions remained to wait for Al Dobbs before we started work at the site. It seemed like over-kill, and we were anxious to finish with our obligations to Beth Dillon. Any enthusiasm we had for our work at the Buehl ranch, had evaporated. The ghoulish history of what we uncovered was too far afield from archaeological science. My usual joy derived from "digging in the dirt" had become revulsion.

Mark sulked, swishing a stick around in circles in the sand and made complaints as we waited for our 'protection detail' to arrive. When Mark grumbled, "It's about time," thirty minutes passed between the time we left Al chasing media at the gate and Mark spotted his car rounding a cypress head.

After his cruiser rolled to a halt, Al's first words weren't hello. "Did you see her?"

"See who?" I asked.

"The Buehl woman."

Mark grinned, "Did she have any clothes on?"

Al didn't see any humor in Mark's comment. He frowned. "Yeh, she wore clothes. She also had a high-powered rifle with a scope propped up in the front seat of her ATV. I asked what she intended to shoot with it. She said varmints. I told her to make sure they had four legs and to stay away from the dig site," Al shivered, "Uoooeee! That skinny little woman gives me the creeps!"

"Is that why it took you so long to get back here?" Mark asked.

Al nodded. "I watched for a good ten minutes to be sure she didn't head back this way." He pointed east. "She went into the next pasture, but I intend to keep my head on a swivel. I don't trust either of the Buehls. You two need to take a good look around before you crawl into those holes you're digging."

Mark and I walked toward the Jeep. Al yelled a parting warning. "When I drove back here, I saw some tire tracks that weren't from your Jeep, Buehl's ATV, or my cruiser. Be careful. Are you both working in the holes you were yesterday?"

"Yes," I answered.

"Good. You're a little more than fifty yards apart. I'll split the difference so I can watch you both. I'll check in with each of you once every hour. That okay?" Al asked without needing an answer. He smiled, "Mind if I ride over in the Jeep? I'm afraid I'll get the cruiser stuck in the soft sand. Damned near did yesterday."

"No problem," Mark said.

Al jerked his thumb at the patrol car. "Good. Let me get my .308 and my entertainment. I hope you folks finish next week. I'll use up all the puzzles in my Roku book by then and I'd have to buy another one."

~ ~ ~ ~ ~ ~

Mark parked the Jeep half-way between our two excavations.

"You sure are making it easy on me," Al observed. "Can I help you tote things?"

I answered for Mark and me. "No. All we need is our back packs and tools. You just keep us from developing any new holes in our bodies." I looked around the unimproved pasture where the archaeological site was located. A few heavy thickets of palmettoes, gall berries, and scrub oaks provided great shooting blinds less than a hundred yards from us. My old sergeant in the Corps would have called it "a sniper's dream."

Mark gathered his work implements and strode toward his pit while I decided what I did and didn't need. He reached his excavation while I was a quarter of the distance away from reaching mine. He yelled, "Son-of-a-bitch! Somebody has filled my damn dig with some of the sand I've dug out of it."

I quickly looked at my pit. Shoe prints were everywhere. When I got close enough to see into the hole, a foot of sand had been dumped in it. I yelled, "Someone's done the same thing to me." I stared at the evenly distributed sand with a piece of tubing stuck down into it.

Mark cursed again, turned to return to the Jeep, and yelled, "I left my shovel in the Jeep. Chessie, you want me to bring you yours?"

"I brought mine with me." It was then that I noticed an entrenching tool stuck in the sand overburden pile several feet from my pit. It wasn't one of my tools or one that belonged to our group. Strange! Every Marine has carried one like it at some time in their tour. The handle was smooth and polished looking, an appearance wood gets when frequently used. It took me back in time for an instant. The smell of freshly dug earth drifted to my nostrils. I half expected to hear gunfire.

Crack! I did hear gun fire! Training and instinct took over as I dropped to the ground and flattened against it. My eyes focused on the Jeep in time to see Al Dobbs slump over in his seat. Everything seemed to be happening in slow motion. Mark crouched low as he sprinted the last few yards to his pit and threw his body into it.

Immediately after he disappeared, I heard a scream…then the familiar *snap, snap, snap* of shots fired from my Glock. The question, who fired them?

I looked for Al, but he'd disappeared, I assumed he'd taken cover by getting lower inside the Jeep's body. The alternative…I wasn't prepared to face that.

The crack of the high-powered rifle caused my head to swivel toward the sound. It came from a group of tightly spaced cabbage palms fifty yards away. Another shot zinged over my body and struck the entrenching tool on the other side of the pit. The pit! I had a ready dug foxhole. I didn't wait for the sniper to take another shot. It took three rotations of my body to get to the safety of the hole. I let myself tumble into it as I heard another bullet zip by.

As I dropped toward the sand, two hands, one clutching a large knife, emerged from the earth that covered the bottom of the pit. Immediately, they were followed by the screaming face and upper body of Billie Mulhee. I saw the knife move toward my throat. A quick blocking move with my arm deflected the threatening blade from my carotid artery, but not enough to keep it from doing me serious damage. The knife nicked my throat, barely enough to draw blood, but buried deep into my right shoulder below my clavicle.

Mulhee screamed something again, I don't know what. She pulled the blade from my shoulder, and we were immediately engaged in a life-or-death struggle for control of the knife. I got both my hands on her wrist holding the blade. She tried to twist free, but I pushed her back into the sand, our bodies and faces crashing together. We looked into each other's eyes from two inches apart. The hate was mutual. She tried to bite my face, but I maneuvered my arm in front of her mouth while still clutching to the wrist that held the knife. I felt her teeth sink into my forearm.

My superior strength and size began to overpower her. She made a move to free her hand and I crushed her arm against her forehead. I knew I had to do something quick. The wound in my shoulder was severe enough that I knew I'd lose consciousness soon. Using Billie's head as a fulcrum, I pushed down as hard as I could. I heard her scream, and her bones break as she dropped the knife. The world swirled as I grabbed the knife and drove it deep into her rib cage.

Before I could pull the blade from her body, the deafening shot from a rifle came inches from my ear. My foggy mind tried to figure where I'd been shot before I lapsed into unconsciousness.

Chapter   68

The setting was so familiar. I was carrying my lunch tray to my seat at the Vero Beach High School cafeteria. The suggestive stares and comments from male classmates were bad enough, but the jealous, catty, and snide remarks from my school sisters were worse.

Amazingly, Al Dobbs was suddenly walking at my side. He whispered in my ear, "Don't pay any attention to them. The boys want what you won't give them, and the girls are jealous of what you have."

"What's that?" I asked.

"Big tits and a great ass!"

I looked again and the face wasn't Al's. "That's not like you Al," I explained to the eyes staring at me. Those eyes were housed in an unfamiliar face. I decided that I'd wandered into a masquerade party and the older man's concerned features were part of his doctor's costume.

"Nurse Cather, go tell her brother she's awake," the fake doctor told another party goer dressed in scrubs. I watched her disappear through a door that had been decorated to duplicate a hospital room entrance.

"How do you feel? Are you in pain?" the fatherly voice came from the fake doctor.

"Hell no! I feel fine," I said. When I tried to move, the reality I laid in a bed in white sheets entered my unclear mind. Huge bandages covered my right shoulder and arm. Things began to make sense to my drug impaired thought process. "Where in the fu---" that wasn't lady-like, "Hell am I?"

"You're at the Cleveland Clinic Indian River Hospital." The father figure informed. His countenance was professional, neutral. As I watched him clinically watch me, the reason for my being in the hospital struggled into my thought process. Buehl's ranch. Mark. Billie Mulhee. Al Dobbs. Gunfire. The knife. The last shot. I took a quick visual inventory of my body. There were no signs of patching a gunshot wound.

I heard familiar heavy footsteps in the hall. Reading! He entered the door and I felt more secure.

"Hey, Sis. I see they have you patched up." He looked at the doctor. "Don't let her give you a hard time Doc. She's a barker, not a biter."

The doctor looked disgusted, turned, and left the room.

While Reading was in that process, my short-term memory returned. I squeezed my brother's offered hand. "Mark and Al?" My eyes completed the question.

Reading smiled, "They are both okay. They got banged up about like you did." He saw the concern remain frozen on my face. "Mark took a spear through his leg and Al got shot in his rear. They're down the hall. You all will be able to visit each other tomorrow."

Another thought entered my whirling mind. "Did I kill her?"

"No," Reading shook his head as he spoke. "Someone else did."

"Who—"

The doctor reappeared and interrupted, "That's enough! You," he pointed at my brother, "Out!" The doctor's face clouded, "You," his finger moved to me, "Lay back and stay still. You're stitched up like a football. I don't want you messing up my needle work."

The doctor winked at me though his face remained serious as a grave.

Reading backed to the door. He asked, "Doc, when can I take her home. I miss her cooking."

"We'll see how she does overnight."

"I'll fill you in on what happened tomorrow," Reading said.

The doctor waved his hand at Reading and commanded, "Good-bye."

Reading and I exchanged, "Love you's" as he left. However, my good feelings dropped a bit as I stared through the door to watch him leave. A uniformed sheriff's deputy sat outside my door.

Chapter   69

"How's your shoulder?" Millie Lane asked, the concern in her voice, genuine. Four weeks after my confrontation and struggle for life with Billie Mulhee the arm remained tender. I'd been very lucky. The knife missed tendons that could have destroyed part of my shoulder's function. I provided my standard answer, "It's healing very well. I'll recover completely."

I sat with eight others at one of our favorite gathering places, The Roarin' Gator. The place was decorated for rednecks, but appealed to over-age Yuppies, its largest clientele. Besides Millie and me, Mark, Reading, Beth Dillon, Al Dobbs, Celeste Anders, Bill Worthington and his wife held down chairs around the large circular table. The occasion of our gathering…the completion of the Buehl ranch project.

The celebration covered several areas. The final papers, completing the sale of the ranch from Buehl to Dillon took place two days before. Sheriff Travis pronounced a close to the spectacular criminal case on the same day. Mark and I completed our final excavation in the afternoon. We all had lots to celebrate. Beth could start her development. Bill and Reading could move on to other cases and away from the daily dodging of the press,

Worthington's wife, Evelyn, could celebrate having a normal life with her husband, Celeste had her monster story, and Millie had her large life-changing commission and had the hopes for a new boyfriend. Mark and I felt we had the most to celebrate; we would not have to return to the sands of the Buehl ranch!

Beth Dillon asked me, "How did it feel to stick that knife in Mulhee? After all, she was trying to kill you."

"I didn't feel anyway. Relief maybe…that she wouldn't kill me." I thought for a few seconds, "Guilty, after I learned she was dead."

"You didn't kill her, for the hundredth time!" Reading growled at me. "Laurie Buehl did."

Evelyn Worthington asked, "What did happen out there? Bill never discusses the sheriff's business with me. But in this case, I want to know." Everyone turned to Reading. He shook his head and said, "One last time."

"When Mark, Chessie, and Al arrived at the dig, three members of the cult were in hiding, waiting on them. Mulhee and the professor, Williams, from South Carolina hid in the pits. We suppose the third person, the Weber guy from Gainesville, covered them with a thin layer of sand. Then he hid in a clump of cabbage palms with a rifle. The idea was to kill all three. Al was to be collateral damage, just because he was there. Williams tried to stick a spear in Mark."

Mark interrupted, "Bad aim and bad spear. He got me in the thigh, but the spear broke right after it started to penetrate. I had Chessie's gun in my hand as I dove in the pit and shot him before he could try anything else."

Reading continued, "Actually, Weber started everything. He shot and hit Al, right in the butt." Al sheepishly held up one finger. "Al's rifle's strap got caught on the Jeep seat under him. He had to raise up to get it loose. Weber shot him again." Al pointed to his rear and held up two fingers.

"Al was pinned down, and here, it gets iffy. We think Weber shot at Chessie. That's when she crawled into the pit and Mulhee tried to kill her with a knife." Reading looked at Worthington. "Should I tell Travis' version?"

Bill nodded.

"Okay. Laurie Buehl says she was close by and heard the shooting. She claims she saw Weber shoot Officer Dobbs, got a good shot at Weber, and she shot him. Then she says she drove her ATV up to where Mulhee and Chessie were fighting, and she blew Mulhee's brains out...from a foot away." Reading glanced at Bill again. "Buehl said she thought she was saving Chessie's life."

Beth Dillon said, "It doesn't sound like you're convinced, Reading."

"It doesn't make any difference. That's what Travis has said happened. That's what happened."

Anders laughed. "Don't worry, I won't print that. I only report the truth."

Bill Worthington suggested, "If we can find the slugs that were shot at Chessie... Well, that might make things different. The Bahamas have an extradition treaty with us."

"Why the Bahamas?" I asked.

Beth answered. "I gave the Buehls the check for the property day before yesterday morning. They were on a plane to Nassau that afternoon."

"And...that's the end of it?" Evelyn asked.

Reading and Bill stared at each other. Bill answered, "Not exactly. Travis hasn't closed Wilbur Carson's murder case. There are leads on it. But I can't discuss them. However, some might tie into the Vidar case. Like Weber. He supposedly died in the mass cremation. We found an engraved watch that belonged to him in the ashes. He obviously didn't die. The question is..." Worthington shrugged his shoulders.

THE END